W9-AVS-034

Accelerated
Reader
ATOS 5.0 – 5

THE GHOST ROADS

The RING OF FIVE

THE GHOST ROADS

Eoin McNamee

WENDY
LAMB
BOOKS

Text copyright © 2012 by Eoin McNamee
Jacket art copyright © 2012 by Scott Altmann

All rights reserved. Published in the United States by Wendy Lamb Books,
an imprint of Random House Children's Books,
a division of Random House, Inc., New York.

Wendy Lamb Books and the colophon are trademarks of Random House, Inc.

Visit us on the Web! randomhouse.com/kids

Educators and librarians, for a variety of teaching tools,
visit us at RHTeachersLibrarians.com

Library of Congress Cataloging-in-Publication Data
McNamee, Eoin.
The ghost roads / Eoin McNamee. — 1st ed.
p. cm. — (Ring of five)
Summary: "The nefarious leader of the Ring of Five, Ambrose Longford, is still
determined to control both the Upper World and Lower World. But Danny and his
friends at Wilson's school for spies stand in his way. As Danny struggles with his
role in the spy world, Longford is attempting to bring down the other members of
the Ring, to usurp all of its power. Or is he?"— Provided by publisher.
ISBN 978-0-385-73821-7 (hardback) — ISBN 978-0-385-90714-9 (lib. bdg.) —
ISBN 978-0-375-98592-8 (ebook) [1. Fantasy. 2. Spies—Fiction.] I. Title.
PZ7.M4787933Gho 2012
[Fic]—dc23
2012001197

Printed in the United States of America

10 9 8 7 6 5 4 3 2 1

First Edition

For Gabriella, Imogen and Michael

The prime minister looked at the file on the desk in front of him. It was massive, and he had only scanned the first few pages, but even that had been enough to shake him to the core. The top pages of the file had been recently printed, but as he went back through it, the paper grew older, brittle and yellowed with age. The bottom section was composed of parchments and cracked vellum. But each report, whether modern or ancient, asserted the same thing: There was another world, existing parallel with his own. A world of danger that threatened to invade his own, if the documents were to be believed. The files had been closed for many years, but their opening had been triggered by strange happenings—the sightings of men and women with wings flying in formation across the countryside, the sudden assault on a military base by a group of creatures with one brown eye and one blue. Inexplicable events that had brought Harris, the head of his secret service, to his door.

"I have grave news," Harris said, his face filled with concern. "My predecessors, going back hundreds of years, have always passed on an instruction: if winged men are seen in the countryside, then this file has to be passed to the prime minister."

The prime minister had read the first pages of the file with growing incredulity.

"This other world has always existed?" he said now.

"Yes, sir. There have always been discreet contacts between the Two Worlds, but things turned sour. The Lower World, as the other is called, sought to take over this one. After terrible conflict, a treaty was signed between the two, forbidding almost all contact."

"And now?"

"The treaty has been broken. The Lower World is free to attack ours."

"Who are they?" the prime minister asked. "Are they all . . . evil, winged . . . things . . . ?"

"No, Prime Minister, that is where our hope lies. We have allies sworn to fight evil, those who have resisted for hundreds of years. Men and women of integrity and valor. I will introduce you to one!"

Harris stepped out. The prime minister went to the window and looked down on the blackness of the river below. Who knew what foul secrets were concealed beneath its inky depths?

He heard the door creak behind him. He turned, half expecting to see a winged creature, but the door had opened to a pleasant-faced man, someone who looked like he might be a schoolteacher, with a ready smile.

"Here he is," the secret service chief said, "the leader of the freedom fighters in the Lower World, our best hope in these dark times."

The prime minister stepped forward eagerly, his hand outstretched.

"Welcome," he said, "welcome to our country . . . I mean to say, our world. . . . I am the prime minister."

"I'm very pleased to meet you," the man said, his voice low.

"And you are?" the prime minister said.

"I am Ambrose Longford, leader of the Ring of Five, and, I hope, your ally in this battle."

"Of course, of course," the prime minister replied. "All our resources are at your disposal. What can we do?"

"Thank you," Longford said, taking the seat the prime minister offered. "Time is indeed short. The opposition is well organized, and I am sad to say that their ringleader and chief troublemaker was born in your world."

"Who is he?" the prime minister asked. "So we can track this menace down."

"His name is Caulfield, Danny Caulfield," Longford said, "a boy with enormous power, bent on dominating your world and mine. He leads a gang from a school for spies known as Wilsons, a place of such infamy that it must be erased. Caulfield is half human and half Cherb. The Cherbs are evil beings, foot soldiers of the Ring of Five. Some say they can be redeemed, but believe me, they cannot."

"And this . . . this Danny Caulfield, what are we to do

with him?" the prime minister asked. The whole situation was outside his experience; he felt helpless.

"Many times I have tried to bring him to the side of righteousness," Longford said, "and each time he has returned to the embrace of darkness. It pains me to say the words, as it must pain you to hear them, Prime Minister, but there is no other way. This scourge must be dealt with for once and for all. We must pool our resources to this end. This menace must be eliminated!"

"How do you propose to stop him?" the prime minister asked.

Longford's eyes flickered, and his mind traveled to a secret prison fifty miles away, where a plan to do just that was unfolding. But the prime minister didn't need to know everything. Knowledge was power, after all.

"We are working to that end, Prime Minister," he said, "working with all our might. A trap has been laid. This Danny Caulfield was reared here in the Upper World. The people he has regarded as his parents are in our custody."

"Though of course they are not his real parents," the secret service chief broke in, "but rogue agents!"

"He purports to hate them, but he has in fact a sick regard for them," Longford said. "They are the bait in the trap!"

"This Ring of Five you mentioned," the Prime Minister said, "it must be a wonderful organization!"

Longford inclined his head modestly, concealing a small, sly smile. Besides himself, the Ring of Five consisted of some of the most wicked beings it had ever been his pleasure to know.

"A fine body of men and women, toiling selflessly in the cause of peace," Longford said.

"Splendid," the prime minister said. "I hope to meet them someday."

You will, Prime Minister, Longford thought with secret delight and malice. Someday soon, you will!

At the secret prison Longford had been thinking about, things were not going well for Agent Pearl, the woman who had been hired to look after Danny by pretending to be his mother. When Danny had found out the truth, he had been devastated by the betrayal, but if he had glimpsed Pearl at that very moment, he would have realized how much she cared for him, how far she was prepared to go to save him and how much she longed to see him one more time— although she could hardly see at all now, after the beatings, her eyes were so bruised and swollen. She sensed rather than saw the interrogator enter the cellar where she had been for . . . how long? Time had lost all meaning.

"Water," she whispered through parched lips. "Water, for pity's sake." She would have reached out her hands to beg, but they were tied behind her. The interrogator touched her cheek gently and she flinched from him.

"Such a pretty face," he whispered, "and such a shame to see it like this. Why, even your own son would barely recognize you. But he's not your son, is he?" The man's voice changed. "So why won't you tell me where he is?"

She trembled and waited for the blow to fall. Danny was at Wilsons Academy of the Devious Arts; that was all *she knew. Could they touch him there? Probably not, but she wouldn't take the chance. She emptied her mind and waited for the pain to begin again.*

In another cellar in another part of the same military building on the outskirts of a nondescript town, her partner, Agent Stone, swam into consciousness. He too had been tortured, but he had not seen his torturer for several days. He had even been fed, an anonymous hand placing a dish of rough but edible stew just inside the door.

He sat up. Something had wakened him. There it was again. The scrape of a key. More food? The door creaked open; then he heard quiet feet walking away.

The door was open!

He went over to it, moving painfully. The corridor outside was empty. A trap—it had to be. He would be shot trying to escape. And yet if they had wanted to kill him before now, they would have done so already. There was nothing to stop them. Perhaps he did have a friend in this secret prison. Hardly daring to hope, he stepped out of his cell.

Ten minutes later Agent Stone stood in an empty foyer, its lights dim. He had moved with great caution. Once, he heard footsteps and shrank into the shadows. A secretary had crossed in front of him, carrying an armful of files. She did not look up.

He peered through the partly open door. He could see the night sky, but he could also see barbed wire and watchtowers surrounding the building. How was he to escape? At the possibility, however remote, of freedom, the face of his partner sprang unbidden into his mind. Agent Pearl! Was she in the same building? Was she even alive? He half turned to go back, but then, as if she were beside him, he heard her voice in his head.

Never mind about me. Find Danny. Look after him!

He heard the rattle of an engine outside. An old black taxi trundled around the corner and stopped in front of the building entrance, blocking the view from the watchtowers. The back door swung open.

"Get in, you fool," came a deep, gravelly voice. In a flash Stone analyzed the situation. He didn't know the taxi driver. Hurt though he was, Stone was still a trained operative, and his training stood by him. Inching open the door of the building, he ducked to the ground and rolled toward the cab, then dived into the back and hit the floor. The door slammed.

"Stay down!" The taxi roared toward the gate. The engine slowed, and Stone heard voices.

"Where are you going this time of the night, Fairman, you old goat?"

"You know I don't answer for my comings and goings," the rough voice said. "Out of my way, sentry!"

"Charming, I'm sure," the sentry said. "Go on, get out of here."

The cab started forward. Stone waited for the shout, the thud of bullets against the bodywork, but none came. He was free.

"Who are you?" he asked. "Why are you helping me?"

"My name is Fairman," the taxi driver growled. "My taxi travels between the world you know—the Upper World—and the secret Lower World, unseen by you Upper Worlders for many years."

7

Stone could not suppress a shiver of excitement. He had researched the existence of a Lower World, and Danny had confirmed it to him. Now he was to go there! His excitement vanished as he thought of Pearl, still being held prisoner.

Don't worry, Pearl, I'll find Danny; then I'll come back for you. *He made the promise in his mind, even if Pearl could not hear him. If he had lifted his head and looked right as the cab left the military base, he would have seen a poster of Danny pasted to a wall. On it was written:*

WANTED FOR CRIMES AGAINST HUMANITY.
EXTREMELY DANGEROUS. DO NOT APPROACH.

But Stone did not look. He was thinking of his next move.

"What part of the Lower World are we going to?"

"Where do you think?" Fairman said. "The school for spies. Wilsons."

1

WANTED.
EXTREMELY DANGEROUS.

Danny's life had changed forever on the night that the same black cab had appeared at his door, supposedly to take him to ordinary boarding school, but in fact to sweep him away to Wilsons Academy of the Devious Arts in the Lower World. From being an unhappy student at an inner-city school, he had been plunged into a world of spies and winged messengers, intrigue and betrayal. The skinny boy with the triangular face and two different-colored eyes had been inducted into the Ring of Five as the fifth member in his first term at Wilsons. He was supposed to be there as a spy acting on behalf of Wilsons, but part of Danny Caulfield's soul belonged to the darkness, longed to betray and hurt. The members of the Ring could join their minds to read each other's thoughts, and would have spotted Danny as a double agent were it not for the fact that he was partly one of them. He had broken away from the Ring eventually, but still, at night, when the lights of Westwald, the city of the Ring, could be seen across the turbulent waters of the sound, he could feel the warm, treacherous allure of his old allies. The presence of Ambrose Longford, head of the Ring of Five, was a shadow at the edge of his consciousness. He did not know that Longford was at that very minute plotting to capture him, but deep down he felt that the man's attention was somehow focused on him. . . .

But today the sun was shining, and the ancient school looked rather less brooding than it usually did. In fact, Danny thought, it felt like home, more than anywhere else he had ever lived. Part of him wished he could stay there forever—the good side of him longed for home and family and security. But the other side of his mind, the part that plotted and spied, knew that this was only a lull, and that the Ring of Five was restless and dangerous.

For the moment, his attention was on more immediate matters, for he found himself perched precariously on the roof of an old summerhouse, pleading with a very pretty but very dangerous siren named Vicky. She was examining a globe about the size of a tennis ball.

"Vicky, please, it's not mine. Dixie will kill me." The roof flexed under Danny's small frame.

"Oh, you took it from her, did you?" Vicky said with an unpleasant grin.

"I just borrowed it to check something."

"A likely tale," Vicky said. Her eyes narrowed. "You're up to no good."

"No, I swear, I was just looking at it."

"I know what you were doing," Vicky said. "You were trying to find your way out of here."

"No," Danny said crossly, although that was exactly what he had been doing. The glass ball was a Globe of Instant Positioning, which could be used in the way a GPS in a car was used. He had borrowed it (at least, that was the word he had chosen) from his friend Dixie's bag and had brought it to the quiet little summerhouse in the woods to study it. He had left it on the windowsill for a moment, and when he turned back, he found that the siren had made off with it.

He saw movement on the path behind her.

"That dress is very pretty, Vicky," he said.

"Thank you," she said, "but you're not going to butter me up like that."

"No, really," he said. "Sets off the color of your hair."

"You think so? Well, that's very nice, 'cause it'll make it a lot easier for me to sell this globe in Tarnstone."

"I don't think so."

"Why not?" Vicky sneered, holding up the glass ball. Behind her a figure shot through the air and a hand grabbed the globe. Startled, Vicky fell backward, slid down the roof and landed with an enraged shriek in a gooseberry bush.

"Thanks, Les," Danny said as his good friend landed

at his feet, holding the globe. Les folded his wings, dusted the sleeve of his threadbare coat and looked at Danny, his gray eyes somber in his thin face.

"Yes, well," he said, "I've been practicing that move with the wings. Might come in useful in this war everybody says is coming. But what are you doing with Dixie's globe?"

"I kind of borrowed it," Danny said.

" 'Kind of borrowed' means 'kind of stole.' "

"Maybe," Danny said, "but, Les, I've got to be able to move between the Two Worlds on my own!"

"You're a spy, not a thief, Danny."

"I know that."

"So give it back."

"I will." Danny looked into the depths of the globe. He could see the summerhouse and the bulk of Wilsons Academy of the Devious Arts half a mile away through woods and shrubbery. Farther to the north was the town of Tarnstone, and beyond that, the sea inlet that separated Wilsons Island from the Ring of Five and Cherbs on the other bank of the Sound of the Lower World. If you looked south, however, you could see only darkness, the darkness of time and space that separated the Lower World from the Upper.

"What's wrong?" Les said.

Danny shook his head. He didn't want to talk about the two people who had pretended to be his parents for years but who had turned out to be secret agents, paid to look after him. (How much had he been worth? he won-

12

dered.) Now he knew that his real parents were the spy Steff Pilkington and a Cherb woman, both dead before he'd had a chance to know them.

His bogus parents, Agent Stone and Agent Pearl, said they had learned to care about him. Danny didn't trust them, but they were the only way he had of finding out what had happened to his real parents and how he had ended up in the agents' care. He *had* to talk to them again!

But first he had to find them.

In the globe he saw two small figures standing by the summerhouse, and a few hundred yards away, the retreating figure of the siren. Then he froze.

"What is it?" Les said.

"Stay very still," Danny said. "Don't move a muscle." He passed his hand over the surface of the globe, making it zoom in on the summerhouse.

"There," he whispered. Behind them, in the trees, something moved, and there was a flash as though sunlight shone on steel.

"Armed?" Les whispered.

"Looks like it."

"What do we do?"

"Wait." Danny got the globe to zoom in farther. The watcher in the trees was clear now, sitting astride a bough. A boy, Danny thought. He couldn't see the face, but there were leaves in his hair, and he had a large tear in his coat. In his hand was a long knife.

"Can you do what you did to Vicky?" Danny said. As

he spoke, the boy in the tree turned to look behind him, as though sensing that he was being watched. Les drew a sharp breath.

"A Cherb!" he exclaimed, for he had seen the face of their bitter enemy, with its one blue eye and one brown, its pointed chin and ears—very similar to Danny's own appearance.

"I'll take care of him, don't worry," Les said grimly. His parents had been killed by the Cherbs in the last of the many wars between Wilsons and the Ring of Five, the Cherbs' masters. Before Danny could stop him, or warn him about the dangers of an armed Cherb, Les shot off the ground like a bullet and crashed through the leaves and branches, sending twigs and leaves flying. There was a thud of bodies meeting, followed by a loud grunt. Two shapes plummeted through the foliage, the Cherb hitting the ground first, rolling and coming up with the knife in his hand. Les landed beside him, dazed, and Danny could see he was in trouble. He felt frantically in the pockets of his overcoat for the old revolver concealed there, but the Cherb sprang toward Les, caught him by the hair and pulled his head back, exposing his throat. The knife flashed.

"Nala!" The word exploded from Danny's mouth. The Cherb halted.

"Nala, no! He's a friend."

"No Cherb is a friend of mine," Les said. Nala looked at him.

"Nala, please," Danny said, inwardly cursing Les. The Cherb met Danny's eyes. He looked weary, fright-

14

ened. Slowly he lowered the knife, pushing Les's head away and spitting on the ground. Les stared at Danny, puzzled.

"You making friends with Cherbs now?"

"I didn't tell you—I met Nala on the last mission. He helped me."

"I hate Cherbs," Les said. "They killed my parents."

"I know, that's why I didn't tell you."

Les got to his feet, eyeing the Cherb with hostility. Nala raised his knife again.

"Cut it out, both of you," Danny said. "There's something strange going on."

"You can say that again." A voice cut across him. It was Vandra, a small, pale girl with two pointed incisors just visible on her lower lip. She looked like a vampire, but she was the opposite. The fangs were used to inject antidotes and medicines rather than to steal blood, for a physick was a healer. Vandra had been a friend to Danny from the start, and once he had gotten over her intimidating looks, he'd found her warm and loyal.

"Is this the Cherb you and Dixie met on your mission?" Vandra said.

"Everyone knew but me?" Les said.

"Never mind that now," Vandra said. "What's he doing here?"

"Probably trying to kill us in our beds," Les said. Nala kept his gaze fixed on Danny.

"Stop it," Vandra said. Danny walked toward Nala, ignoring the deadly blade. The Cherb had backed away when he saw Vandra, until he was against a tree.

15

"What *are* you doing here, Nala?" Danny asked. "Why have you come to Wilsons?"

"Nowhere else to go," Nala said. His look was hard, but Danny could hear the fear in his voice.

"Why?"

"They try to kill Nala."

"Who's trying to kill you?" Vandra said. Despite her sometimes fearsome appearance, she was full of compassion, even for a deadly enemy.

"Cherbs, Ring, they hunt Nala. Nala make friends with Danny and Dixie. Is not allowed."

"What isn't allowed?" Danny said. "To befriend an enemy?

"No," Nala said, "friends not allowed."

"How do they stop people being friends?" Vandra asked.

"Not people," Les said. "Cherbs."

"If friends with other Cherb, they cut off hand," Nala said. "For friends with people, they kill."

There was a long silence. Danny knew how vicious the Cherbs could be, but this was the first he had heard of these laws.

"Nala has nowhere else to go."

"That's not our problem," Les said.

"It's my problem, Les," Danny said, "if my friendship caused what happened."

"He can stay in the summerhouse for the time being," Vandra said firmly. "I'll get some food for him later on."

"You're not serious?" Les said.

"I am."

16

"You're on your own, then," Les said. He glared at Nala and stalked off.

"Go inside," Vandra said. "You'll be safe here."

That's what you think, Vicky mused. The siren had heard the commotion and doubled back to hide in the shrubbery. A Cherb at Wilsons! She hugged herself in delight. This was a juicy morsel of information, a very juicy morsel indeed!

2

PESTERING THE DEAD

Looking out the window of the library of the third landing, Master Devoy, the principal of Wilsons, had never seen the school so busy. An air-raid shelter had been built on the lawns beside the school and its windows sandbagged. The Storeman had gathered all the weapons in the school and was cataloging them so they could be distributed. Starling (her real name was Cheryl Orr, but everyone thought of her by her spy name) and Master Brunholm, the vice principal, came and went at all hours of the day and night, trying to gather information on when an attack might come. The treaty between the Two Worlds had been broken, and only Wilsons stood between the Upper World and the Lower World, with the Ring of Five and their Cherb armies. There had been reports of Cherb raiding parties on the outskirts of the nearby town of Tarnstone.

Devoy glanced upward as a raven fluttered through the rafters of the library of the third landing, engaged in some business of its own. The ravens of Wilsons went their own way, paying no attention to human affairs. Down below, Devoy saw Danny come out of the shrubbery and cross the parade ground at the back of the school. The boy was the key to everything. He was the Fifth, the final member of the Ring. He was also possessed of extraordinary destructive power, coveted by the Ring and its allies. Devoy understood that good and evil, fidelity and treachery, waged war within the boy, and all their fates might depend on the outcome of that struggle. Danny was inching closer to the truth about his birth and upbringing, and Devoy knew that the truth might well turn him toward the Ring.

"Sometimes I think it would be better just to put a bullet in him. Then no one could make use of him." Devoy did not need to look to see that Marcus Brunholm had appeared behind him. Brunholm made a point of using secret entrances whenever possible.

"Admit it, Devoy. The only reason you don't do it is that we need his power more than the Ring does. We're in big trouble."

"What's he doing?" Devoy said. Danny had stopped to talk to his friend Dixie, but there was something wrong.

"They're up to something sneaky," Brunholm said. "I can tell."

"They're students of spying," Devoy said drily, "they're supposed to be sneaky."

19

"Yes, well," Brunholm said, "there's another matter I'd like to bring to your attention. This power of Danny's, the power of the Fifth, as they call it . . ."

Devoy turned sharply. Somehow membership of the Fifth had uncovered a mysterious power in Danny, something that welled up inside him, capable of unleashing a huge destructive force.

"What do you know?"

"I researched it in the Library of the Antiquaries . . . ," Brunholm said.

"Not like you to study, Marcus."

"I thought we might use the power in defending Wilsons."

"Ah. Continue."

"The power is a rare side effect of a union between Cherb and human—in this case, Danny's parents. The changes on a genetic level were so profound that an effect not dissimilar to nuclear fission can emerge from the very atoms of the child. A human atom bomb, in other words."

"Luckily, such unions are almost unheard of. Cherbs despise humans."

"Perhaps. But it was not always so. In the ancient days there were many such marriages. Any children these couples had were examined at birth for signs of the power, signs now lost to us."

"And if the signs were found?"

"The power was too dangerous to control. Eventually it consumes the holder, and those near to it. Indeed, in extreme cases whole towns were lost."

"Did anyone learn to control the power?"

"No one . . . Any child who showed signs of having it was left outside to die."

"But is there no cure, Marcus, no antidote?"

"In one old document I found what purported to be a cure."

"Purported to be?"

"If death can be said to be a cure," Brunholm said grimly, "for the words were 'The Fifth may be washed of his power . . .'"

"Yes?" Devoy said. "And saved?"

"I haven't finished," Brunholm said. "'The Fifth may be washed of his power only in the waters of death.'"

Far below Devoy and Brunholm, Dixie was staring at Danny with her mouth hanging open.

"You have Nala in the summerhouse?"

"I didn't know what else to do."

"If anyone sees him, they'll kill him, or worse!"

"Worse?"

"Can you imagine what Brunholm would do to him to get information on Cherb troop movements?"

"I can't think about it now, Dixie. I have to go to the Butts." The Butts were the network of underground passages beneath Wilsons. The traitorous dead of several centuries had found refuge there, and they roamed freely. Once, Danny and his friends had tried to sneak through the Butts and had encountered the dead. A cold hand had thrust a ring into Danny's shirt. The ring bore the entwined initials "S" and "G." Steff and Grace—Danny's parents.

"Whoever or whatever gave me that ring knows something about my parents. I need to find out what I can."

Danny had learned who his real parents were, but he had struck a wall of silence when he attempted to find out how they had died. Both Devoy and Brunholm had said they did not know, and the detective McGuinness, though he had tried, hadn't been able to find out anything.

"I want to go with you, Danny, but I'm afraid of the dead." Dixie shivered, and Danny remembered with a pang of guilt that he had allowed her to be taken by the dead as a servant on their last mission, although he had rescued her in the end.

"You don't have to go far into the Butts, just come as support," Danny said. "Les is mad at me over Nala, and Vandra flat refuses to go anywhere near the Butts."

"I'll go with you to the entrance, but no farther." Dixie flickered, disappeared and reappeared twenty feet away. She possessed the Quality of Indeterminate Location, and when she was nervous, she couldn't control it.

"Let's go, then."

The entrance to the Butts that Danny had chosen was a nondescript little door beside a buttress that shielded it from view. Danny picked the lock in seconds.

"Good luck, Danny," Dixie said. "I'll stay here. I promise."

"Thanks, Dixie." Danny was nervous. The dead of

22

Wilsons were, after all, the cheats and traitors of history who had proved themselves capable of any betrayal. He patted Dixie on the shoulder and plunged into the darkness.

At first the air was musty, but not unpleasantly so. But as he penetrated the maze in the foundations of the building, the air grew colder and the odor changed to a sweet smell of putrefaction, as though something were rotting in the shadows. Danny shivered. His torch caught something glistening in the dark. He shone the beam on a jelly-like mold on the ground, which heaved and writhed as though something, or someone, was trapped within.

Dark thoughts flitted through Danny's mind. He found himself thinking about his own death. He imagined a mournful procession to a graveyard at dusk, a new grave dug among ancient tombstones. . . .

"Stop it," he said firmly to himself, but the dread would not go.

Every twenty yards or so, he stopped and called out "Hello," but no answer came, save for a swarm of blow-flies that appeared out of nowhere, fat, slow-flying things that caught in his mouth and nostrils. He batted them off, trying not to think of what they might have been feeding on.

"Hello!" he called again and again, with the same result. You're going about this the wrong way, he thought. If you were one of the traitorous dead, you'd be the one who was wary of a stranger.

He stopped and turned off the torch. The blackness around him was absolute, and the silence pressed down like a weight. He fought the panic rising inside, the feeling that he would be consumed by the nothingness around him. Then, at the farthest range of his hearing, a sound . . . someone whispering. . . . There it was again. Voices, cold and far-off. Another noise—dead leaves, perhaps, or scurrying feet. Ice stole through his veins. The noises stopped, but he knew, though he could see and hear nothing, that someone or something stood very close to him in the dark. A person, but not a living one, for a living form would not be able to quiet its breathing in the absolute stillness, and whoever was beside him made no sound.

He felt that he had been standing there forever, assailed by dark thoughts and evil imaginings, waves of horror sweeping through him. Just when he thought he could take no more, a bony hand touched his arm and he felt his insides turn to water.

"What do you need from the dead?" The voice was mournful, rasping, full of terrible regret that could never be assuaged.

"Nothing. . . . I mean . . ."

"Nothing!" The voice was scornful. "What does a child know of nothing? Wait until you have walked the halls of the dead and breathed their stench and misery before you talk of nothing!"

"I'm sorry . . . ," Danny began.

"Sorry . . . sorrow . . ." It wasn't a voice any longer, but a low moan like a winter wind blowing across a moorland at night.

"The ring," Danny managed to gasp. "We were in

the Butts and someone put a ring in my pocket. A ring with initials on it . . . 'S & G' . . . Steff and Grace . . . my parents . . ."

There was a long silence; then his dead companion spoke.

"Steff and Grace. The living child comes among the dead to seek his parents. Who has heard of such a thing?"

Danny tried to ease himself away, but the bony grip tightened.

"What do the dead long for? What do they dream of when the stillness of the tomb descends? What one thing would they take from among the living to succor the endless night of death?" The words echoed in the damp stone chambers of the Butts and fell away. Silence returned. Despair gripped Danny. The silence stretched on and on.

"It's a question." The voice said abruptly.

"What?"

"It's a question. What one thing would the dead take from among the living to succor the endless night of death?"

"I don't know."

"Speak!"

"I don't know!"

"Well, for me, it would be a cup of tea," the dead voice said, "a cup of tea and maybe a plate of muffins."

"*Tea?*" Danny managed.

"With milk and sugar."

"Who *are* you?"

"Name's Hinault, James Hinault, former professional spy, and a damn good one until I got caught coming out of the judge's wards with the verdict in the Schiele case under my coat."

"Who was Schiele?"

"It doesn't matter, sport, he's been dead for a hundred years or more."

"What did they do to you—when they caught you, I mean?"

"Hanged me high, then had me drawn and quartered for good measure."

"Drawn and quartered . . . doesn't that mean . . ."

"They butchered me like a prize hog, but the Guild of Spies got hold of the body and stitched it up again. It was in the contract, and I'd paid my dues. Always did, no matter what. But never mind that. Let's go somewhere a little cozier. Talking with the living is a little frowned upon in the Butts, you might say."

"Cozier?" Danny couldn't imagine anywhere in this damp, cold underworld being cozy, but Hinault kept his grip on Danny's arm.

"Can I turn on the torch?" Danny asked.

"Keep it off for a minute," Hinault said. "You drew enough attention to yourself going through the tunnels earlier."

Danny heard the click of a lock and a hinge squeaking. He was led through the door, which closed behind him.

"Put on your torch now," Hinault said.

Danny found himself, to his surprise, in a railway carriage—a luxurious carriage with leather seats, brass fittings and faded velvet drapes where the windows had been.

"Previous owner was a railway enthusiast," Hinault

26

said. They sat down. Remembering what the dead man had said about being hanged, drawn and quartered, then stitched up, Danny turned reluctantly toward him. Hinault's face was battered, and one eye was missing. His head lolled to the side at a strange angle on a neck that was longer than it should have been. Stitches in coarse thread on his throat disappeared below his collar, and his body was lumpy and lopsided like a badly stuffed sack. Hinault stared at him with his one good eye, and Danny wondered shakily whether he would ever get out of the Butts.

"So," Hinault said, "what's this all about?" Danny took the ring from his pocket and showed it to him. "Steff and Grace Pilkington—who would have thought it?"

"Did you know them?" Danny sat forward.

"'Fraid not," Hinault said, "but I heard they were killed. You see, the dead don't have much to do with the living unless they're on their way here, when they do become of interest, if you follow."

"But . . . Steff and Grace aren't here," Danny said.

"No," Hinault said, "only the faithless end up here, those with nowhere else to go."

"Then who gave me the ring, and why?"

"Who gave it to you I can't tell, but the why might be more interesting."

"What do you mean?"

"There's a great silence around your parents' death," Hinault said. "The silence was even commented on down here."

"I know!" Danny exclaimed. "No one will tell me anything!"

"Think about it, sport. Cherbs and humans get together, marry, have children. There's a lot of folks who
would have an interest in stopping that kind of peace.
You get peace, then there's awkward questions about why
there was war in the first place, and who kept it going
and why. Take it from me, many a person has been killed
for less."

"Then why give me the ring?"

Hinault edged closer and dropped his voice.

"There are rumors of a rebel movement—the S and
Gs, they're called. Very secret, but they're trying to show
that there can be peace between Cherbs and humans. I
heard they were trying to contact you. Some say you're
not to be trusted, others say you're the last hope to lead
the Two Worlds away from war. Now. I've said enough."

"Please," Danny said, "who are these people? How do
I find them?"

But Hinault would say no more. Danny pressed him
again and again. He had let the torch fall away from
Hinault's face, and it was only when he lifted it again
that he realized his mistake: you did not pester the dead.
Hinault's face was fixed in a rictus, his one good eye red-
rimmed and staring, staring for a moment, then rolling
back into his head so that only the white was showing.
Then the mouth opened, wider than any mouth should
open. Danny had a vision of rot and putrefaction, such
things as human eye should not fall upon; then he was enveloped by a smell that was more than a smell, a hideous,
clinging fog of odor that made him retch. Last came the
sound, a screech as though the gates of hell had opened

and a legion of the damned rode out with foul war cries to destroy the earth. Gagging, choking, holding his ears, refusing to open his eyes for fear of what evil he might see, Danny reeled from the railway carriage, driven before the stench and noise, blind to all save panic.

He had no idea how long he had spent in the tunnels, when finally a voice sounded in his ears, distant but familiar.

"Danny . . . Danny!"

Somehow he followed it to the source and found the entrance he had used to enter the Butts. He pulled at the latch, then sprawled out into the fresh air, panting, his nostrils full of hideous odors, his mind assailed by visions of the dead.

"Danny . . . it's Dixie. . . . Are you all right?"

"Yes." He gulped great lungfuls of fresh air. "I think so." He shook his head, trying to rid his mind of the thoughts of the dead.

"What happened?"

"Dixie, you know how nothing is ever the way it looks in Wilsons? And when you find out what's really going on, the truth is always worse than you thought it might be?"

"I know what you mean. I think."

"Well, what if the truth *wasn't* as bad as you thought? What if there were *good* secrets?"

"Danny, what are you talking about?"

He shook his head, but his eyes were shining. The S & Gs, he thought, a secret force for good!

3

THE SKELETON OF A MESSENGER

A mile away, Fairman's taxi pulled up outside the gates to Wilsons. Agent Stone woke from his uneasy doze with a start.

"Get out!" Fairman snarled.

"Where am I?" Stone said.

"Wilsons."

"Wilsons? The school for spies? I'm actually in the Lower World?"

"I'm a taxi driver, not a tour guide. Get out."

Stone climbed out of the taxi. He was exhausted, hungry and thirsty, his body bruised and torn, but none of that counted for anything. He barely noticed the taxi pulling off. Despite everything he had been told and had read about another world, some part of Stone had resisted admitting its existence. Now here he was, standing in the Lower World! He swayed as a wave of fatigue struck him; then he started to walk into the growing dusk.

As soon as the taxi had rounded the next bend, the driver reached for the car radio.

"This is Fairman," he growled. "Your bait has been delivered."

Despite his wonder at finding himself in the Lower World, Stone was desperately tired. The avenue to Wilsons snaked and turned so that he had no idea how far he had to go, but he knew he couldn't walk much farther without rest; the temperature was falling, and in his present condition a night outside could be fatal. Then he caught a glimpse of lights through the trees, the lights of a great building flickering as the wind tossed the trees. Wilsons, it had to be.

He looked at the avenue, which appeared to be heading away from the building. He would take a shortcut through the trees! Using his last reserves of energy, Stone plunged into the forest.

Nala, the Cherb, sat on the veranda of the summerhouse. He was used to the cold stone walls of Grist, the fortress of the Lower World, and the forest around him and its noises made him nervous. He was used to disciplined Cherb life and its unforgiving laws and had never experienced freedom. He had been tracked from Grist by fellow Cherbs, who hunted him as he fled, sleeping rough and stealing food to survive, and his nerves were stretched to the breaking point. He had come to Danny not because he had absolute trust in him, but because he had nowhere else to go. And he had seen the hostility in Les the Messenger's eyes, If Nala wanted to stay alive, he had to be alert.

His eyes darted among the trees. He heard the sounds of a bird roosting and some night creature rustling in the leaves, and above those, the sound of someone plunging through the forest, panting, moving fast directly toward the summerhouse. Nala reached into his boot, took out a short knife and turned to face the threat. A man, half stumbling, half running, broke from the cover of the trees, saw the summerhouse and changed course for it. Nala shrank back into the shadows, but there was no way to avoid confrontation. The man was on the steps, one foot on the veranda. Nala stepped out of the shadows.

"A real Cherb!" Stone's face lit up in wonder. "I really am in the Lower World. "He reached out with one hand as though to touch Nala, to verify the fact that he existed. It was too much for the Cherb. He leapt out and plunged the knife into Stone. The man gasped and fell to his knees.

"Nala, is that you?" a voice whispered. Danny appeared from the shrubberies, a bag of food under his arm, and took in the scene.

"What happened?" Danny dropped the bag and darted forward. In the dusk he could just make out the features of the man lying on the ground.

"Dad!" he cried out. He spun round to Nala and saw the bloodied knife in his hand.

"What have you done? Look at him!" Danny crouched down. Nala raised the knife. It had tasted blood once that night. It could do so again. But it was not to be. A spotlight blazed in the darkness.

"Halt, or die where you stand! Put down the knife, Cherb! Now!" It was the voice of Master Brunholm.

Slowly Nala lowered the knife. Detective McGuinness stepped out from behind the spotlight and handcuffed Nala. Devoy moved into the light and knelt beside the wounded man.

"Get Jamshid and the physick," he said. "Have this man brought to the apothecary."

"I'm going with him," Danny said.

"You're coming with me," Devoy ordered. "Mr. McGuinness, escort Mr. Caulfield to my study."

"He's my . . ." Danny started to say "father" but stopped himself.

"Yes," Brunholm said, "and he's severely wounded, thanks to your stupidity in concealing a Cherb on the premises!"

McGuinness stepped forward. Danny knew that deep in his mind lay a limitless power, and that if he chose to use it, none could withstand him. Stone groaned, and blood bubbled on his lips. Danny felt all fight drain from him, replaced by despair. When McGuinness took his arm, he did not resist.

Twenty minutes later Danny stood in Devoy's study, a grim-faced McGuinness behind him. The door burst open and Devoy entered. He sat down at his desk without looking at Danny.

"Mr. Devoy," Danny said miserably, "Agent Stone . . . How . . ."

"His condition is very grave," Devoy said. "He was weak to begin with, and the wound is deep. What were you thinking of, bringing a Cherb into the heart of our defenses!"

"I didn't bring him, he came on his own."

"Perhaps," Devoy said, "but you should have informed us straightaway."

"He helped me and Dixie when we were escaping from Morne."

"So that's the Cherb you were talking about," Devoy said. "I understand a little better now."

"Do you?" Brunholm appeared from a secret entrance. "I don't. A Cherb is an evil, a blot on the face of this world to be exterminated. Even if this Nala did help you, it was only to further some end of his own."

"He was scared," Danny said.

"A rat in a trap is scared," Brunholm said, "but it's nonetheless a rat for all that."

"You put us all in danger by not telling us about the presence of this Cherb."

"In cahoots with him, I wouldn't be surprised." Brunholm sniffed.

"In light of your behavior, you are suspended from all classes and defensive activities at Wilsons," Devoy said. Danny looked at the floor miserably.

"Make sure you are available for interrogation at all times," Brunholm said. "If we can't find you on the premises, it will be evidence that you have gone to the other side."

"Can I go to see him now?" Danny asked.

"Who?"

"Agent Stone."

"Get out of here," Brunholm snapped.

Danny ran from Devoy's office to the apothecary. He met Vandra at the door. She looked grave.

"How is he?" Danny gasped.

"Not good," she said. "Jamshid is operating now. The knife pierced the main artery to the heart. He is very weak, Danny."

"I didn't mean this to happen," Danny said despairingly.

"I know you didn't."

"At least it teaches me something."

"What's that?"

"Why try to do a good thing? It always comes back to hurt you," he said bitterly.

"I hope that's not all you learn from it," Vandra said gently.

Danny sat outside the apothecary long into the night. Vandra waited with him, and was joined by Dixie and Les, who sat down silently and still would not meet Danny's eyes. As the hours stretched on, Dixie fell asleep first, followed by Les. Finally even Danny closed his eyes. Only Vandra stayed alert. And when tiredness threatened to overwhelm her, she was joined by Toxique. The serious, dark-haired boy had worked with the apothecary to make sure there was no poison in Stone's wound. He came from a long line of assassins and had an instinctive understanding of death. He looked at Vandra, and his look said much.

Danny was wakened by a gentle hand on his shoulder. He opened his eyes. It was Vandra. A solemn Jamshid stood behind her. Danny got to his feet. Jamshid motioned and he followed. They passed under the skeleton of a Messenger in flight suspended from the ceiling and went through a doorway. Toxique watched them with mournful eyes.

Stone lay alone in the infirmary. His breathing was shallow, his color dreadful. Danny stopped in the middle of the floor, but Jamshid touched him gently on the shoulder and urged him on. Danny went alone to the bed. He touched Stone's hand. The skin was cold. Danny looked back at Vandra. The tears in her eyes told him all he had to know. He touched the man's forehead, smoothing his hair back. Stone blinked once, twice, then his eyes opened. The ghost of a smile touched his lips when he saw Danny.

"Hey, Danny." His voice was barely audible. "I saw a Cherb!"

"I'm sorry." Danny's voice broke.

"Sorry? Sorry for what? You've shown me incredible things—Seraphim . . ." Stone started to cough. A thread of blood ran from the corner of his mouth. Jamshid stepped forward, but Stone waved him away.

"It is I who should be sorry. I should have spent more time with you. . . ." Stone looked suddenly agitated. He grabbed Danny's sleeve and tried to sit up.

"Agent Pearl . . . she's in trouble. She's at a government facility. You're the only one who can help. . . ."

Stone fell back on the pillow, his chest rising and falling rapidly. He lifted a finger slowly and pointed into the darkness behind Danny.

"What's that?" he said so faintly he could barely be heard. Danny followed the pointing finger.

"It's a skeleton," he said, "the skeleton of a Messenger."

"A Messenger? A real Messenger? How marvelous." A smile of wonder lit Stone's face; then he turned his head to the side and breathed no more.

"Dad?" Danny whispered, but there came no answer.

For several minutes no one moved. It was Vandra who broke the spell. She put one arm around Danny and with the other pried his hand out of Stone's grasp.

"He's gone, Danny," she said. His friends surrounded him. He felt Dixie's hand on his shoulder, the brush of Les's wings. With kind words and touches they led him away, under the shadow of the mournful skeletal Messenger. They brought him back to their dormitory, the Roosts, where his friends gathered around him until dawn touched the eastern sky. They spoke to him, but he would not reply. There was a cold light in his eyes that worried them. When they went to bed and woke again halfway through the morning, he was still sitting in front of the stove. Les put his hand on Danny's shoulder.

"You have to try to get some sleep, Danny," he said.

"It's a trap," Danny said. His eyes were cold and hard.

37

"What?"

"A trap, and Pearl's the bait."

"What do you mean?"

"I can sense it, Les. I could nearly hear the jaws of the trap shutting when Stone told me that they were holding Pearl. They want me to try to rescue her so they can get their hands on me."

"How do you know? How can you be sure?"

Danny looked into his friend's eyes.

"Because it's what I would do in their place."

Stone was buried in the old Wilsons graveyard, a place of shadows and mystery, where you felt, as Dixie said, that you weren't sure if the dead were really asleep. His grave was beside a small triumphal arch where an eternal flame burned to the Unknown Spy. Devoy made a short oration. Danny watched, dry-eyed and silent, as the coffin was lowered into the grave. He stepped forward and laid a small bunch of flowers he had gathered in the forest on the coffin. Everyone's eyes were fixed on the flowers. When Dixie finally looked around, Danny was gone.

In the small jail in the master's quarters, Nala sat alone, shackled to the wall. He had heard Brunholm talking about "the interrogation of the prisoner." Nala knew what interrogation meant in Grist, the Ring of Five fortress in Westwald, and how few survived it. All his life the Cherb had known nothing but pain and cruelty, and he expected nothing different from Wilsons. He knew that the torturer would not accept his first answer, even if it was the truth. The torture would continue to make sure that every scrap of information was forced from him. He had tried to pick the lock from the inside, but it was no use. It was a Lock of Ineluctable Closing, which was unpickable. Nala sat back in the darkness and waited for the hurt to come.

4

CRUEL ANGELS

Gabriel the Messenger was disturbed. He had heard about the Cherb killing the man from the Upper World, of course. The whole of Wilsons was in an uproar. Several of the elderly Messengers were so afraid they had hidden themselves in a wardrobe and refused to come out. But that wasn't what worried him. The Messengers had once been a noble breed, but they had become timid. Several times in the past Gabriel had managed to summon courage from them, but now, with the threat that the Lower World would invade the Upper, they appeared to have resigned themselves to slavery and even death. "That's what will happen if the Ring of Five takes over Wilsons!" Gabriel had cried, but his protests had fallen on deaf ears. He had taken it upon himself to hold daily defensive flying classes, but only Daisy, a small, feisty Messenger, had turned up. Every evening they exercised. Daisy, who had always been a good flyer, had built up impressive strength, but what good would the two of them be against a Cherb army?

"Come on, Gabriel," Daisy said, "aerial combat. I'm waiting!"

Gabriel smiled weakly. His wings stirred the air and he rose off the ground. Daisy rose as well, moving toward him slowly and menacingly; then, with astonishing speed, she shot straight up, twisting her body as she went. When she reached the top of her climb, she dived, spiraling, picking up speed. It was the Von Richtoffen dive, as Gabriel well knew, and very difficult to defend. He could see the look on Daisy's face: she wasn't going to pull out. Just as he was bracing himself to leap into a counterspiral, he caught a movement out of the corner of his eye. He hesitated a fraction of a second too long. Daisy's eyes widened in alarm, and he hit the ground with a crash that drove the breath from his body.

When he opened his eyes, Daisy was gingerly picking herself up and Danny was standing over him—a different Danny from the one he remembered. The uncertain, clever boy who had first come to Wilsons was gone. This boy looked hard-eyed and sure of himself, and there was a hint of impatience in the way he was looking down at Gabriel. Painfully Gabriel clambered to his feet as Daisy hobbled toward him.

"Danny." Gabriel held out his hand. "I'm sorry for your loss." Danny shook his hand distractedly.

"I need your help," the boy said.

41

"Of course," Gabriel said, "what can I do?" He knew that the boy was the Fifth and that he had extraordinary powers. Other Messengers often muttered that Danny was too dangerous to have around. "Nonsense," Gabriel told them, "we need to harness that power to defend ourselves. We should be helping him. I'm going to help him, anyway."

Now Gabriel had the feeling that he was going to have to live up to that promise.

"I have to get to the Upper World," Danny said, "and you're going to take me."

Gabriel stared at him. He had not flown to the Upper World for many years. He did not even know if his wings would carry him. He was too old and weak.

"Well, Gabriel?" Daisy was half smiling at him.

"I'll . . . I'll do it," Gabriel said, "if I can!" Danny nodded curtly. Daisy clapped her hands.

"I'll need you as well, Daisy," Danny said. "Here's what I want you to do."

Daisy's expression changed when Danny stood close, murmuring into her ear.

"I can't," she said, "I can't! I'll have to leave Wilsons if they find out!"

"They won't find out," Danny said. "I have a plan."

"But why?" Daisy protested.

"Because I need to. You don't have to know anything more. Are you with me?" Daisy bowed her head.

"I will help you," she said in a small voice.

"Let's go."

* * *

Nala had slept. The long pursuit had left him fatigued in body and mind. As he slept, he dreamed of Brunholm. The man was banging nails into his arms, snarling, "How many in the Cherb army? How many? How many?"

"No, stop!" Nala moaned, but the sound of the nails would not stop. Bang. Bang. Bang. Nala rolled over, holding his head, then sat up. The noise was not in his dream; it was real. They were coming for him. He squeezed into the corner of his bunk, his fists raised, then realized that the noise wasn't coming from the door but from the window. Impossible! He had looked out the window earlier. It was many floors from the ground, set into smooth rock. But still the sound went on, and as Nala stared, a pane of glass flickered and then was gone.

"Nala!" He heard a familiar voice. "Come to the window!"

Nala crept closer and peered out. Danny!

"Help me get rid of the rest of this glass. Use this." Danny handed him a rubber sucker and a glass cutter. Nala knew what to do with the sucker and cutter, but how was Danny managing to hover outside the window?

Quickly Nala worked at the glass, using the sucker to hold the pane while he cut around the edges, then carefully lifted the glass and put it on the floor of the cell. He stuck his head through the window. Danny was sitting on a male Messenger's back; a female Messenger hovered a few feet away.

"That's the last pane," Danny gasped. "Can you squeeze through, Nala?"

Nala saw the female Messenger move into position underneath the window. She looked old and frail; a gust of wind pushed her sideways and she had difficulty in getting back into position. Nala hesitated, but his dream of torture came back to him. Wriggling like an eel, he squirmed through the small opening and climbed onto the Messenger's back. She sank in the air a little, but then, with strong beats of her wings, she rose and banked left gracefully. With Danny and the other Messenger following, they drifted down through the darkness.

After a few minutes of flight, Nala was aware of trees around him. A branch brushed his face and then they were down. He slid off. They had landed back at the summerhouse.

"There isn't much time," Danny said. "I'm going on a mission in the Upper World. I need someone who can work undercover, and who can steal. I know you can do these things."

"Steal what?" Nala said.

"Not what," Danny said, "who. A person."

"Why not ask your friends?" Nala said.

"Because my only friend with a talent for stealing has wings—he stands out too much."

Nala spoke quietly. "Tell me real reason."

"What do you mean?" Danny said.

"He means there's something more to it," Gabriel cut in unexpectedly, "and you need to tell him what it is."

"All right," Danny said, turning to face Nala again,

his voice cold. "You're expendable. I can't afford to lose any more of my friends, but I can afford to lose you."

Gabriel studied Danny. He knew that the harsh words hid a world of pain and loss. But Nala merely shrugged— cruelty and mortal danger were part of a Cherb's life. He had simply wanted to know what he was getting into.

"We'll have to go at night," Danny said. "We need to have a look at the place from the air and figure out a way in."

"Then we had better start," Gabriel said, "if we want to get there before dawn. The night trade winds will carry us quickly over, but it is a long way, perhaps too far for you, my dear?" Daisy looked at him and snorted.

"Don't 'my dear' me, Gabriel. I was flying missions to the Upper World before you ever sprouted a wing feather. I can take care of myself. But I have to ask you, Danny, are you doing the right thing? The school needs you in this grim time."

"The school did without me before, they can do without me again. I've lost enough. I'm not going to lose any more."

"We've no time to waste!" Gabriel spoke urgently. "On my back, Danny!"

Danny clambered on while Nala leapt lightly onto the space between Daisy's wings.

"When we cross over, where do we go?" Gabriel's wings started to beat.

"East," Danny said, "fly due east."

Barely visible in the darkness, the two Messengers and their burdens rose into the air and turned, picking up speed as they cleared the treetops. They had just reached the edge of the forest when another stealthy shape rose into the air from a copse behind the summerhouse and set off in pursuit.

Danny could not say how he knew they were above the shadowy border country between the Two Worlds, but he sensed that the almost trackless wilderness was below him.

"What's it like?" he asked Gabriel.

"What?"

"The land below us, the border country that divides the Two Worlds?"

"Who knows?" Gabriel said. "It has the characteristics of a physical place. You can walk in it, you can drive across it, as you have done with Fairman, but there is more to it than that. Some people say it exists as much in the mind as it does on the ground."

"You mean like a dream?"

"Or a nightmare," Gabriel said. "There are those whose job it is to patrol it. A strange breed. They speak little of what they see and do there."

Gabriel fell silent and Danny looked down, trying to pierce the darkness below, a darkness composed of more than mere night. It felt timeless, as though hours and minutes did not mean the same thing there. When he traveled in Fairman's taxi across the waste, he always fell asleep, but now he stayed awake for what felt like the whole night and into the following day, and yet the darkness around him did not change, and when they reached the other side, the moon was still high in the sky, meaning that the journey could only have taken an hour or two.

Gabriel slowed and waited for Daisy, who had fallen behind. Danny could see she was struggling.

"Do you need a rest?" Gabriel asked. She shook her head. "Due east it is, then. And the wind is with us." The Messenger shaped his wings and caught an updraft. He soared into the sky. A second later, Daisy did the same.

Thirty miles away a nervous official sat hunched over a radar screen in the control tower of a small airport. The airport was closed for runway repairs. The man had every reason to be on edge. A tall, shadowy figure stooped over him, a man with a gaunt face who had to be seven feet tall. He was wearing a large rucksack on his back—or at least, that was what it looked like; he was draped in a cloak, so the man couldn't see what was making the bulge near his shoulder blades. He was accompanied by a stocky figure who wore a baseball cap low over his eyes. The tall man did not speak, but he gave off a dry, unpleasant odor.

The air traffic controller worked for a covert government agency and had been in many strange places, but this was the oddest of all, shut in a disused control tower at night with this pair who spoke only to each other, their voices harsh and guttural. They had been told to look out for two contacts that would suddenly appear in a quadrant of the sky. The man hadn't believed such a thing could happen. Flying objects did not appear just like that.

But at 3:35 a.m., two objects had appeared on the screen in front of him, two green blips moving more slowly than any aircraft he had ever known. The men behind him muttered and pointed to the radar screen, then fell silent again, intent on the green dots.

What were the objects? UFOs, perhaps? In the world of spying the man belonged to, there had recently been many strange rumors, warnings of an unidentified threat. There was unprecedented cooperation with foreign intelligence services, which had been on high alert for weeks now. The word "invasion" had been whispered, but an invasion of what, and from where? There had been sightings of winged figures, and one terrified pilot had spoken of a flight of "cruel angels" that had cut across his flight path. Could it be a form of extraterrestrial life?

The prime minister had sent messages down through senior officials, asking for calm. He spent much time closeted with a close advisor, a quiet, studious-looking man named Ambrose Longford, who was thought to have unique knowledge of the situation. The air traffic controller sighed. He certainly hoped it was true.

"Where are they going?" the squat man growled.

"I don't know," the controller said, "but on that trajectory, they'll be over Kilrootford in twenty minutes."

The man nodded in satisfaction. The controller kept his eyes on the screen. Kilrootford was a top-secret installation that did not appear on any maps. He was amazed that these two knew anything about it.

The squat man addressed him now. "Watch them. Do not let them out of your sight!"

The controller did as he was told, feeling a drop of sweat trickle between his shoulder blades. The men made it hard for him to focus. In fact, they broke his concentration to such an extent that he didn't see the single green dot moving slowly down the screen, ten miles behind the first two.

Danny had known that it would be cold at high altitude, but he was not prepared for the bone-chilling winds. His coat kept his body warm, but he had long ago ceased to feel his feet, and he was sure his ears were frostbitten. He looked back at Nala. The Cherb was wearing only a light leather jerkin, but he didn't look cold at all.

"Is it me, or is it freezing?" Danny called over Gabriel's shoulder.

"Getting colder," Gabriel said tersely. "There's trouble up ahead. He pointed toward towering clouds up ahead, their edges a menacing black. "We can't fly around or over them—too big—and even if we turned back, we couldn't outpace the storm."

"What do we do?"

"Hold on," Gabriel said grimly, "hold on!"

The wind struck first, buffeting them backward and forward. Then Danny felt a terrifying lurch of vertigo as they flew into an air column, shooting hundreds of feet upward in seconds, then plunging back down. Hail came next, huge, bruising spheres of ice striking his face and hands hard enough to break the skin. As they went deeper into the cloud mass, Danny could see lightning flashing blue in the bowels of the storm. Once, he caught a glimpse of Daisy and Nala: the female Messenger's face fixed, her wings laboring, the Cherb motionless on her back. Then cloud swept between them and the storm closed in, rain this time, hard and black, drumming down on Danny and Gabriel, updrafts buffeting them so that they barely knew which way was up, until one violent gust blew Gabriel across the sky, his wings momentarily powerless to hold them upright.

Gabriel dipped sharply and Danny found himself holding a handful of feathers. With a cry he slipped sideways and back, unable to find another handhold on the lurching Messenger beneath him. He fell backward, losing all sense of where he was. The maelstrom of the storm above and the abyss below were one and the same, and there was nothing he could do about it. As fear paralyzed him, a firm hand caught his collar and shoved him upright. He grabbed a handful of Gabriel's hair and regained his seat. Nala released Danny's collar and sat back, expressionless. Daisy, panting, and with rain streaming down her face, winked at Gabriel.

"This is fun, what?" she said as an updraft caught her wings and sent her spiraling off into the storm again. Danny thought he could hear Gabriel sigh before they too were taken wind.

Dawn was showing in the east when they finally flew clear of the storm, exhausted and bedraggled. In the distance they could see the glow of a city and, far to the north, headlights moving on a great road. Below them was an anonymous cluster of buildings that would have looked like a medium-sized factory were it not for the watchtowers, the spotlights, and the barbed-wire fencing that surrounded it.

"Kilrootford," Danny said, "that's where we're going."

"I'll bring you in from the north," Gabriel said. "There's some cover in those small hills over there."

As they glided in, Danny scanned the defenses in front of them. Two rows of barbed wire and a guardhouse at the entrance. A car pulled up. The driver showed identification; then the car was thoroughly searched.

How was Danny to get in? And once he was in, how did he get Agent Pearl out?

Gabriel glided to a halt in the middle of a copse of small trees at the top of the hill. A moment later Daisy landed. Nala got off her back and looked around suspiciously. There was an old stone building farther down the hill.

"We can use that as a base," Danny said. "Whatever happens, we'll have to wait for nightfall to get into Kilrootford."

They walked down to the building, which proved to be a locked holiday cottage. Nala had it open in seconds. The cottage was cozy, and there were tins of food in a larder. Nala curled up on a sofa and instantly fell asleep.

"You two need to rest," Danny said to the Messengers.

"No," Gabriel said, looking at the sky. "The weather has changed, there's a bit of low cloud we can use for cover. We'd better get back."

Daisy nodded agreement. "A bit of excitement is all very well, but you do start to miss your own things after a while." She looked thoughtfully down at the sleeping Nala. "He never flinched through the whole storm, used his weight to keep me balanced."

"He's a Cherb, Daisy," Gabriel said sadly. "The only reason he kept you balanced was to save his own skin."

"Perhaps," she said. Danny followed them outside.

"Thank you," he said.

"I wonder if you'll thank me at the end of this." Gabriel put a hand on Danny's shoulder. "Take care of yourself, my boy."

"And take care of the Cherb," Daisy said sternly. "Even if you are using him rather than being his friend, he has put his trust in you, and that is a bond you must not break."

Trust? A bond? Danny thought wearily as he watched them take to the air. What did those words mean? People threw them about without thinking.

He went back into the house. He sat down on a chair opposite the sleeping Nala and reached for the television remote control.

The news came on. The prime minister was onscreen. Danny's tired eyes barely registered him. Then he sat up. Directly behind the prime minister was a familiar face, looking sad and concerned. Ambrose Longford! Danny turned up the volume.

". . . there have been rumors and incidents of actual sabotage. We suspect that the terrorist group responsible is being sponsored by a foreign power, and we will regard another attack as an act of war."

The screen showed images of burning oil refineries, sinking ships, a town center devastated by bombing and people weeping. Danny's mind raced. What was Longford up to? Over images of soldiers deploying on the streets of small towns and of warships at sea, the prime minister announced a national curfew.

"Citizens are urged to report any suspicious activity. Foreign agents are active in our cities and countryside." Behind him Longford nodded sagely.

Forget about all that, Danny thought. Look after yourself and your own!

As dawn broke over the deserted airbase, the tired controller took off his headset.

"There," he said tiredly. "Two foreign objects landed close to the base and took off an hour later. That's all I can do."

Conal, the chief of the Seraphim, evil brothers to the Messengers of Wilsons, nodded to his companion. Rufus Ness, general of the Cherbs, nodded back. They were both members of the Ring of Five and needed no further communication. The Cherb's strong hands circled the controller's neck. His death was swift and silent.

"It's the boy," Conal said, "of course it is."

"Yes," Ness said, "but how do we get him to use his power in our interest?"

"It doesn't matter whose side he uses it on as long as he uses it. It doesn't matter to us which puny band of humans believes themselves to be in charge, as long as the Ring of Five are in control of them. That fool of a prime minister tells Longford everything and accepts all the advice he is given. The Fifth will give us enough to push things over the edge."

"How do we do that?" Ness said. "How do we make him use his power?"

"We are already halfway there. The agent the boy thought was his father, the bait in our trap, has been killed by a renegade Cherb, according to my sources in Wilsons. The boy doesn't have the strength to control the power of the Fifth. Sooner or later something will tip him over the edge, and his power will wreak untold devastation. Plans are already under way to connect him to a hostile foreign nation. If the Fifth will not join us, he must be made to work in other ways."

Conal and Ness went outside. A high-powered car awaited them. They drove off into the dawn light. Behind them, unheeded on the computer screen, the green lights representing the two Messengers continued on their way. The mysterious third point of light had disappeared.

Nurse Flanagan looked across the table at the sleeping man. She had bumped into him, ostensibly by accident, at a gala film screening earlier that evening. Nurse Flanagan knew how to make a man interested in her, and this man had invited her back to his lavish apartment for dinner.

It was, she had to admit, very impressive. She was well briefed. She knew that the man—the head of intelligence of a foreign power—was known for his corruption, but she hadn't realized just how wealthy he had become.

Before she could act, she'd had to wait until he had dismissed the cook, the serving staff and finally the butler. Her quarry had drunk a lot of expensive wine and had begun to flirt with her, but Nurse Flanagan had been in the spy business for a very long time, and she knew a subtle and cruel operator when she saw one. It was very late before she could open the secret compartment in her ring and tip the white powder into his wineglass. It took ten minutes for the sedative to render him unconscious. Then she set to work.

She removed a set of plastic sheets from her handbag and applied them to various surfaces around the apartment: door handles, tables, the undersides of chairs, windowsills. She left them there for a few minutes, then carefully removed them and put them back in her bag. She then took a sealed package from her pocket. She went to the freezer in the kitchen and concealed the package in the very back, under a packet of frozen shrimp.

Satisfied with her evening's work, she touched her glossy red lips with her fingertips, then placed her fingers on the man's forehead. She would never see him again. She put on her coat and pulled down her hat. The security cameras in the lobby of the building would show only a woman slipping out the front door and disappearing into the awakening city.

5

BLOCK X

Danny slept fitfully for several hours. When he awoke, Nala was sitting at the front window gazing intently at the installation below them.

"No way in," he said shortly.

"After dark . . . ," Danny began, but Nala cut across him.

"Trip wires. Body-heat sensors. Infrared detectors. We try, we die."

"We're going to try anyway," Danny said roughly. Nala shrugged again, as if to say it was all the same to him.

"I'm going to find something to eat," Danny said.

* * *

In the prime minister's country residence, Ambrose Longford drained the last of his morning coffee and brushed a few crumbs from his lap, then checked his watch. It was time. He rang a bell on the table beside him and a secretary entered: an elegant woman with bright red lipstick and a swaying walk. There was little sign of the fur-draped seductress who had left a man drugged and sleeping in his apartment the night before.

"Perhaps you would telephone Kilrootford, Nurse Flanagan," Longford said. "It's time to send them out. And tell the squad to deal with Agent Pearl in two hours' time. It's important that the timing be right."

"Of course," Nurse Flanagan said.

"I presume your night's work was satisfactory? It was well within your capabilities."

Nurse Flanagan smiled and executed a mock curtsey, then closed the doors behind her. She lifted the telephone and dialed the number carefully. There were no phones in the Lower World, so she was still getting used to the concept.

"Hello," she said into the receiver, "this is Professor Longford's office. Please activate the patrol. And begin the proceedings in relation to the prisoner. We expect them to be completed in two hours' time, but ensure that the events are synchronized."

Longford checked the coffeepot and poured the last cupful. He put another log on the fire, then leaned back in his chair, savoring the exquisite sensation of watching a plot long-hatched coming to fruition.

* * *

In the woods behind the holiday cottage the patrol moved quickly in absolute silence. They were masked, wearing full body armor and carrying silenced machine guns, although they knew that one of the targets was to be taken alive. The four men and two women moved as a single machine. They were the elite, and they did not contemplate failure.

Danny had found a few tins of sardines and some dried biscuits. It wasn't a combination he would normally go for, but he was starving, and it tasted good, if rather odd. He found a metal tray and carried some of the food in to Nala, who looked up in surprise. He obviously hadn't expected Danny to share.

Outside, the elite squad moved to the front and rear exits of the house. At a signal from the leader the kitchen window was smashed and a stun grenade hurled in. Danny whirled, half deafened by the explosion. Nala dropped to his hunkers as the house doors burst open and the room filled with yelling figures in ski masks.

"Down! Down! Down!"

Rough hands grabbed Danny and forced him to the floor. He managed to turn his head. Nala had dived behind the sofa. He stuck a foot out, tripping one of the squad and hitting him on the head with a glass lamp. The man groaned and lay still. Nala grabbed the man's gun and opened fire. Another attacker went down, bleeding from the legs. One of the squad aimed his gun.

"No!" Danny tried to squirm out from under the

man who held him, but the grip was strong. In slow motion Danny saw the trigger finger tighten. Flame blazed from the muzzle. Nala took the shot full in the chest, the power of the round lifting him off his feet and flinging him against the back wall. He fell to the ground, convulsed once and was still.

It had happened again. Everyone who got close to Danny or became his ally was taken away. He could feel the blood pounding in his ears, and a red mist formed over his eyes. The power was rising in him, the power of the Fifth, against which none could stand. He would destroy them all this time. They would never take anything from him again. The power kept rising in him. . . . He would let it build this time, to maximize the destruction.

Two of the squad dragged Danny to his feet and searched him, though he knew they would find nothing in his coat. Only Danny had access to its hidden pockets.

He was thrown back to the ground then, and cord was wrapped around his wrists and tightly cinched. A heavy boot crashed into his side, and he knew it was revenge for what Nala had done. Danny was able to crane his neck to see that the two fallen squad members were being attended to. Attend all you like, he thought. In a few minutes' time none of it will matter.

He was calm now, filled with terrible power, his decision made. He watched the soldiers move around him with huge detachment. When a small blond girl appeared beside the television, he barely blinked. The appearance was so unlikely that it was moments before the elite squad reacted and one of the women shouted and brought up her weapon. The gun blazed fire, but the blond girl was no longer there. Instead, she was standing by the door. Bullets stitched up the wall, but this time the girl appeared right beside the woman, snatching the gun and disappearing. At the same time the skylight above their heads crashed open and a winged figure burst through, grabbing two of the remaining weapons as they were raised to fire. But there was still one gun left.

Danny watched these events unfold with a certain admiration for the attackers' skill coupled with mild regret that their courage didn't really matter. It's Dixie and Les, a small voice said in his head. You can't unleash your power on them. But he'd seen Nala gunned down. He had to do something. Besides, there was still one armed squad member left. The man's hard eyes had picked out Les; his gun barrel swung upward. There was no time to disarm him. They were all too far away. . . .

From out of nowhere a small figure struck the man behind the knees. He went over backward, the gun discharging harmlessly into the ceiling. Nala! Confusion gripped Danny. Nala was dead! Momentarily he lost hold of the power seething within him. He felt as if his temples would burst as he fought to control it. With a supreme effort he restrained it, his whole body shaking, the desire to destroy receding. . . .

He had done it. They were safe from his power, at least. Then he saw that Nala had trained his gun on the squad members and his finger was tightening on the trigger.

"No!" Danny screamed the word. More than a word. Some of the residual power had remained unsuppressed and burst from his mouth as he yelled. The windows shattered. Part of the ceiling collapsed. The hardened members of the elite squad fell to the ground. Dixie flickered in and out of view. Even Nala whimpered and dropped the gun, while Les flew in an aimless circle.

Danny found that he had snapped the ties around his hands. He grabbed the battered revolver from one of his hidden pockets and trained it on the squad as they got slowly to their feet. Les, recovering quickly, hovered five feet above the ground, a gun in each hand pointed at the soldiers.

"Don't move," he said slowly. "Danny, you nearly burst my eardrums."

Without a word, Nala ran to tie up the squad members. Dixie helped.

"Where did you two come from?" Danny gasped, amazed.

"Followed you," Les said cheerfully. "I carried Dixie. I've been practicing my flying. You want to work on your navigation, Danny. Couldn't believe it when you flew into that storm. We just went around it."

"We thought you'd try to rescue your . . . the other agent who brought you up," Dixie said.

"Sometimes for a spy you're pretty transparent," Les said.

"And there are other people around here not transparent at all," Danny said. "Nala, I saw them shoot you in the chest!"

Nala reached inside his jerkin and brought out the steel tray that Danny had given him with food on it. "When I hear them come in, I do this," the Cherb explained. Danny looked at the tray. It was pocked with bullet marks, but none had penetrated.

"What are we going to do with this lot?" Dixie said.

"Bullet here," Nala said, pointing to the back of his neck.

"Cut it out, Nala," Danny said. "First of all, Dixie and Les, you have to go back. This is not your fight. You're needed at Wilsons."

"Forget about it, Danny, that's not going to happen. We're here for good."

"I've lost too . . . too many people."

"Think about it," Dixie said, serious for once. "You reckon it's any less dangerous in Wilsons? If and when the Cherbs invade, the place is finished."

"I'm betting that whatever happens in the end, you'll be involved with it," Les added. "Besides, things happen when you're around. This is what I think. . . . You were lured here to a trap. They let Stone go—because I can't see any other way he got out of that place. He was the bait. And the trap would have worked if we hadn't helped. You need us, Danny."

Danny looked at his friends, a plan forming in his mind.

"Okay," he said, "but here's what we have to do. They were expecting two prisoners, so that's what we'll give them. Dixie, come here."

* * *

Pearl lay awake in the darkness. The men had left her alone for two days now. Her body was racked with pain and sleep was difficult. She drifted in and out of consciousness. Sometimes a dream brought her back to the time when Danny was small. She would remember bathing him, reading him stories and chatting when he came home from school, and would smile in her sleep. But waking always brought pain and fear. The men would come again.

And indeed her cell door did clang open that morning. Two men entered and she shrank against the wall. It had always been two men in the days of torture. But this time they laughed at her feeble protests. They made her stand against the wall and measured her. Then they weighed her on a portable scale. Finally they put a tape around her neck, recording the results carefully in a notebook. When they went away, she lay down again. She had no illusions about the place she was in. She would never see the sun again, but she longed to see Danny's face one more time. She tried to find a comfortable space for her broken body in the hope that sleep would bring perhaps one more sweet memory.

At Wilsons Academy for the Devious Arts, Master Brunholm yelled into Vandra's face.

"You will tell what you know, or I'll bring that so-called assassin friend of yours in and get it out of him."

"He doesn't know anything," Vandra said.

"A few days locked in the Butts and we'll soon find out if you're telling the truth! Where are they?"

"I told you a thousand times, I don't know!"

"Has Danny gone over to the other side?"

"Leave her alone, Marcus," Devoy said. "What's done is done. They are gone. The physick had nothing to do with it." Brunholm made a gesture of disgust and Vandra took it as a dismissal, almost running from the room.

"I nearly had her admitting her guilt," Brunholm said angrily.

"Forget about it. We must think about what is going on. With the Treaty Stone broken, I had expected a Cherb invasion. But nothing has happened. Are the Ring of Five up to something else?"

"We need to send someone to Grist to find out what's happening," Brunholm said, "but who do we have who we can trust?"

"The student body is weak, and there are many we can't trust. Starling's cover was blown in Grist. I suspect we would be sending her to her doom."

"Then it must be the physick."

"She may be needed here."

"If the Cherbs invade here, there will be no need of a healer. We will all be dead."

"She can't be sent alone."

"Then Toxique must be sent with her."

Brunholm grimaced. "He's not fit for undercover work. He jumps at shadows. He'd scream if a mouse ran over his toe."

"But he also has the gift of anticipation. He knows when things are going to happen."

"Bah, we're clutching at straws here."

"Straws are all we have, Marcus."

Devoy went to the window and stared west as though he could penetrate the clouds that lay between Wilsons and the great Cherb fortress of Grist.

"Halt! Who goes there?" The sentry was taking no chances. Kilrootford had been on the highest state of alert for weeks now. They were all jumpy and on edge. The escape hadn't helped matters. Heads had rolled in the upper division. The other prisoner's security had been doubled. The sentry had seen her when they'd brought her in. She was a sad blond lady.

"Nice-looking," he'd said to one of his colleagues.

"She won't be by the time they've finished with her," the other man said with an unpleasant laugh.

"Outland patrol," came the reply now. The sentry lowered his rifle a little, but a different kind of tension crept in. He had been told to expect a patrol, but they were early. They weren't due to pass the gates for another thirty minutes. The elite squad were the best, it was fair to say, but they were arrogant and aloof, and he didn't like dealing with them.

He could see them clearly now, walking in the dusk. There were four figures. Two were prisoners—a bedraggled blond girl and a skinny boy being prodded along at rifle point by two ski-masked squad members. Then the sentry's mouth fell open. The thin boy had something growing from his shoulders, a feathery mass. . . . No, they couldn't be. He rubbed his eyes. The boy definitely had wings. Proper curving wings rising proud of his shoulders.

The sentry had read accounts of winged figures being spotted, but like most people he had dismissed them as being as probable as crop circles or alien abductions. Now one of these winged figures was trudging down the road toward him.

"What you got?" He directed his question at one of the ski-masked figures, trying to sound nonchalant.

"Got a report of intruders in the south quadrant," one of the figures replied. "Found this freak and the girl when we got there. We need to get them straight to the lab."

"Can't let you do that." The sentry's voice was nervous. "Orders. I was told you'd be coming in with one or two prisoners but that I wasn't to let you in until eight o'clock, and then I was to direct you to block X."

"Whose orders?"

"Direct from the prime minister's office. Longford himself."

"This won't wait."

"It will have to."

Under the ski mask Danny was puzzled. He presumed that the sentry was expecting the real elite squad (who were now tied up in the holiday cottage) to bring in two prisoners—Danny and Nala—but why was the timing so precise? The only answer was that something was due to happen when they were finally permitted into the complex. He knew it wouldn't be anything good, and the only way to thwart it would be to get in *ahead* of time.

"We have to go in," he said. The sentry gripped his rifle.

"Orders . . . ," he began. He never finished the sentence. In a few minutes he was trussed up tight, gagged and hidden in a corner of the sentry box.

In block X the door to Pearl's cell opened. She was hauled to her feet and her arms were pinned behind her back.

"Where are you taking me?" she said, but there was no reply. Just before they got to the door a black mask was put over her eyes. Blindfolded and tied, she was frog-marched along, only odors reaching her behind the mask, and they were odors that had become familiar to her since she had been brought to this place. Sweat, blood, fear, loneliness.

"Where are you taking me?" she asked again. For her pains she received an open-handed slap to the side of her face that made her reel in pain. She got the message. No more questions.

Danny and Nala kept their ski masks on, although Les had made them lower their rifles.

"I don't want that Cherb pointing anything at me," he said. If Nala was offended, he didn't show it.

"I don't understand it," Dixie said nervously. "There should be more security around. "Even at the gate, there was only one sentry."

It was true. They were walking through the complex with ease. No one challenged them. In fact, no one was there to challenge them. They were the only people on the neat paths leading from one nondescript building to another. Dixie tried to peer through windows, but the ones that didn't give onto dormitories or canteens were frosted glass.

"I don't like it," Les said. The sinister air of the deserted camp only increased as they went through unlocked gates channeling them toward a large, windowless building at the farthest reaches of the camp.

"Sanitize," Nala growled from under his ski mask.

"What?"

"They sanitize camp."

"What, like a cleaning thing?" Dixie looked puzzled.

"No," Danny said, "we learned about it with Brunholm. It's where one side withdraws everyone from a location. It's to give a team like us a clean run in without anybody challenging them."

"Why would they do that?"

"Because something nasty is waiting for them when they get there," Les said grimly.

"We have an advantage, though," Danny said. "They're not expecting us for another thirty minutes."

*　*　*

Pearl could tell from the sounds around her that she was in a large, echoing room. She was shoved toward the center of it. She banged her shins off a step.

"Up!" She climbed what felt like rough wooden steps and found herself standing on a creaking floor.

"You're early." Another man's voice joined the ones she had already heard. A shiver ran down her spine. There was an inhuman coldness to the tone.

"No matter. Prepare her." Pearl was puzzled as something was placed on her shoulders, a large necklace or cowl of some kind. Hands worked at her nape and she felt a tightness around her neck, constricting her breathing. Her legs weakened and a whimper escaped. She knew where she was now.

It was one of the pleasanter parts of the day in the Upper World, Longford thought. The hour when people had drinks in the drawing room—preferably before a roaring log fire—preparatory to going in for dinner. He looked at his watch. Perhaps twenty minutes before the call that would throw the informal dinner session with the government into consternation. He sipped his whiskey and soda, then looked up with a pleasant smile as the prime minister entered the room.

"This is it," Les said. "Block X." He tried the door. It wasn't locked. He looked nervously at the others, then opened the door and walked into a well-lit hall that looked like the foyer of a clinic.

"Smells like a hospital," Dixie said.

"I've got a feeling this isn't a hospital," Les said in a hoarse whisper.

"Search the place quick," Danny said. "Check that security camera, Dixie."

"Check the what?"

"Never mind," Danny said, frowning when he realized that the surveillance camera had been unplugged.

"What's going on?" Les said.

"They can use those things to watch us," Danny said.

"They can?"

"Yes, and record. The only thing is that others can break into the loop and watch as well. The camera's unplugged. They're making sure that whatever happens here isn't witnessed by anyone else."

"This is worse than I thought," Dixie said. They looked around.

"Whatever it is," Danny found himself whispering, "there's a lot more at stake than just one life."

"Yes, but we're responsible for that life, so let's go," Les said, and they set off down the main corridor, moving fast, acting as a team, checking rooms as they went. The first few rooms were full of ordinary-looking electrical and measuring equipment, but Les drew in a sharp breath as they came to a row of cells. The first door was open. There was a bed in the middle of the floor with manacles on it. There were thumbscrews and electric shock wands on a rack on the walls, and rubber hoses and

70

pliers on a table. They moved on to the next cell and the next. Each was the same. When they came to the last one, Danny looked down at the table. Entwined in the chains at one end were several blond hairs.

Danny felt the power rise in him again, an angry wave of terrifying strength. He forced his mind to remain cool and clear.

"If you want to rescue her, you have to stay in control," Dixie said urgently. Danny turned and ran from the room. The others followed. The corridor widened. They heard voices from behind double doors at the end.

Longford pushed his soup bowl away and turned toward the foreign minister, a red-faced man with a mustache.

"Do you not agree with me, Longford?" the foreign minister asked. "The country is riddled with terrorist cells. If we allow them to infiltrate us any further, we are doomed. We must strike back, and strike hard!"

"I appreciate your point, but we must be moderate," Longford said smoothly. "We cannot allow our enemies to dictate what we do. And we cannot be sure of their intentions. Of course, if there was a major incident, then that would change my view." He slid back his cuff and looked at his watch. Only minutes remained.

Danny hit the double doors at a run. They crashed open. The group around the structure at the center of the room whirled around. Danny skidded to a halt, staring in horror. The wooden structure was topped with a scaffold. A hemp rope hung from a wooden crossbar, and a slight figure stood underneath, a noose tight about its neck. As everyone turned toward the noise, the figure also moved, and Danny saw golden hair stir.

"Mum!" he cried out. Pearl, with a supreme effort, shook her head so violently that the blindfold slipped down. Her blue eyes met Danny's and locked on them, and in that moment all was understood, all was forgiven. The masked man standing beside Pearl grasped the lever that would trigger the trapdoor, sending Pearl hurtling into oblivion.

"No!" Danny cried as the power rose in him like a great wave. With a noise like the gates of hell being wrenched open, the lever crashed back.

6

AN ARROW POINTING NORTH

Longford looked at his watch again. Ten minutes had elapsed. He knew it might take a while for information to reach the prime minister's residence, but he was impatient. Others were poised to move into place once he had received the news.

"Excuse me," he murmured, rising from the table. The foreign minister was still talking. The man was an idiot, Longford thought, but he wouldn't be around for long. Nurse Flanagan would make a much better foreign minister.

Longford crossed the paneled hall outside the dining room and went into Nurse Flanagan's office. He raised his eyebrows. She shook her head. No news.

"Send Conal in for an aerial reconnaissance," he said,

"Danny will have broken. I know the boy's mind. It is not strong enough to contain the power."

Vandra and Toxique stood outside the library of the third landing at Wilsons. They had been summoned to a meeting with Devoy.

"Probably your dad back to make sure you've killed again," jeered Exspectre, a small, pale boy. Toxique's assassin family had their doubts about his willingness to follow the family trade.

"Don't be stupid, Exspectre," said Smyck, the ringleader of the group opposed to Danny. "Toxique couldn't even squash an ant without crying about it."

"Never mind them," Vandra said to Toxique, "we'd better go."

Toxique couldn't stop jumping from foot to foot and asking Vandra if she knew what they were wanted for.

"Please stop it, Toxique," she begged, "you'll find out soon enough. Toxique. Toxique! What is it?"

The boy had fallen to the ground, holding his head and moaning. Vandra dropped to her knees beside him.

"Talk to me!" she begged. "What's wrong?"

"Something . . . something terrible is going to happen. . . ."

"Where?"

"I don't know. Not here. Danny . . ." Toxique cried out as pain gripped him.

* * *

To Les it felt like an hour passed between the moment the executioner pulled the lever and the terrible crash of the trapdoor opening. Pearl plunged downward with a despairing wail, echoed by a terrible cry from Danny. Les turned away. Only Nala kept his eyes fixed on the scaffold. The small group of soldiers at the base of the structure seemed at a loss. In the distance a siren sounded. Danny turned to Les with tears in his eyes.

"They're all gone," he said. "I can't hold the power in. Run, Les! Take Dixie and Nala."

"I'm not running," Les said.

"Then I can't help you," Danny said calmly. A volcano was growing inside him, grief and power mingling in an all-consuming rage. Nala stood to the side, ignored. Only he had stayed alert, staring, listening.

"Where's Dixie?" Les swung around suddenly. "She was here a moment ago!"

Nala sprang forward, running toward the base of the scaffold. A black curtain, erected for the purpose of concealing the hanging body within, barred his way. He plunged through it.

"What on earth is he doing?" Les said, glancing nervously at Danny. Suddenly the curtain fell aside and they could see the scene within. Dixie was desperately supporting Pearl's legs, stopping the noose from doing its foul work. Nala had grabbed the woman's legs at the other side.

"Stop, Danny!" Dixie cried. "Stop whatever you're doing and help us!"

Les reacted first. Dixie was staggering, and Nala

wasn't tall enough to get a proper grip. If Dixie fell, the rope would snap Pearl's neck. Already Pearl was gasping for breath.

Danny bent his head to concentrate. He knew that the power would tear him apart if he did not master it. Now . . . now . . . the fractions of seconds felt like hours, for the power of the Fifth distorted time itself. It was too much. He could hold it for seconds, minutes perhaps, but he could not put it back.

He lifted his head and took in the situation under the scaffold with a glance. That, at least, he could help. In one swift movement he took the Knife of Implacable Intention from his inside pocket and threw it. The knife did exactly as its owner intended it to do: just as Dixie's knees buckled, it flashed in front of Pearl's face, severing the rope, and she fell, sobbing, to the floor.

The soldiers went for their guns, but Danny unleashed a fragment of the power welling within him. The men tumbled to the floor, the gallows itself swayed, and the executioner fell to the ground with a sickening crunch.

"Get out of here now!" Danny yelled. "I can't control it!" The soldiers grabbed the executioner and bolted for a trapdoor leading to a tunnel. Before they could react, the trapdoor slammed shut, locked from the inside. Danny's mother looked at him groggily. He saw her wounds, her eyes swollen and bruised. The power raged within him. He took Pearl in his arms.

"Outside!" The others followed him as he raced out of the building, giving orders as he went. "Dixie, disap-

76

pear and reappear outside the wire. Les, can you carry my . . . Agent Pearl?"

Les put his arms around Pearl's waist and lifted her.

"She weighs less than Dixie," he said quietly.

"Wait," Danny said, "take Nala first."

"I stay with you."

"No," Danny said. "You'll die. Les, you must lift him out." Les looked at the Cherb in disgust.

"Please," Danny begged. "He saved Pearl. She would have died."

With a disgusted look on his face Les rose, grabbed Nala by the shoulders and hauled him into the air. Nala didn't struggle.

"I wait for you," he said quietly. Les flew back over the fences, Nala dangling beneath him. Danny writhed in pain.

"Go, Dixie!" She started to protest, but his expression frightened her. "Please," he moaned. Dixie hesitated, then disappeared.

Danny knelt and took Pearl's hand. She turned her head. He could see the glint of blue through her swollen eyelids.

"What's happening to you?" she whispered.

"Talk to me," he said, "tell me what I was like when I was small."

"When you were small? You remember the time you made a race car out of the old bath in the garden? I found you with a saucepan on your head. You were convinced you'd driven to the North Pole."

"Keep talking," Danny pleaded. Pearl spoke of his childhood, of baths and bedtimes, of toys and teddy bears, until the moment when Les plucked her gently from the ground and took off over the barbed-wire fences of the camp. When Danny saw that they had reached a safe distance, he bowed his head, weariness overtaking him. He no longer had to resist.

Ten miles away, Conal, flying hard, saw a blue flash and heard a boom rolling across the hills. He smiled grimly. The first part of Longford's plan had come to fruition.

Two hours later, helicopters hovered over the base site, spotlights focused on the desolation below. No buildings had been left standing. The fence posts that once held barbed wire were charred sticks. Teams of heavily armed special forces combed the wreckage. Firemen directed their hoses onto smoldering rubbish. It would have been impossible to keep it quiet: the force of the blast had shattered windows for miles around. Television news helicopters replaced the military choppers over the site as the air force began to focus its attention on the countryside and woods around the base.

Silent residents stood in clusters in nearby towns and villages. There had been rumors of a possible terrorist attack, but they had never thought it would come to their quiet backwater. None of them had any idea what the installation had been used for, or what and whom had been carried by the trucks that drove through at night. They stayed outside until their radios and televisions told them that there might be one or more dangerous fugitives in the area; then they went into their houses, locked their doors and waited for dawn.

High in the hills above the wreckage, Dixie and Les lay on their stomachs, looking down.

"What have you done, Danny?" Dixie said.

"He can't have survived," Les said, glancing back at a semiconscious Pearl. In a nightmare flight from the installation, they had half dragged, half carried her this far. She knew little about what had happened; she was tormented in mind and body.

"Of course he survived!" Dixie said fiercely. "But what are we going to do?"

"The only place Pearl will be safe is Wilsons," Les said. "I could fly back and get help, but I don't know which way to go. What's that damn Cherb doing?"

Nala had tumbled a pile of logs onto the ground and was arranging them in a triangular structure.

"Shelter," he said.

"What's that?" Dixie asked. Something fluttered across the clearing behind them.

"I don't know . . . ," Les answered. With a suddenness that made them both jump, a raven alighted in front of them. It did a strange little dance up and down, then flew off a few yards, looking back expectantly.

"It wants you to follow," Dixie said. The raven did an impatient jig.

"Yes, but where?" Les said.

79

"Wilsons?"

"We can't be sure." The raven looked at them in exasperation as Dixie thought. It came back toward them, picked up a mouthful of twigs and with incredible speed laid out a "W" on the ground, with an arrow pointing north.

Behind them, Nala had started laying boughs of pine across the logs.

"We'll wait here for you," Dixie said. Pearl moaned as if at the memory of some recent pain. "I wish Vandra was here. Hurry, Les!"

Les hesitated, but the raven rose off the ground, fluttering its wings in his face.

"All right, all right, I'm coming," he said. "I'll bring back enough Messengers to get you and Pearl and . . . the Cherb, I suppose."

"What about Danny?"

"If Danny is still alive, he'll go his own way now," Les said. "He's a danger to himself and everyone around him." He turned to Nala.

"Here, you—make sure nothing happens to them. If it does I'll hold you personally responsible."

With that Les took off. The raven flew in front of him, then sped up, flying fast and true between the tree trunks, heading for the open sky. With a wave to Dixie, Les followed.

A hundred miles away a group of grim-faced policemen gathered in a back street. At a signal from their leader they moved out into the open. Half of them went to the back entrance of an exclusive apartment block, half to the front.

The intelligence chief had just settled himself on his satin sheets and turned out the light when a mighty crash shocked him awake. He grabbed the handle of the bedside cabinet, where he kept a Magnum revolver, but before he could open it, men's hands had tumbled him onto the floor, a gun barrel pressing between his eyes.

The men knew exactly what they were looking for. One of them went straight to the freezer in the kitchen, reached into the back of it and pulled out a sheaf of documents in a plastic bag. In the living room white-overalled technicians unpacked their instruments of detection. They glanced up as Nurse Flanagan, looking radiant, stepped over the threshold. The freezer package was handed to her. She went to the hall table, picked up the telephone and dialed carefully, still slightly wary of the instrument.

"Hello? Ambrose?"

In the backseat of a black limousine, Longford received her news with pleasure. He replaced the receiver. The great web he had spun was gathering in its prey. The phone rang again. A clipped military voice informed him that an unidentified flying object had been detected in the area of the destroyed Kilrootford military installation.

"Scramble air cover," Longford said. "Shoot it down."

Now it was his turn to make a call. He dialed a

number. In the intelligence chief's apartment one of the crime-scene technicians answered his mobile. He nodded, then went to one of the other technicians, who were lifting fingerprints from every available surface. The man stopped what he was doing, walked to the hall telephone and began to brush fingerprint powder on it.

7

SEEK AND DESTROY

Toxique had gotten over his strange mood, and when Vandra asked him what had happened, he muttered that it was all over now anyway and it didn't matter. By the time they were summoned into the library of the third landing, she had pushed it to the back of her mind. Devoy and Brunholm were waiting for them.

Devoy motioned for them to sit.

"In the great days of Wilsons we would have the cream of adult spies to call upon," he began, "but alas, those days are long over. Yet the danger is graver than ever. We have no armies to oppose the might of the Cherbs. We have only our wits."

"We have to know their deployments!" Brunholm said. "We are deaf and blind. There could be whole divisions on standby waiting to invade. The Ring has stopped all shipping traffic between Westwald and Tarnstone. Our best agent, Starling, has been unmasked. Wilsons must get someone into Westwald."

"You mean me and Vandra?" Toxique said.

"Yes, of course," Brunholm snapped. "There isn't anyone else."

"Well, that's a vote of confidence if ever I heard one," Vandra said drily. Her thoughts were with Danny. What would he do now? What would he say? She knew that this mission in Westwald was fraught with danger, but it was especially dangerous for her and Toxique. Vandra did not have the skills the others had, nor did she have the capacity to lie so essential to a spy. And Toxique . . . as a spy he was a positive liability.

She made up her mind. She would go alone. The second she made her decision, a raven who had been sitting unseen in the rafters began a raucous cawing.

"What the devil . . . ?" Brunholm said. But Vandra studied the raven closely. It hopped down to the top of a bookcase and its black eyes met hers.

What should I do? she thought. Should I take Toxique? In reply the raven flew back to the rafters. A second later a white glob dropped from above and landed right on top of Toxique's head.

"Ugh!" Toxique took out a handkerchief and wiped his head as Brunholm looked on with malicious amusement.

"We'll go," Vandra said. For better or worse, the raven had indicated that Toxique should go with her.

"Splendid," Devoy said. "There's no time to waste."

* * *

Danny skirted the back gardens of the little village. He was weak, his limbs shaking. All he wanted to do was lie down and sleep, but he knew he had to get away from the ruins of Kilrootford. The destructive power that had poured through him had been appalling. He had seen the soldiers guarding Pearl run away, but he had no way of knowing if there had been anyone else in the buildings before the terrible fury of the Fifth had blown through the place like a burning wind, leaving nothing standing— except, of course, the source of the destruction: Danny himself.

When he came to and saw the flattened base and the felled trees, he felt sick. It looked like the old pictures of Hiroshima or Nagasaki after the atom bomb had been dropped on them. He'd started to run, half blinded by smoke from the smoldering wreckage, his breath coming in great racking shudders.

He had no idea how long or how far he had run before he tripped on a stone and fell face-first into an icy stream. He lay there, barely gathering the strength to turn his head away from the water. He could hear helicopters over-head, circling, and he knew they were searching for him. He staggered to his feet. He needed to sleep, but first he had to find cover.

Keeping under the trees so the helicopters wouldn't see him, Danny made for distant lights. He found himself passing houses in the suburbs. There was a warm teatime glow to the lit windows, and he imagined people his own age inside, watching TV, doing homework, playing games on the computer. It made him feel unutterably lonely, and he found himself creeping closer and closer to the houses, until in the end he was under a living room window. He lifted his head carefully. The family—mother, father, two girls and a boy—was gathered around the television.

Danny's stomach lurched. The images on the screen were of Kilrootford. A somber-looking anchorman came on. At first Danny couldn't hear what the man was saying, but then the mother turned the volume up. In a few seconds, Danny wished she hadn't, for he found himself looking at his own face on the screen.

". . . police are seeking terrorism suspect Danny Caulfield. Caulfield is wanted for questioning regarding the outrage. The public are warned not to approach him. He is known to be extremely dangerous."

They've got that right, Danny thought; then he stared at the television in puzzlement.

"A foreign spy known to be closely associated with Caulfield has been arrested and held for questioning. The man is a senior representative of a foreign power whose president has referred to the matter as an act of war.

"The prime minister, however, has said that the man's apartment contained multiple fingerprints belonging to Danny Caulfield, as well as documents linking the conspirators."

Danny saw footage of a handcuffed man being led from an apartment block. He had never seen the man before in his life, he was sure. But he recognized the sweeping nature of the conspiracy against him, the dramatic scope of it. Only one man had the ambition and cunning to lead such a conspiracy: Longford. Danny had to get to him and put a stop to his schemes.

Stop him and replace him, a cold little voice whispered in his mind.

Stop it! Danny thought, shaking his head.

Another helicopter crossed the sky. He shivered. It was getting cold. In the distance he heard a police siren and knew he had to get under cover. He continued along the back of the houses. Dogs were barking. He spotted a coal shed, so he pulled the door open and crept inside. An old quilt lay on the floor. Danny wrapped it around himself and lay down. He was utterly drained. Where were his friends, he wondered, and had they survived?

You don't need them, the cold little voice said. *You don't need them.*

Danny was too tired to fight voices in his head. He fell into a fitful sleep.

If he had but known it, Les was very close to Danny— about five hundred feet above his head. The raven flew fast and was hard to see in the dark. Les's wings ached as he fought to keep up. The night was clear and Les was glad of it, knowing nothing of radar, nor of the fighter jets that had been scrambled to intercept the lone object flying slowly away from the mayhem at Kilrootford. The raven ahead of him did not slow but allowed a thermal to carry it upward. Les rode the thermal in turn, allowing it to carry him a thousand feet upward. He had never flown at this altitude before, and he looked in awe as he crossed great canyons between the night clouds, the full moon casting mile-long shadows on the ground far below. Lost in the majesty of the night, Les forgot all save for the beat of his wings and the night currents that bore him.

Half a mile behind, four F-16 jets flew in formation while the squadron leader confirmed his orders. His headset crackled.

"Order confirmed. Seek and destroy."

"Is there an option to engage and force the unidentified craft to land?"

"Negative. Seek and destroy. Be aware that the target will have no heat trace. Heat-seeking ordnance is useless. Engage with gunfire from close range."

"Roger. Alpha One, take the lead."

The F-16 on the port side of the flight peeled off. The pilot armed the twin Gatlings slung under each wing. The target was moving so slowly, it would be like firing at a stationary enemy on the ground. But he had been told to take no chances. To approach from ahead, using the moonlight for cover. At briefing they had been told that the target had unknown capability. That it was to be "terminated with extreme prejudice."

As Les flew through the cloud canyons, he became aware of a distant whistling noise, something coming up fast behind him, darkness on the wing. His own wings beat as they had never beaten. Ahead of him the raven flew on without looking back. Les remembered what had been said at Wilsons: *The ravens have their own purposes.* The noise behind him grew louder. Without looking around he knew that death lurked somewhere behind him. There was a cloud a few hundred meters in front of him. If he could make it that far, the cloud might hide him. In front of him the raven flew at the same steady speed. If the fate of the young Messenger behind him was of concern, he did not show it.

Suddenly, Les realized that the cloud was drifting away from him. He would not make it. The sound behind him was deafening now. He gave himself up to the darkness.

Ten miles away, the fighter squadron kept station. The squadron leader was a stickler for discipline, and the pilots knew the consequences of getting out of formation. The seconds ticked by. The squadron leader's headset crackled.

"Confirm acquisition and destruction of target."

"Roger. Please await advisement."

The squadron leader switched channels.

"Alpha One, status of mission?" There was a long pause. The squadron leader was about to snap a repeat query into his face mike when the reply came. Alpha One sounded puzzled.

"Must be some kind of false reading, sir."

"What do you mean?"

"Well, there's no target, sir."

"There must be something. I can see it on the radar in front of me."

"Yes, sir, there is something—a large flock of birds, but nothing else."

"Birds?"

"Yes, sir. Look like ravens or something. Odd to see them flying at night."

"Roger, Alpha One. Break off contact. I'll report back."

The F-16 banked and turned away from the flock of birds. Through the wall of feathers around him, Les heard the roar of its jet engine. The ravens had formed a perfect flying cocoon around him, concealing him from view. Les didn't know what the danger was, but he was glad of the shelter. What kind of place was the Upper World, he thought, where death could seek you in the sky at night?

There was a single caw, and at that signal the ravens broke away. Within a minute they were a distant shadow. Les, still feeling vulnerable, was glad to see the dark earth below.

As the limousine swept through darkened streets, Longford listened to the wing commander's report with eyes narrowed.

"Birds?" Longford's tone was icy. "What kind of birds?"

"I'm not sure, sir." The wing commander sounded nervous. There was a muffled consultation on the other end of the line.

"The pilots believe they were ravens, sir."

"Ravens?" Langford's voice was low and dangerous. "Did the pilot not consider that the ravens might have been concealing something?"

"No, sir," the wing commander said with a nervous laugh, "what raven would be able to keep up with a flying aircraft? How could they have concealed something, unless it was another bird or, er . . . something else. . . ."

"Relaunch the aircraft!" Longford ordered. "Fire into the birds, destroy them and whatever they are hiding! And next time, if there is a next time for you, complete your mission exactly as you are told."

"Yes, sir!" His palms damp, the wing commander replaced the phone and turned to the radar operator.

"Status report on target!" he snapped.

"It's gone, sir."

"Gone?"

"It just disappeared off the radar. One minute it was there, next it was gone."

Devoy had trained his face never to change expression, but sometimes it was difficult. Now that the borders were open, the Treaty gone, it was vitally important that the Messengers resume their former function as couriers between the Two Worlds. But most of them had allowed themselves to fall into comfortable ways, despising the very flight that had distinguished them in the past. Devoy had been heckled when he addressed them.

"Deliver messages? I never heard such a thing! What does he think we are? Who's going to pay for it, that's what I want to know?"

He ached to remind them that once, in the recent past, they had flown to the defense of Wilsons, but they had erased that disgraceful episode from their memory. The Seraphim, Devoy knew, showed no such qualms. Almost nightly he could sense them above Wilsons, wheeling in the wind, probing the school for weaknesses or flying to perform some foul mission in the Upper World. Depressed, he left the Messengers squabbling among themselves. He knew he could rely on Gabriel and Daisy, but that wasn't enough. They had just returned from one dangerous mission and were about to embark on another that night, bringing Toxique and Vandra across the sound to Grist.

Devoy made his way toward the Gallery of Whispers. If you whispered a question at one end of the gallery, an answer would be whispered to you from the other. But you never got a straight answer from the gallery. You had to work out the meaning.

The gallery was dark and quiet, surrounded by marble pillars reaching up to shadows above.

"Where is Danny?" Devoy spoke against the wall. He waited for his voice to resolve itself into whispers, circling the pillars and carved alcoves of the gallery. The answer when it came was not in a form Devoy had ever experienced. There was a rustle, and he turned expectantly. A raven flew fast and hard at him from the far end of the gallery, swift and brutal as a thrown stone, claws raised toward Devoy's eyes. Only at the last minute did Devoy manage to cover his face with his hands. The raven's claws tore at him, and he felt blood spurt from the backs of his hands. Without hesitation, the raven shot up and out through a broken pane in an elaborate stained-glass window showing the night sky.

"What . . . ," Devoy murmured, studying his torn hands, "what is your answer?"

"The raven attacked your eyes," a quiet voice said from the shadows, "then it flew into a window depicting the night sky. Perhaps you should use your eyes to look at the night sky."

The school detective, McGuinness, stepped forward.

"Here." He took two field dressings from his pocket and quickly wrapped them around the wounds on Devoy's hands.

"Thank you," Devoy said. "Shall we go onto the roof?"

It was a clear, cold night. It was always windy on the roofs of the school. Tonight an east wind swept down toward the sound, the lights of Tarnstone and the far-off glow of the enemy stronghold of Westwald, dominated by its fortress, the Grist.

"Nights like this are invigorating," Devoy said with satisfaction. "They clear the mind."

"I hear you had a difficult time with the Messengers," McGuinness said. "Don't be too discouraged. They are difficult to awaken, but when they do wake . . . well, you have to remember that they are born of the same stock as the Seraphim. And speaking of Messengers, look!"

Devoy followed McGuinness's outstretched arm. A

solitary raven arrowed across the night sky, followed by a winged human, flying erratically.

"Knutt!" Devoy called out. "Down here, boy!" At first it seemed as if Les had not heard; then he lurched sideways and plummeted toward the two men. Les struck a roof peak hard, lost control and rolled down the slope, bits of slate and roof creating an avalanche in front of him.

"Look out!" McGuinness thrust Devoy out of the way. Les slid past them, toward the low, crumbling parapet at the front of the building. McGuinness could see that the boy's wings were hopelessly tangled. He dived full length and caught Les just before he went over the edge.

He turned Les over. The Messenger's breath came in great sobs.

"Looks like you got some kind of answer," McGuinness said.

An hour later, Les sat in front of a fire in the library of the third landing, drinking tea and eating muffins while he told Devoy and McGuinness what had happened at Kilrootford.

"But you don't know where Danny is," Devoy said. Les shook his head.

"You should have seen the place when he was finished with it," Les said sadly. "Don't reckon anyone could have lived through that."

"But Danny isn't just anyone," McGuinness said.

"No," Devoy conceded, "although it might be better for all if he was gone."

Les looked at him, aghast.

"I'm sorry, Les, I don't really wish it, but he is volatile and very dangerous. How many people died at that camp? Danny is a weapon—a weapon that will turn against the hand of anyone who tries to use it."

"Well, maybe you shouldn't try to use it!" Les's eyes were flashing. "Maybe Danny knows what he's doing!"

"Les may be right, you know," McGuinness said.

"If I were Longford," Devoy said, standing up and appearing to tower above Les, "then I would say throw Danny to the dogs and be done with it! But I am not Longford. I will do my utmost for him, and will, as I must, try to use his power if I can. But I fear it may turn on us."

"On that matter," McGuinness said, "we had better get Danny's mother and the others back here. He'll be more inclined to defend Wilsons if he knows she is here."

"I agree. I have already summoned Daisy and Gabriel. They can bring Dixie and Pearl back. We will have to defer Vandra and Toxique's infiltration of the Grist to another time."

"And the Cherb boy?"

"He will have to take his chances, I'm afraid."

"He will not." Les stood up, swaying as he did.

"You are in no condition to go. I thought that you, above all people, would have no cause to love a Cherb."

"Protecting him was the last thing Danny wanted me to do," Les said defiantly, "and I'm not letting my best friend down."

"Very well," Devoy said, "but if you fall behind, the others will not wait for you."

"I won't fall behind."

"Get some rest. You leave at dawn."

Vandra and Toxique were disappointed to get the news that their mission was postponed. Now that they were to stay, Brunholm tried to equip them with large pistols and sharp knives to defend Wilsons, but both turned them down.

"I'm a healer," Vandra said. Brunholm turned to Toxique.

"I thought you were supposed to be an assassin," he jeered.

"Do you think if I want to kill someone I need your gun or your knife?" Toxique said with a gleam in his eye that made Brunholm step back.

"Steady, steady, no need to threaten me."

"But no one threatened you, Mr. Brunholm," Vandra said sweetly.

"What about our friends?" Toxique said.

"Knutt is back tomorrow night."

"Les," they breathed together.

"What about the others?"

"Still alive, by all accounts. Apart from the Fifth. Nobody knows what happened to him."

Vandra and Toxique turned anguished expressions on each other and raced for the Roosts.

The firelight flickered on Pearl's sleeping face. Dixie had torn off a piece of her skirt and was using it to mop the woman's brow. There was a rustle from the entrance to the teepee. Dixie turned in alarm, but it was only Nala. He carried a skinned rabbit in each hand and his pockets were stuffed with moss. He laid the rabbits down and knelt beside Pearl. Her face and arms were covered with cuts and abrasions, and there was a bad cut on the back of her head. Several of her fingers were twisted out of shape. Nala wet some of the moss and applied it to each of the serious wounds. He packed it into the cut on the back of her head. Then he took a small bottle from his pocket. He took the stopper out and Dixie could smell something sweet. When the lip of the bottle touched her mouth, Pearl writhed and moaned, but Nala persisted, and when he laid her head down again, a little color had returned to her cheeks.

Dixie hadn't waited. She had made a little spit over the fire and was turning the rabbits on it. Nala had ignored her until now, but she sensed some approval in his look.

When the rabbit was cooked, they ate with their bare hands. Dixie realized to her shame that she had eaten her whole rabbit, while Nala had left half of his in case Pearl woke.

Dixie found herself staring into the fire and drifting. Wind rustled against the outside of the teepee, but no draft got through. Imagine, she thought. I'm in a teepee in a wild wood with a Cherb and an injured woman, and there's a manhunt going on outside, yet I feel cozy. But the moment that thought crossed her mind she heard the rotor-chop of a distant helicopter—the pursuit had not been given up. Still, she was warm, and safe for the time being.

In his coal shed, Danny was neither warm nor safe. The damp had seeped into his bones and he couldn't sleep. Far off, across the fields, he could hear dogs howling. Had they found his trail? He could not stay here.

He crawled out of the shed and flitted down the back alleys. The dogs were closer. The mournful clamor of bloodhounds made the hairs on the back of his neck stand up. He moved onto wasteland. As he passed a deep drain, he heard a whimpering noise. He tried to force himself to go on, but the whimper came again. *Go on, stupid,* the cold voice in his head said, but Danny could not pass another creature frightened and alone in the night.

He turned back and looked into the drain. In the darkness at the bottom, something stirred. He slid down the side of the drain, the lip giving way so that he landed up to his knees in evil-smelling mud. He reached out and an eager little tongue licked his hands. A dog! He bent down to lift it and realized that one of the dog's legs was trapped. He felt around under the vile water and found its paw. Barbed wire had formed a noose around it, and every time the dog tried to escape, the wire tightened. Danny had to use both hands to free it, soaked up to his armpits now. The dog struggled free. Danny clambered up the side of the ditch, slipping and slithering, the dog tucked under one arm. He almost made it the top of the bank and freedom, but as he reached out to drag himself up, a powerful torch clicked on, shining directly into his eyes. Danny looked around desperately, but there was nowhere to run.

8

EEL GUTS

Les flew in front of Gabriel and Daisy as they crossed the dark wasteland. He felt light-headed, and everything was very distant.

When Les had insisted on going on the mission with Gabriel and Daisy, Brunholm had brought him to Jamshid, the apothecary.

"Do something with this damn boy," he'd growled, "give him something for energy. He needs to fly a long way tonight."

Jamshid looked at Les dubiously.

"Not much muscle mass. If I put too much strain on the heart . . ."

"Then it's not much loss," Brunholm said. "Get on with it!" Jamshid shrugged and turned to a chest of drawers. He took out two vials of clear fluid and poured both into a test tube. The mixture immediately turned a violent blue.

"Stop!" A girl's tremulous voice rang out. It was Vandra. "What are you giving him?" She snatched the vials from the apothecary's hands. "Lirmodium sulfate and salgisium tartar! You could kill a Messenger with these."

"They used to give them to Messengers in the old days," Jamshid said, "if a communication would not wait. They knew the risks!"

"But Les doesn't."

"It's my choice, Vandra," Les said. "I'm going to do it."

"Fair enough," Vandra said, her normally pale face flushed. "I want to get Dixie back as much as you do, but these two can't go around shoving stuff down your neck without telling you what it is."

"Thanks, Vandra," Les said, touching her arm lightly, then taking the test tube from Jamshid and downing the contents with a grimace.

That had been three hours ago, and now Les felt as if he was floating through the skies. Gabriel and Daisy had trouble keeping up with him. They crossed the dark wasteland quickly. As Gabriel flew, old knowledge came back: what altitude to maintain in order to catch wind currents, how to use thermals to gain height instead of stressing tired wings. Finally they looked down and saw car headlights moving along roads, the glow of distant towns on the horizon.

"When we get close we'll have to watch out for their flying machines," Daisy said.

"We'll fly at treetop level, that's the way to do it," Gabriel said. Les felt light spots of rain on his face.

"The rain will help conceal us," Gabriel said. On they flew, into the rain, confident that no one could see them. They had never heard of radar. They had no way of knowing that three dots were now being tracked across a radar screen, nor that the scream of jet engines was shattering the night calm fifty miles away.

Danny remained frozen in the beam of the powerful torch. He couldn't see who was standing behind it, but the hand was steady. He had to do something. Carefully he slipped his left hand under the belly of the dog he held in his right. If he could reach the pistol in his coat . . . A sudden pain seared through his hand. He slipped and almost fell back into the drain. The dog, freed, leapt from his arms and ran into the darkness.

"Good boy, Fionn," a strangely accented girl's voice said. Danny looked down at his hand.

"The mutt bit me," he said in disbelief. "I rescued it."

"You salved your own conscience. That doesn't buy you even a dog's loyalty," the girl said. Her voice was hoarse but there was a rough music to it. "But I thank you nonetheless. They said that the dog was gone. That I was to bow my head to my fate. But I did not. I searched for it and I am rewarded."

"Can I get out of here now?" Danny asked.

"Who's stopping you?"

Danny painfully eased himself out of the drain. The

dog darted forward, snarling. It was an ugly little terrier with stumpy legs, a head that was too big for its body and patches of color on its face that made it look as if it were perpetually snarling.

"Do you mind taking the torch off my face?" Danny's eyes were smarting from the glare.

"It's you." The voice was wondering.

"I don't know what you're talking about." How was he going to get away from this girl? "Can I see your face, since you can see mine?"

In answer the torch was lowered to the ground and a small girl walked into the beam and squatted down. She had blue eyes and bushy blond hair and wore a pink top and white jeans.

"Who are you?" Danny asked.

"My name is Beth. And I know your face."

"They're looking for me, then?"

"Who?" She seemed confused.

"People. Because of the base."

"Why would they be looking for you because of that?"

"Never mind. Where did you see my face?"

"I'll tell you if you come with me."

Danny hesitated. He didn't know anything about the girl. "Come with you to where?"

"To our camp. It's down the road a ways."

"Camp?"

"We're travelers. Gypsies to you." The little dog darted forward and snapped at Danny's trouser leg before running back and hiding behind Beth's legs.

"It would be the better part of you to come with me," Beth said. "I can see you're foundered with the cold, and if you're on the run from the peelers, they'll spot you in a crowd—you're covered in mud. Make up your mind."

Beth stood up and walked away. Danny thought quickly. He was alone and he needed a friend. Perhaps he could use her to get away and then dump her. As if the dog sensed what he was thinking, it snarled at him.

"Leave him be, Fionn," Beth said.

"I'll come," Danny said.

"Let's go, then."

Beth's camp was a collection of caravans strung out along a canal bank. Washing hung from scrubby bushes, and there were piles of scrap on the towpath, but the caravans themselves were new and modern. Two piebald ponies were tied to a tree, looking downcast in the rain.

Danny slipped and slid on the muddy ground, but Beth picked her way through the muck without getting so much as a spot of dirt on her white trousers. She led him to the newest of the caravans and ran up the steps. Fionn darted underneath and bared his teeth at Danny.

"Come on," Beth called over her shoulder. With a wary eye for Fionn, Danny followed Beth into the caravan.

The caravan site might have been dirty and muddy, but the interior was completely different, spotless and well lit, if rather cluttered with brightly colored trinkets and gleaming china. An old lady sat on a small floral-patterned sofa, carefully positioned in front of a large, gleaming television set. Her skin was wrinkled, but her brown eyes were shining and alert, and they immediately fixed on Danny.

"You have brought us a guest, Beth," she said. Her voice was low and musical.

"I found him down a ditch, Nana," Beth said with a laugh. "I didn't know what to do with him. Then I saw the face on him."

"Step closer, young lad," Nana said. Danny moved nearer. As he did he realized that there was a theme to the collection of china, to the decorative plates on the walls, to the brightly colored stuffed cushions scattered over the sofa.

Each item was adorned with a picture of a raven.

"The blue and the brown," Nana said, wonder in her voice. "The ravens spoke of it."

"The ravens." Danny glanced nervously toward the door, but Fionn stood there, a growl in his throat.

"They speak to me," Nana said, "of other lands, dream places, perhaps. They said there would be a sundering. That evil would come wandering. There would be a boy with eyes like yours who does not know if he is the future of the world or the ending of it."

"What else did they say?" Danny asked.

"Nothing that is fit for your ears," Nana said sharply. "But they did give instruction about you."

"What was that?"

"That we must look after you and hide you, for you are to be hunted like a dog, and those hunting you do not come to offer you their mercy. That you are a knife which might turn in its wielder's hand, a grief bringer, full of treachery, but we must help you all the more for that."

"He doesn't look all that treacherous to me," Beth remarked with a sniff.

"And yet betrayal wells up in him," Nana said. Her words were harsh, but her expression was full of compassion.

"Maybe if we feed him, he won't be as treacherous," Beth said, grinning. In a few minutes she had stew in a pot in the compact kitchen. When it was ready, Danny tucked in. Nana looked on in approval.

"When all is done," she murmured, "a hungry boy is a hungry boy."

There was a firm knock on the door. Beth opened it. Danny heard a brief, angry conversation; then a man pushed past Beth into the caravan. He was tall and thin, with a straggly beard and inquisitive darting eyes. He stopped dead when he saw Danny.

"What stranger is in the camp without me knowing?"

"A stranger who gets a welcome in my caravan whether you know about it or not, Sye."

"These are bad times, Nana. Outsiders bring trouble, and there's trouble enough without them."

"Be that as it may, I will do as I am bid by the ravens."

"Ravens! What do they want? Ravens interfere."

Nana got to her feet and moved stiffly across the caravan until she was standing directly in front of the man. She was shorter than he, but such was her authority that Danny thought she looked at least a foot taller. The man took a step back.

"If you want to tell the ravens how much trouble they bring, then do," Nana told him. "If you want to lie awake at night listening to ghost voices whispering, then I will cede all these things to you. Do you want to listen to the ghosts?"

Nana cocked her head to one side as though listening. For the first time Sye looked uncertain.

"They are coming," Nana said.

"No!" Sye said. "Stop. We will keep the boy. I don't want to listen to the dead!"

Danny could see that Sye was genuinely frightened.

"I'm not afraid," Danny said. "I've talked with the dead lots of times."

This was too much for Sye. His eyes rolled in his head and he started muttering very fast, backing out of the caravan and bowing in the direction of Nana and Danny. Within seconds the caravan door slammed and he was gone.

"What was he saying under his breath?" Danny said.

"Prayers and invocations against evil. Powerful enough in their own way, but not as powerful as a well-told lie."

"A lie?"

"Of course. I cannot summon the dead like that. They come and go as they choose."

"I see." Danny turned at the noise of a distant siren.

"There was an explosion the other night," Nana said slowly, looking at Danny, "and now they are hunting hill and dale for someone. You?"

"Did the ravens tell you about the explosion, Nana?" Beth asked.

"No, silly," Nana said, "I saw it on the television. But they were telling lies about it."

"What lies?"

"They said that many people were killed." Danny looked at her, stricken.

"No, son, don't look at me like that. No one was killed. I would have heard them. When the living are bidden suddenly around here, I hear their laments as they make their way toward the river."

"The river?"

"The dark stream that carries the dead to their final destination."

Danny felt a shiver run down his spine. Another siren sounded, closer this time.

"Peelers, peelers!" The cry went up all over the camp. Danny looked out the window. A police van with flashing blue lights blocked the entrance to the gypsies' encampment. The travelers gathered at their caravan doors, watching sullenly as policemen in riot gear emerged from the back of the van. An important-looking policeman with braid on his cap got out of the passenger seat. Sye approached in a curious, hunched-over, wheedling manner.

"You'll not get nothing here, Inspector, sir. Nothing, sir. We're only poor travelers trying to make our way in the world."

"I know what you are," the inspector said brusquely. "Thieves and liars. Out of my way."

The policemen spread through the encampment. They seemed to take delight in breaking things, throwing washing on the ground and trampling it, kicking over cooking pans and teapots.

"They've no right to do that!" Danny said indignantly.

"They do what they like with us ones," Beth said.

The inspector stood in the middle of the camp.

"Attention!" he shouted. "According to records, there should be seven males between the ages of ten and twenty in this encampment. I want them all here now."

Slowly, children and teenagers started to emerge from the caravans. As each reached the policeman, he put his hand under their chin, tilted their head upward and examined their eyes. When he had examined the last one, he turned to his men.

"Go through the caravans! Search every last corner."

Drawing batons, the men stormed into the little caravans. There was the sound of breaking crockery. Bedding and clothing were thrown out the doors into the mud. They went methodically through each caravan, arriving last at Nana's. A policeman threw the door open. Nana met them. Her cheeks were wet with tears. She tried to speak, then turned away, making a choking noise. A red-eyed and red-nosed Beth put her arm around her.

"What's wrong with her?" one of the policemen said roughly.

"My sister," Beth sobbed. "She fell into a drain. She is lost to us."

A figure in a dress lay on the sofa. The face was muddy and the eyes were covered with two coins.

"What's with the coins?" one of the policemen whispered.

"Gypsy traditions," another whispered back. "They're to pay the ferryman to cross the river of death."

"What's going on here?" The inspector burst in. "Why aren't you searching?"

One of the searchers pointed wordlessly toward the corpse. The inspector went over.

"What's all this? Looks dead, all right, but it could be a trick." He motioned to Beth.

"Take those coins off!" he said. Nana sobbed. "Quiet. Do as you're told. I'll see those eyes!"

Beth went over to the body, glaring reproachfully at the policemen. She gently lifted the coins from the eyes. The inspector leaned over eagerly, then stepped back in revulsion. The sockets where the eyes should have been were bloody and suppurating.

"The rats got to the body before we did," Beth said, replacing the coins carefully and smoothing back the corpse's hair.

"Leave them," the superintendent spat. With looks of disgust on their faces, the policemen backed out. A few minutes later the van started. Danny sat up.

"Yeuch," he said, feeling his eyes. "What is this stuff?"

"Eel guts," Nana said. "I knew the peelers would want to see your lovely eyes."

"Smells rotten," Danny said. Beth gave him a cloth to wipe his eyes.

"You look good in a dress." She grinned. Danny shot her a dirty look.

Nana waited until she was sure the police were gone; then she gave Danny a towel and bar of soap.

"Strip to the waist," she said, "and wash yourself at the pump."

Danny was going to protest, but a glint in her eye warned him not to. As he stood shivering at the pump, he was aware of eyes watching him from the other caravans, eyes that were neither hostile nor friendly, but simply appraising.

When he got back to the caravan, Beth was in bed on the top half of a bunk.

"You take the bottom half," Nana said. She turned her back while Danny undressed and climbed between the clean cotton sheets, which smelled of lavender. He wondered how far he could trust the travelers and tried to stay awake to watch for any trickery, but within minutes he had slipped into a dreamless sleep.

Nana sat long into the night after the two young people had fallen asleep. She was old, and sleep did not come quickly to her. She had hidden her shock well when she had seen Danny. The ravens had warned her that there was turmoil in the other world and that the entity they called the Ring was plotting to destabilize both worlds. She had believed them, of course, but she hadn't really expected the boy to appear. Nor, when he did come, did she expect him to look so like his parents, with his mother's eyes and his father's watchful manner.

9

CAPTAIN STRANG

If Les and the others had known they were being watched, they might have stood a chance. Conventional heat-seeking missiles were useless against them, as they left no trail of heat. They were small and so not easily seen. The pilots could not lock on to such tiny slow-moving objects. Clouds and rain might have assisted them, but as the war planes approached them at speeds the people of the Lower World could only imagine, the moon came out.

"Good," Gabriel said, "it'll help us find them." He adjusted their course slightly so that they flew along the southern bank of a reservoir, the water gleaming silver.

"You know," Daisy said softly, "I'd forgotten how lovely it is to fly by moonlight."

The jet fighters approached so fast that the Messengers had no time to take evasive action. One minute the skies were empty, the next they were full of roaring death. A howl unlike anything they had ever heard bore down on them. Gabriel's concentration failed and he veered sharply left, tangling wings with Les in the process. They both dropped like stones. It saved their lives. Both pilots concentrated on the sole remaining target.

Daisy had been a champion flyer when she was young, and all her skill had not deserted her. She did not know what the danger was, but she reacted nonetheless, turning into a swift barrel roll so that the startled pilot of the first jet saw his hail of tracer bullets miss the target. Daisy lacked the strength and agility for another roll, so she veered sharply sideways and down. It was almost enough. Red-hot tracer bullets from the second fighter streamed by, singeing her feathers and whistling off into the darkness, save for one bullet, slightly misshapen in manufacture or by the rifling of the gun barrel. The bullet tumbled through the air, moving more slowly than the others but still quickly enough to do terrible damage. As Daisy soared clear of the other bullets, it followed its untrue path and struck her in the breast. She cried out in pain.

Les and Gabriel had gotten clear of each other. They heard Daisy's cry and looked up. She was falling gently toward them, her wings beating feebly. As one, they rose and caught her on either side.

"Gabriel," she gasped. "Oh, my dear."

Behind them the jet fighters banked. The leader was furious. He wouldn't miss this time. The jet engines screamed. They were almost within range. The pilots grasped the gun control on each joystick.

"Please . . . ," Gabriel said, oblivious to the screaming jet engines.

"It was wonderful, wasn't it?" Daisy smiled weakly.

"Wonderful?"

"To fly together in the moonlight one more time." Daisy smiled without pain, put her head on one side and died.

Time stood still. Only a few hundred meters away, the fighter pilots lined up their targets. The lead pilot's fingers tightened on the trigger. Just as he was about to fire, something fluttered at the corner of his vision. He could not see what it was, but Les, watching, frozen in horror, could. A flight of ravens had appeared, flying straight at the jets. At the last moment four of the birds peeled off, two going left, two going right. Without hesitation each bird flew straight into the air intake of an engine, two to the first fighter, two to the second.

The ravens were destroyed instantly, but the blocked intakes denied air to the screaming engines. The planes shuddered violently. Before the pilots could throttle down, the engines shattered, fan blades breaking off and scything through casings and piping. All thought of their enemy forgotten, the two men fought the controls of the doomed machines. At the last moment two ejector seats fired. The planes plunged downward, one catching fire as it plummeted. The pilots floated free of the heavy seats, which jetted upward. As they fell, the two men glimpsed in astonishment an elderly winged lady being supported by a lad and an old man. Then they dropped out of sight.

"Look out!" Les shouted. A heavy pilot's seat was falling on them. Les thrust Gabriel away. The seat plunged between them, striking Daisy and carrying her downward.

"No!" Gabriel flew after the seat and Daisy, going like the wind. But it was too late. The heavy seat carried her frail body into the water of the reservoir below. There was a mighty splash and then no more. By the time Gabriel and Les reached the surface of the water, nothing remained save for a single feather.

"Gabriel . . . ," Les said, appalled.

"No," Gabriel said in a fierce, grief-stricken voice. "She would not have us wasting time mourning her. We will grieve for her when we return. We will think of her when the clouds travel across the moon at night. Now we have work to do."

Gabriel hovered and plucked the feather from the surface. A tear rolled down his face and he dashed it away angrily.

"Now, Les, now we fly like the wind!" he exclaimed,

His wings beat the air, and Les could barely keep his position, such was their force. Gone was the dusty old Messenger. This was a magnificent creature like some angel of vengeance from an old book. Another beat of the great wings and he was gone. Les shot after him. The surface of the water, ruffled by the wing beats, stirred again and was still.

* * *

Dixie was concerned about Pearl. She was no longer feverish, but she'd opened her eyes several times and whimpered with fear when she had seen Dixie and Nala.

"I help wounds," Nala said.

"I know, Nala, and thank you, but it is the wounds to her mind I worry about," Dixie told him.

She went outside. Her eyes searched the night sky. Where was Les? And where was Danny? Was he even alive? She looked through the trees to where the land sloped into the valley below. A line of torches was moving slowly but surely toward them up the slope.

"Nala!" she called out. The Cherb was beside her in an instant.

"We must go," he said. "They be here soon."

"We can't, Nala! Pearl can't be carried over this ground. But you go. I'll take my chances with Les."

"If you stay, I stay," Nala said.

"You will do as I say and go," Dixie said firmly. Nala folded his arms and looked at her, making a strange noise. Dixie realized that he was laughing.

"I don't think it's very funny," she started to say, and found herself laughing as well, as the full ridiculousness of her situation took hold. Stranded in the wilderness, hunted, dirty and bedraggled, stamping her foot like a child when one of the deadly Cherbs didn't do as she wanted. They laughed until their sides were sore, and when they were done, Dixie knew that she could never think of the Cherbs in the same way again.

"Let's get her ready to move," Dixie said eventually. "If . . . when . . . Les and the others come, we'll need to go quickly."

Nala went into a stand of willow and emerged with armfuls of flexible willow branches. With lightning speed he wove them together to make a kind of harness.

"Will hold her to Messenger," he said. There was a great noise above the trees and Dixie ducked down, thinking it was one of the helicopters—machines she did not understand at all—searching for them. But when she looked up, Gabriel was standing on a large bough above their heads, Les beside him. At least, it looked like Gabriel, but he had changed. This Gabriel looked like a Seraphim, tall and haughty, his wings held stiffly away from his body. There was a remote look in his eyes, which looked golden, like an eagle's.

"Thank goodness!" Dixie said. "You're safe." Then she saw the look on Les's face.

"What is it?"

"Daisy. We lost Daisy." Dixie stared at them, stricken.

"We cannot dwell on it," Gabriel said, his voice harsh. "We still have a little time before the sun rises. Let us use it."

Nala was thinking the same thing, his eyes on the line of torches coming up the valley. He darted into the shelter and emerged, carrying Pearl effortlessly. Gabriel floated to the ground. He examined the harness, then instructed Nala to fit it to him. He lifted off the ground to try it.

"That will do. Come, Les." Dixie looked around. It had finally dawned on her.

"But there are three of us! You can't carry us all. I'm not going anywhere without Nala."

"I think Nala has made the decision for you, Dixie," Les said. She looked around, but Nala was nowhere to be seen.

"We must go, Dixie," Gabriel said. "You will not help your friends by dying here."

The dawn sun spread light on the eastern horizon. It caught the edge of Gabriel's wings and they flashed golden. Dixie bowed her head, and after a moment climbed onto Les's back. They rose into the air and began their journey home.

It was an uncomfortable journey. They flew so low they were almost in the trees, and where there were no trees Gabriel found a ridge to fly along, even at one point flying alongside a railway viaduct. They didn't know they were in no danger. The prime minister had grounded all military flights in the area until they had discovered the nature of the weapon that had brought down two of the most technically advanced fighter jets in the world.

Once, an old man looked out of his window as he rose in the dawn and saw—what? Winged shapes as if from a dream. A little girl went to the bathroom and saw something from the hallway window, but when she woke her parents and spoke of it, they told her to go back to bed, and when she woke in the morning, she'd forgotten what she had seen. Flitting like ghosts across the landscape, the two Messengers and their cargo reached the frontier between the Upper and Lower Worlds and disappeared over it.

* * *

Ambrose Longford was also awake in the dawn. He was pleased by the way things had gone at Kilrootford. The foreign power had put its troops on high alert. He wondered if Danny had been consumed by his own power. He thought not. The power of the Fifth would be building inside the boy again, and he did not know how to control it. Longford had no doubt that it would be unleashed again. When it was, he would be in position to exploit it.

In the meantime, all was going well. The country, indeed the world, trembled on the brink of war, with Longford poised to use the chaos to gain control. But that was not enough. It never had been. Control of one world was no good without absolute control of the other. The Ring of Five had served its purpose. It was time to act. He lifted the phone.

Ten miles away, in a small, though perfect Palladian mansion, Nurse Flanagan stretched luxuriantly in satin sheets. Bed was delicious, but so many little treats awaited her when she woke. There was her own Cordon Bleu chef to cook breakfast. After that perhaps a facial, or a mas-sage, and then of course there was that handsome ten-nis coach . . . She sighed. There was so much on offer it was hard to know where to start. Then she heard noise, a crash from the hallway, pounding feet on the stairs, hammering on the bedroom door. She sat up in alarm as the doors burst open. Suddenly the room was full of men pointing guns at her. . . .

A policewoman stepped forward.

"Come quietly. We don't want to use force. Your fingerprints were found in the apartment of a known terrorist associate."

Nurse Flanagan threw back the covers. They wouldn't dare shoot her down in cold blood. Her silver derringer was in the bedside cabinet. She reached out for the handle. The policewoman reached out her hand too.

Nurse Flanagan's torso arched as forty thousand volts hit her. Her body convulsing, she fell from the bed onto the floor, but even as her body revolted, her mind was clear. They had planted Danny's fingerprints in the foreign representative's apartment. But she had been sure to wipe everything she had touched, and the night before, she had worn gloves. Then it came to her: the telephone. She hadn't wiped the telephone. Before the Taser was turned on her again, she remembered who she had called. Longford!

Vandra was miserable as she lay in bed in the Roosts. All her friends were gone on missions. She didn't know when or if any of them would be back, and her own mission had been postponed. The sound of her fellow pupils breathing was irritating her, and a third year, Vanessa Odile, was snoring loudly. Besides, Vandra couldn't sleep knowing her friends were out there, in danger. After an hour of tossing and turning, she crept out of bed and, pulling a blanket around her, slipped out the door onto the little balcony that ran around the front of the Roosts. She shivered and pulled the blanket around her shoulders, then stepped back into the shadows as the door of the boys' Roosts opened and a furtive figure exited.

The cloaked boy passed so close to her she could have touched him. Whoever it was, he was up to no good. Vandra waited until the boy had reached the ground; then, taking the steps two at a time, she followed.

The shadowy figure moved swiftly toward the driveway, staying underneath the trees. Vandra had to run to keep up. Soon she was breathing hard, and she realized with a guilty pang that she had not been keeping fit. A shadow detached itself from a nearby tree and a cold, clammy hand tightened around her neck. She struggled, but her arms were held to her sides in a grip like iron. She knew that if she did get free, she was a long way from the school. Her screams would not be heard, and she could not outrun her opponent. She stopped struggling, and at that very moment, a familiar voice spoke and the grip at her throat slackened.

"Funny, I usually foresee these things."

"Toxique!" Vandra cried out. "What are you doing?"

"Could ask you the same thing."

"I couldn't sleep and I saw someone sneaking around. What's your excuse?"

"A little more complex than that, I'm afraid," another voice came. Agent Starling stepped out from under the trees.

"Er, I've been doing a bit of training with Agent Starling," Toxique said guiltily.

"Have you?" Was everyone devious at Wilsons? Vandra wondered.

"Well, I thought I had to," Toxique said defensively. "They're always giving missions to Danny and Dixie and Les. I want to prove that I can be as good a spy as everyone else."

Vandra had often had the same feelings. If she admitted it to herself, it was the reason she felt down about the mission being suspended.

"I was sending him to Grist on his own," Starling said gently. "I am of the opinion that your chief talent is as a healer, Vandra. It is too precious in these times to be risked on a mission."

"But Toxique," Vandra said, hurt by the deception, "he'll scream or something like that! They'll catch him."

"He has to learn not to do it. But time is short. Come with us as far as Tarnstone. A boat will take Toxique to Grist."

"I thought there were no boats."

"There are no official boats, but there are always smugglers. I have a boat that will bring Toxique across tonight. I paid dearly for it. But we must be there on time. Come with us as far as Tarnstone."

Without waiting for an answer, Starling went in under the trees. She started pulling at branches, and Vandra realized that a car was concealed there. Starling started the engine and pulled the car onto the driveway without turning on the lights.

"Well?" the woman said. Toxique jumped in. Vandra paused, then slid into the passenger seat.

Twenty minutes later they were on the outskirts of Tarnstone. With trading suspended, there was no money circulating in the town. Even late at night, Tarnstone was always busy with revelers, but tonight no one moved. They sped through the suburbs toward the port and soon found themselves among vast empty warehouses and deserted wharfs.

"It's down here," Starling said, easing the car between two warehouses. She stopped and flashed the headlights twice. The signal was returned with two flashes from a torch. Starling started forward again. They emerged onto an old wharf strewn with packing cases and winches and other marine junk. They eased around the debris and found themselves at the water's edge. A man stepped out and raised his hand.

"Get out of the car," he said. Vandra didn't like any of it. The man whose features she couldn't see; the dark, silent dock, oily water lapping against the piling. Nor did she like the look of the long, thin smuggling boat, powerful engines throbbing, that bumped gently against the dock.

"Get on board," the man said.

"Where's Captain Strang?" Starling said suspiciously.

"Captain Strang is no longer in charge of this vessel," a familiar voice said. "I am."

Vandra turned in horror. Toxique whimpered.

It was Rufus Ness, the ruthless general of the Cherbs.

10

A CHAIN OF LIGHTS

Ness didn't carry a weapon. He didn't have to. A group of heavily armed Cherbs appeared from behind an old shipping container. Ness flashed his torch three times. Another torch answered from the roof of a warehouse. Then another, and another. All the way down the wharf, torches flashed in answer. Starling turned pale.

"Yes, Agent Starling. You have thwarted us for years. But now we have infiltrated the entire waterfront."

"A bridgehead," she said dully.

"Yes. Even now the expeditionary force is embarking in Westwald. By morning Wilsons will be ours. In the meantime, this is by way of thanks for the years you held us up." Ness stepped forward and clubbed Starling on the side of the head with the heavy torch. She fell without a word. Vandra rushed forward to her. The Cherbs laughed and jeered. Vandra looked at them with hatred, wishing them all dead. She tried to examine Starling's wound, but two Cherbs picked the woman up carelessly and threw her onto the deck of the smuggler's boat. Vandra and Toxique were bundled roughly after her.

"So much for my career as a spy," Toxique said miserably. Ness and his men stepped down onto the boat and cast off. The powerful engines roared, the boat's stern dug in, and the boat roared out of the harbor and into the channel.

They sped past the ruins of the old railway bridge where Vandra had once fled Westwald with Danny and her other friends, a long time ago, it seemed. The wind stirred Vandra's hair. The Cherbs had their attention fixed on the far shore, so she was able to creep forward to Starling. She felt her pulse. It was strong. There was an open gash above her ear, the blond hair matted with blood. Vandra tore a strip off her blouse to staunch the blood. As she reached down, Starling's hand gripped her forearm.

"I'm going to stay down," she whispered. "Try to tell me what's going on."

Vandra crawled on her hands and knees to the bow. The boat was traveling fast now on a choppy sea, and spray was coming over the bow, stinging her face as she lifted it above the thwart. She held her breath. The entire Westwald shore was a wall of light. There were boats drawn up on the beach, flat-bottomed boats with a shallow draft, and Cherb soldiers were filing onto them. Vandra tried to count the soldiers. Perhaps a thousand? Most of them were on board now, the craft well loaded down.

The spray was coming over the sides of the smuggler's craft now as well. Ness laughed, his face slick with salt water.

"A good fresh night for a new beginning, a new order!" he shouted. The smuggler's boat was built for speed, not for stability in high seas, and it corkscrewed violently as it slowed. One of the Cherb soldiers, his face green, turned away from them and leaned over the gunwale. The others looked worried.

"Sir," one said, "these autumn gales in the passage. They blow up very quickly. All shipping ceases."

"Nonsense!" Ness roared. "All the forecasts are on our side. I have assurances, charts and graphs. Cast off the fleet!"

There was confusion onshore. Many ropes were cast off, but others were left tied. The shallow craft carrying the Cherb soldiers turned in the rising wind. Voices carried to Vandra's ears across the water. Toxique stood at the rail, his hands gripping it as if he would never let it go.

"What is it, Toxique?" Vandra asked, though she knew his gift of telling the future and she dreaded his answer. Frozen to the rail, he did not speak.

Onshore they had finally cast off the ropes and the invasion craft had set sail. Vandra looked out toward the open sea and saw ranks of whitecaps leading off into the darkness.

"To Wilsons!" Ness shouted over the sound of the sea. "To Wilsons and glory!"

The troop carriers eased out into the main channel. At first it wasn't too bad. The storm had moved closer and lightning flickered on the horizon, but the invasion craft had gathered way and were making good time. The smuggler's boat moved in alongside them. Vandra could see the faces of the troops. They didn't look like the battle-hardened Cherbs who had thrown them onto the boat. These were younger, and they didn't look tough or brave.

The only time, Vandra realized, that she had ever seen Cherbs was when they were in uniform. She had never imagined them in school, doing homework, being told off by their mothers.

"The youngest-ever invasion fleet," Ness boasted. "My own personal choice." His words were carried away by the wind. The Cherb who held the wheel of the boat handed it over to another and came forward. He brought his weather-beaten face close to that of his leader and spoke quietly, but Ness erupted in a fury.

"What? Turn back? After all these months of work, to abandon surprise, all because of a little wind? Begone, you maggot!"

With one blow of his great hand he swept the Cherb over the side. The boy's head appeared once above the waves; then he sank. At that moment a cloud swept across the moon and the night turned black. A moan of fear rose from the Cherb troops. A small searchlight was aimed out to sea from the bridge of the smuggler's boat.

The waves sweeping in were bigger now, and the troop carriers were making little way. One of them was driven against the railway bridge pillars. A railing was torn away, and several young Cherbs fell into the water. Ness looked on, stolid and assured.

"The wind will die down in a few minutes. I have all the forecasts. Take heart. Tarnstone and Wilsons are ours!"

Hardly able to tear her eyes away from the struggling boats, Vandra forced herself to look down onto the deck. While the others were distracted, Starling had crawled into the shelter of the wheelhouse. She looked up and there was a glint as moonlight broke through the ragged clouds. She had a sharp knife in her teeth. She held up one hand: Wait. The time is not yet right.

The moon had only been hidden for a minute, but in that short time the scene had changed utterly. The sea was a maelstrom of white. The troop carriers were making no pretense of forward motion; both were trying to turn back the way they had come.

"No!" Ness roared, his neck bulging. "Stay your course!" Other sailors on the bridge of the smuggler's boat took up the cry.

"You'll broach! Stay your course." But the inexperienced captains had only one thought on their minds.

Vandra was suddenly aware of Starling crouched under the gunwale beside her.

"What's happening?" Vandra said, the storm snatching her words away.

"They should turn into the wind and try to ride out

the storm," Starling said. There was blood and spray running down her face. "They'll broach if they keep on like this!"

"What's broach?"

"Watch," Starling said grimly. She was on her feet, making no attempt to hide herself, for the attention of Ness and the others was fixed on the storm-tossed boats.

As the first one turned slowly, it rolled to port. The troops on board could not keep their feet. They fell to one side, and their weight made the boat list to port. The rail was driven underwater and the list increased. Officers tried to drive the troops back to the other side, but there was too much confusion, too much fear. Water poured into the ship. Panicked Cherbs were flinging themselves into the water. In one last attempt to rescue his ship, the captain tried to turn back to starboard. It was fatal. His companion ship had slewed starboard at the same time. The bow of the first pierced the side of the second with a noise of rending metal and a great wail from the passengers. One boat turned on her side. The other, in what felt like seconds, turned perpendicular in the water, her bow pointed to the terrible raging storm; then she slipped quietly beneath the waves and was gone.

The water was filled with struggling Cherbs. Rufus Ness's face was contorted with fury. From the shore cries reached them across the waves.

"Sir," one of the Cherbs on board shouted, "we can save some of them! Let us get closer!"

"Save them!" Ness sneered. "After what they have just done?"

"Sir," an older Cherb said, "it will take years to train soldiers again. These are our finest."

"Were our finest," Ness said, having to shout to make himself heard above the noise of the storm, the thunder that split the heavens, the cries of the drowning. "If we get in close they will all try to get on board. They'll capsize this ship too!"

"Then call the Seraphim," the younger Cherb insisted, "so they can be plucked from the water. We have fought and died for you for many years—do something for us now. My brother is among the drowning!"

The young Cherb made to grab for the wheel. It was all Ness needed. A pistol appeared in his hand and he shot the Cherb. The older sailor grabbed a heavy wrench and swung it at Ness, striking him on the shoulder. Ness grunted with pain and fired at the sailor. The bullet glanced harmlessly off the binnacle. The sailors saw the row and came running to the aid of their colleague while Ness's men rallied around him.

The fight raged as the cries of the Cherbs in the water started to die away. Starling pushed Vandra into a rope locker and grabbed Toxique, having to pry his hands away from the rail. The sounds of fighting, the grunts and cries, echoed from the deck, which pitched wildly as it drifted with no one at the controls. A body tumbled to the deck in front of them. Vandra gazed in horror at the blood-soaked corpse. Toxique turned away with a choking noise.

"What's going on?" Vandra asked. "What happened?"

"Treachery, I fear," Starling said. "Ness said that he

was told the weather would be good. It's not hard to tell when a storm is coming up the sound. There's a Cherb weather station forty miles away for that very purpose. No. Someone knew that storm was coming but chose to tell Ness that the weather would be fine. I don't like Cherbs, but I wouldn't wish what just happened on them."

"I saw it coming," Toxique said, "blood and water. I saw the sea boiling with bodies."

"But what could you have done?" Vandra said. "We need to get out of here."

A machine gun had clattered to the deck beside the dead Cherb. Starling hooked it with her foot and drew it toward them. The sounds of battle had died down, but the boat was still tossing wildly. The screams of the Cherbs had faded into the distance.

"We could be drifting anywhere," Starling said. "We'll have to take a chance." She rose to a crouch, rolled across the deck and landed on her feet, the gun at the ready.

"No sign of life," she called softly.

"They can't have killed everyone," Vandra said.

"They're Cherbs, remember?" Starling replied, moving stealthily across the deck. Vandra glanced over the side. They had drifted far across the sound. She could hear the boom of surf and see the lights of Tarnstone not far away.

Starling, Vandra and Toxique climbed the steps to the bridge. The metalwork was slick with blood underfoot. When they got to the bridge, Vandra looked for signs of life, but there were none among the bodies nearest to her. Then there was a roar as the engine turned over but did not fire. The starter motor went again. Starling moved stealthily toward the binnacle. Ness was standing beside it, using it for support as he tried to start the engine. His uniform was covered in blood. One hand held his side, and blood welled through his fingers. He was muttering as he worked the starter.

"The weather was fine. . . . I saw the reports. . . . Calm seas . . . clear skies . . . The reports . . . Longford brought them to me himself. . . ."

"Turn around very slowly," Starling said, her gun trained on Ness. She gave a short laugh when he flinched at the sound of her voice.

"Longford gave you the weather reports, did he?" she said. "Do you trust him? Are the reports accurate? Or did he switch them?"

"We are allies," Ness said.

"You are also spies, like me," Starling said. "Our trade is treachery, and this stinks to me. Do you think Longford would give you the wrong weather report by accident? Ambrose Longford plays a long game."

Ness waved his free hand toward the empty sound as if an invasion fleet still sailed it.

"But our army . . . ," he said.

"Not *our* army," she said "*your* army. Did the thought never cross your mind that you might dispense with Longford? Take the whole thing for yourself?"

A greedy expression flickered across his blood-stained face.

132

"Maybe he was thinking the same way," Starling said. "Step away from the engines."

"Stop right there!" Starling whirled around. They had forgotten about Toxique. He stepped past them, and with a speed and dexterity Vandra had not suspected he possessed, he was behind Ness, one arm around his neck, the other drawn back behind the Cherb's neck as if he were about to release a bowstring.

"One blow between the second and third vertebrae and it's all over," Toxique said musingly.

"Toxique! What are you doing?" Vandra looked at him in amazement.

"You pick up a few things when you're raised by assassins," Toxique said.

"Yes, but you . . ." Vandra trailed off.

"Don't have it in me, isn't that what you were going to say?"

"There is a difference between an assassin's craft and murder," Starling said.

"Rufus Ness is responsible for the deaths of thousands," Toxique said.

"Perhaps. But it is not your responsibility to decide his fate, any more than it was his to determine the life and death of those thousands."

"You'll become just like him just the same," Vandra said. "You're not a killer, Toxique. You know that!"

"I don't really, you know," he said with a cracked laugh. He drew his hand back, but just as he launched the killer blow, the keep of the boat grated on shingle. He was thrown sideways. The blow glanced off Ness's skull. Ness

133

swung back hard, so hard that Toxique was knocked off the bridge and over the rail into the water below.

"He can't swim!" Vandra cried. Without hesitation she disappeared over the rail. Seconds later they heard her faint cry from the water.

"Help!"

"Are you going to help her?" Ness smiled grimly at Starling. "Do you have it in you to put a bullet in me first?"

"I want you before the Higher Court for your crimes, Ness."

"But you can't do that without abandoning your friends to their fate."

"Go back and tend to your dead, Ness," Starling said, "and have a chat about the weather with Longford."

Ness's cruel smile turned to a snarl. Catlike, Starling vaulted over the thwart and into the sea. Ness turned back to the engine as the boat grounded once more. This time the engine caught. Wincing in pain, he put the boat into gear. Slowly, then picking up speed, the smuggler's boat became part of the storm.

The water wasn't deep, but Toxique was groggy, washing back and forth in the surf, and it was all Vandra could do to hold on to him and not to be carried out to sea. Starling grabbed him too, and together, they got him onto the shore.

Toxique was merely stunned, and after a few minutes he was able to sit up. Vandra looked out to sea as she tried to catch her breath. To her amazement, through the spume, she saw a chain of tiny lights reaching across the sound.

"What is it?" she asked.

"Not all of the Cherbs were drowned, it would seem," Starling said. "Some of them have found their way onto the railway viaduct. They are showing lights, hoping that someone will rescue them."

"I wouldn't bet on Ness doing it," Vandra said.

"No," Starling agreed. Toxique got shakily to his feet and looked at them guiltily.

"I'm sorry," he said, "I don't know what happened to me."

"Don't worry about it." Starling didn't even look at him. "It comes with the spy job. Nothing's ever cut and dried. Most of the time you don't get to choose between good and bad, you just get to choose between something bad and something even worse. You did well."

Vandra couldn't resist a small smile as she saw Toxique's cheeks flush. Starling didn't normally praise anyone.

"Let's go," Starling said, "it's not much good to escape Rufus Ness and then freeze to death."

They walked along the shore until they came to a fuel depot. There were oil tankers parked up. Starling managed to find a jeep. Remembering a class with Brunholm, Vandra hot-wired it in seconds. They drove back toward Wilsons, weary in body and spirit. On the Tarnstone wharf side they saw flames rising into the night sky.

"The people of Tarnstone have been itching for a

fight," Starling said. "Those Cherbs left on the wharf can expect no quarter."

As they trundled up the Wilsons driveway, another exhausted expedition was arriving from the air. Gabriel lowered Pearl onto the roof of the apothecary. Les landed Dixie beside her and hurried off to find Jamshid.

As if he had always known the group were going to be there, Devoy walked unhurriedly across the roof. He peered over the parapet at the sound of an engine.

"I can tell there are many stories tonight. Cries across water, wings that have ceased beating, the ravens in mourning . . . but come, who can tell me where the Fifth is? Where is Danny?"

They turned their faces away. Danny was lost. Devoy registered their silence.

"Sometimes, my friends, I think other powers run our lives, and what we decide or do not decide counts for naught. But I can do one thing that matters. Hot tea and muffins wait in the library of the third landing, where I will hear your stories, for it would seem that though much wrong has been done tonight, much good may also have come to pass."

11

THE GHOST ROADS

Danny woke to the smell of frying bacon and sunshine through the window of the caravan.

"Wake up, sleepyhead," a mocking voice said. "If you want to be a traveler, you'll have to get up earlier than this."

Danny staggered out of bed to see Beth at work in front of an enormous frying pan.

"Go and wash," Nana said, sitting quietly in front of her large television. Beth handed him a towel and soap. He opened the door and stepped out into a clear, cold morning. He walked across the campsite and noticed an odd thing: the other travelers ignored him, even the children, but he felt as if he was being ignored in a *pleasant* way, if that was possible. He stood at the pump washing while men and women passed only feet away. A grubby toddler steered a toy truck carefully around his feet, then drove on. The same thing happened on the way back to the caravan.

When he shut the door behind him, Nana saw his puzzled look.

"What is it?"

"Everyone's ignoring me, but it's not like they're angry at me or anything. It's just that I'm not there to them."

"It's our way," Nana said. "They are not seeing you. So if it comes to pass that the police seek you and ask of them, did you see this person, they can answer honestly that they have not."

Danny thought about it for a minute, then shrugged. The travelers had a roundabout way of thinking about things, but he wasn't going to start judging them. Besides, an enormous plate of sausages, eggs, fried bread, bacon and hot buttered toast had appeared on the table.

"Tuck in," Nana said. For ten minutes there was silence as Danny ate. He couldn't remember the last time he had eaten proper food, and he felt his mind clear as his body was nourished. As he and Beth ate, Nana moved around them, taking down fragile ornaments and wrapping them, tidying away glassware. So absorbed was he in eating that he didn't realize what was going on. By the time he had finished, half the caravan had been packed away.

"What's going on?" he asked.

"We have to go on the road," Nana said. "We are a peril to the rest of the family while you are with us. Besides, we are too close to Kilrootford. The police will come back. Police always do."

"That's not fair to you," Danny said. "I can find my own way."

"Can you really?" Nana said. "Do you know the ghost roads?"

Danny shook his head. He was about to argue more when he saw an image of Kilrootford on television. He grabbed the remote and turned up the volume. The image changed to a courthouse, a prison van screeching to a halt and the door opening. A woman was led out between rows of hard-faced police.

"Nurse Flanagan!" Danny exclaimed. Nurse Flanagan, as always, looked immaculate, bestowing polite smiles on the dozens of cameramen who aimed their lenses at her.

"The woman was arrested on the basis of evidence linking her to the head of intelligence of a foreign power. However, the key figure in the investigation is still being sought," the newsreader said. A bad Photofit of Danny flashed up on the screen, his forehead misshapen so and his eyes shadowed so that he looked twisted and evil. Beth stifled a laugh.

The story changed then to the "newest terrorist outrage." The smoldering remains of two fighter jets were shown.

"Experts are still examining the wreckage of the two aircraft to determine what kind of weapon was used to shoot them down. In the meantime, talks at the United Nations aimed at preventing the outbreak of war have collapsed."

Danny watched a scrum of reporters at the door of the

United Nations in New York. They surrounded a calm figure who spoke without raising his voice. Longford!

"These talks have broken down for now," Longford said, looking tired but kindly, "but every effort will be made to restart. We must try. The future of the world depends on it."

From five thousand miles away, Danny, to his horror, felt his mind reach out to Longford, could feel his plans, his schemes; he could feel the mind of Nurse Flanagan brooding in prison, her thoughts like the stench of rotten lilies, and that of Rufus Ness, mired in an angry fury. Only Conal's mind was as it had been, a dry and wicked place. Danny knew that Longford was aware of him. On the television Longford shielded his eyes with one hand as though he had felt a twinge of headache, but Danny knew that he was reaching out, trying to find Danny. Danny tried to tear his mind away, but he could not. It would take Longford only seconds to find out where he was. . . .

Suddenly he felt the presence of another mind, earthy and strong, but clean in a way that the others weren't, and honest. The link to the other members of the Ring of Five was cut off.

"Are you all right, Mr. Longford?" one of the reporters asked. An aide stepped forward.

"Mr. Longford has been working tirelessly in the service of peace. He needs a night's sleep." The aide led him away. Danny looked at Nana.

"You?"

She nodded.

"You have chosen strange bedfellows for mind companions," Nana said. "I thought I had better break the chain."

"What's going on?" Beth asked.

"Nothing, pet." Nana ruffled her hair fondly. "Get the van ready, will you? We'll be ready to go shortly."

With a strange glance at Nana and Danny, Beth did what she was told.

"How did you know to do what you did just then?" Danny said. "To get into my mind like that?"

"You do know what a winged Messenger is?" Nana asked.

"Yes," Danny said, "but how do you know?"

"Let the name itself speak to you, Danny."

"What do you mean? Messenger?"

"Yes, Messenger. The winged ones bore messages from one world to the next, did they not? And did not those messages, dispatched by one hand, have to be received by another?"

"I suppose. . . . What, you?"

"People like me. The traveling people's eyes see deep into the world. We have always been servants to those from other worlds—those who come with messages, or those, like you, who come for refuge."

"I'm not here for refuge," Danny said.

"No?"

"I'm here for revenge."

"Revenge is a blade that turns in the hand of the wielder. Will you not draw back?" Danny shook his head. "Well, no one sees all outcomes. But we are servants, though our service is free and gladly given. What would you command of me?"

"I wouldn't command anything of you," Danny said, embarrassed. "You've done enough for me."

"Then you will grant me the boon of allowing me to accompany you on your journey. I am afeard you will not complete it without me."

"You haven't asked where I want to go."

"Where?"

"Longford. I want to find Longford."

"Then let us seek the ghost roads."

It was a strange leave-taking. Once again the travelers pretended they didn't see as Nana's trailer, towed by a van, left the campsite. Beth recited names under her breath, naming each person they saw. The campsite faded away. To Danny, looking back, it appeared to be fading away into history.

They drove for an hour along a busy road. There were army trucks and police jeeps moving in the other direction. Danny was nervous, but Nana drove in a relaxed style.

"Most of the time the police think we're so far beneath them that they don't even see us," Beth said, "which suits us fine."

They reached a turn-off hidden in a clump of trees and drove down it. When Danny looked back, there didn't appear to be an entrance at all.

Nana stopped at a farm gate. She got down and took a

key from under her skirts. She fitted the key to the shiny new padlock on the gate and they drove through. They found themselves on an unpaved but smooth laneway leading off through fields and woods. There was a peaceful air to the place.

"I feel like I just stepped back through time," Danny said.

"Maybe you did step through time," Nana said with a smile, "but not into the past."

Danny didn't know what she meant. They drove slowly down the road, dropping into a valley with a river running through it.

Afterward Danny could not recall how many days they spent on the ghost roads. But he remembered what seemed like many nights of stopping and pitching camp under the stars. Beth showed him how to live off the land, catching fish with his hands ("tickling" them, she called it) or setting snares for rabbits. Though it was cold, they bathed in rivers and wide pools. Nana often joined them, wearing a vast blue bathing suit. Danny was up early in the morning and fell into bed at night, his sleep deep and dreamless. Vandra was a healer, but Nana was a healer in her own way and knew that what Danny needed was to go racing through the fields with Beth, climbing trees and wrestling.

He has the weight of the world on his shoulders, she thought. The weight of *two* worlds. He must be allowed time to be himself, to be a boy.

It was odd, Danny thought; it wasn't as if there were no people on the ghost roads. They saw houses in the distance. Sometimes they'd see a faraway figure working in a field, and they sometimes met another vehicle, the driver raising a grave hand. But they talked to no one.

"What are the ghost roads?" Danny asked.

"They weave in and out and through and around the busy world," Nana said. "Sometimes you will be in a busy place and there will be a ghost road passing nearby, going quietly about its business, and you will not know of it. Travelers on the ghost roads let each other pass without remark."

She did not tell him that there were other journeys to be taken. She could feel the deep power welling up within him, and it frightened her. Her service to him would be to strengthen the part of him that was the boy Danny Caulfield.

She looked with approval on the friendship between Danny and Beth. They spent long hours sitting outside the caravan talking, and Nana did not disturb him. Though sometimes he withdrew from her, and Nana could see that Beth was hurt.

"Child dear," Nana said, when she saw Beth looking sulky one day, "you of all creatures should know what he is going through. Every time he gets close to someone, they die."

"I'm not going to die, Nana!"

"I know that, but take the big long face off you. He needs help."

The weather was fine and cold, but it would not stay that way forever. Danny would not have the time he needed to heal, but Nana could see that he was, half unknown to himself, learning to control his power. But there was another part to him that worried her. Sometimes she saw him looking at them in a sly way. Part of his nature had been twisted. She could sense a part of him that took joy in betrayal, in seeing someone else's pain when they realized what had been done to them. And she feared for Beth.

Brunholm had to wait, fuming with impatience, to debrief those who had returned from the Upper World. Vandra, Toxique and Starling were not allowed to sleep until they had spoken to him.

"So the Cherb army is destroyed!" he declared in triumph.

"But why? That's the question," Devoy said.

"It's obvious. Longford got the weather wrong. You always presume he's smarter than he actually is, Devoy, because he outwitted you!"

Devoy did not answer, but when the others were leaving he asked Starling to remain behind, and they talked until the sun was above the trees.

Les had collapsed on the roof after he had landed. His breathing was shallow and broken. The drug that Jamshid had given him had pushed his system beyond its limits. He had been taken to the apothecary, where Vandra found him. She'd glared at Jamshid and held out her hand. He hesitated, then handed her a jar of brown liquid. Turning away from him, her cheeks coloring as though in shame, she bent her head to the jar. When she turned back, her canine teeth protruded grotesquely and a little of the liquid ran down her chin.

"Sorry, Les," she whispered, and plunged her teeth into his neck. Les screamed. His back arched and his heels drummed on the bed. Taut as a bowstring, his body juddered, then slowly fell back. Five minutes later he was fast asleep, snoring gently. Vandra pulled a sleeve across her mouth.

"Don't ever make me do that again," she told Jamshid softly, and there was something in her brown eyes that made him shudder.

Gabriel went back alone among the Messengers. There arose a great noise from their rooftop quarters when he gave them the news of Daisy. After that, no Messengers were to be seen in Wilsons.

Les slept for four days. The wounds in his neck where Vandra had injected her antidote did not heal quickly, and he would bear scars there for the rest of his life. School routine had reestablished itself. There were classes with Duddy and geography with Spitfire. They heard reports that the surviving Cherbs had been rounded up into prison camps and that Devoy had organized boats to rescue marooned Cherbs from the railway viaduct. Vandra asked the porter, Valant, if this was true, but he shook his head.

"I would have let them drown," Smyck said.

"You weren't there," Vandra said, "what do you know?"

"I know that if I had Rufus Ness at my mercy I wouldn't have let him go to rescue two freaks."

"You weren't there," Dixie said.

"From what I hear, your pal the Fifth isn't about anymore either." Smyck said. "He'd rather spend time with his Cherb pal, by the look of things. What happened to that filthy Cherb anyway?"

Dixie bit her lip, remembering how Nala had sheltered and fed them and dressed Pearl's wounds.

Every night before she went to bed, Dixie went to see Pearl. The agent had recovered a little, but she didn't seem to know where she was, and shrank away from anyone who approached her. Dixie asked Vandra if she could help.

"There is no antidote for her pain—at least, not one that I could inject," Vandra said.

Nor was there any cure for Gabriel's pain. Dixie saw him often, flying on his own, circling the school slowly as though looking for something.

There was a strange mood in Wilsons. The cadets were aware that the Treaty Stone had been broken. Letters from home told them about the war to come—until Brunholm decided that they were getting too much information and started censoring the letters, opening the envelopes and scoring out whole paragraphs with a black pen. This made things worse rather than better. Cadets didn't like knowing that things were being hidden from them.

"In these circumstances, it's better to trust the cadets, I think, Marcus," Devoy said. "Ignorance leads to fear."

But Brunholm insisted. The cadets' annoyance led to increased breaches of discipline, which in turn led to more punishments. The failure of the Cherb invasion was welcomed, although the pupils were aware of the Cherbs who had made it onto the collapsed railway bridge. Both ends of the bridge had fallen in, so there was no way off unless Rufus Ness returned to rescue them, but no rescue boats turned up, and the Cherbs' cries grew fainter every day. The pupils would sneak down to the shore in the evening to look on their enemy, but only Smyck and his allies showed any sense of triumph. The others did not want to see the Cherbs perish abandoned on the freezing ocean, even though they were the enemy. Every evening they went down to look, there were fewer.

One morning, Brunholm called the top rank of cadets into his study. His face was serious.

"The threat of invasion has receded," he said, "but the threat to Wilsons is as great as ever. We have been infiltrated before, and there is no reason to suppose that the Ring will not attack Wilsons this way again. I propose to organize defense committees to seek out and report anything out of the ordinary back to me.

"Spy on each other, you mean," Les muttered.

"To this end I will need a deputy from among you to organize and direct this new activity. Cadet Smyck, step forward."

Grinning at his pals, the tall, pale boy stepped forward. Vandra, Les and Dixie exchanged glances. Having Smyck in charge of spying on his fellow pupils meant trouble.

"Cadet Smyck will be head of the Department of Internal Security. It is paramount that we know what is going on at all times in Wilsons. If you have nothing to hide, you will have nothing to fear!"

"I wonder what Brunholm has to fear," Dixie said moments later as they walked down the corridor toward geography class.

"All this security and spying on each other. What's it really all about? Brunholm keeping an eye on us?"

"Yes, but why now? What's going on in Wilsons that's worrying him?"

"I don't care," Vandra said.

"What do you mean?" Les asked.

"You were supposed to look after Danny," Vandra burst out, "and now he's gone! Maybe he's dead."

"He's not dead," Les said gently.

"I suppose you would know," Vandra said angrily.

"No, Vandra," Les said, "*you* would know."

Vandra bit her lip with her long eyeteeth. It was true. Danny wasn't dead. He was out there somewhere, beyond their help.

Many things worried Marcus Brunholm when he was alone in his quarters, but there was one thing in particular. That morning he had woken, stretched and gotten out of bed to do his exercises, twenty sit-ups every morning. He had brushed his teeth and fetched a crushed velvet suit from his closet. It was only when he'd gone to lay the suit out on the bed that he'd noticed them, carved in a flowing script on the wooden head of his bed, put there during the night as he slept, the initials that he now stood before, tracing them with a trembling finger: *S & G*.

12

THE DARK STREAM

The journey on the ghost roads was coming to its end, and as it always did on those lost roads, a hint of autumn had crept into the air. It was cold when they got up in the morning, cold and fresh, and a hint of brown had started to creep into the leaves. Nana had gone out to a little clearing in the woods to think. She had seen no ravens on the entire journey. It worried her for a while, but she was old and wise enough to put it to the back of her mind. The ravens would do what they wanted, with or without her, and there was no point in worrying about it.

But she did worry about Danny. All she could do was give him space to be himself for a little while. He was a dangerous mixture. Child of a human father and a Cherb mother, to start with. She had to tell him what she knew about his parents, but she was afraid it might unbalance him even more. She sighed.

"I wish the ravens were here to help me," she said.

"What do you need help with?" The voice was Danny's. He had approached her quietly and was watching her calmly. She met his gaze and tried to read his heart, but it was shielded from her. There were two sides to his character, and the treacherous side made her shudder.

Nana thought she saw that side now. Danny was smiling as he watched her, but there was no warmth in the smile.

"What do you know about me?" he asked.

"Why is there a question on your dear lips, child, and none in your eyes?"

"I can tell, you know, when you're keeping something from me."

"Knowing can be dangerous betimes, Danny. It's for the likes of me to judge when you're ready for another burden to carry. The gray hair on my head is hard-earned."

Danny had moved to Nana's side and stood close. She could feel the force of his personality, what he was thinking. . . . If she never returned from this clearing, what would happen? . . . He could lie to Beth; he was a good liar, and she would believe him. Nana closed her eyes.

When she opened them again, Danny was standing moodily at the river at the edge of clearing. He picked up a stone and threw it in. The clear surface of the water rippled and became opaque.

"I'm sorry," he said without turning around. "If I

relax too much, then Danny the Spy finds a way into my head."

"Is that what you call him?"

"Danny the Spy? Yes."

"Hear me now, son. There is but one Danny Caulfield, not two, with all that is right and wrong about him."

"You don't know that."

"I know what I know."

Nana left him on his own in the clearing. Tomorrow they would come to an end of the ghost road. She would have to trust him with what she knew tonight.

Danny had been sleeping for a few hours when he was shaken awake.

"Get up and get dressed," Nana said. "Wrap a blanket around your shoulders. It's cold. You too, Beth."

It was a clear night. Danny shivered and was glad of the blanket.

"Look up," Nana said softly. Danny did as she said. He had never seen so many stars shining bright and cold and clear in the blue-black night sky.

"Come," Nana said. Without talking, Danny and Beth followed. Nana led them into a wood. The path closed in until they couldn't see the sky anymore, but Danny knew it was there, shimmering, majestic. Nana lit a candle, placed it in a small lantern and took them deep into the woods, the path sloping downward. They walked for a long time.

All at once, Danny was aware of steps beneath his

feet. They were descending into the living rock. He put his hand out to steady himself and felt the stone worn smooth, as though multitudes had descended into this place, their shoulders brushing the stone over centuries.

Deep into the rock they followed the stairs, until in the end they came to a little wooden door. It was latched but not locked.

"There'd be no stealing from this place," Nana explained as she opened the door and led them in.

They followed a narrow stone corridor and emerged into a great space. The lamplight did not reach the walls or the ceiling, but Danny had an impression of vastness. In the distance there was a whispering as of many voices, millions, perhaps. He felt Beth inch closer to him and put her hand in his.

"Where are we?" he asked.

"On the banks of the river," Nana said, and Danny did not have to ask what the river was. He already knew.

Silently they followed Nana until they could go no farther. They had reached the river. It flowed dark and powerful at their feet, neither fast nor slow, and they could not see the other side. A black stone jetty jutted out into the water, but no boat stood at its side.

"A boat will come when you need it," Nana said. "This is the river Styx, which you must cross when you have left life behind."

Danny and Beth could hear voices, whispering and innumerable, from the other side.

"Why have you brought me here?" Danny said.

"Two reasons. First, it was where I last saw your

mother and father, as they made ready for their final journey."

Danny felt Beth's hand tighten around his.

"They were long hunted, wounded, poisoned, and knew it was their time."

"What . . . what were they like?"

"Your father was a great spy. He was impatient, would let you down as soon as look at you if it suited him. A liar too. But he fair made me laugh. He'd charm the birds out of the trees."

"And my mother?"

"Serious, a thinker, gentle as the day was long. Beautiful too. She had a tiny waist, and such a dancer as you never seen. But a born spy as well."

"But she was a Cherb."

"You see, you've got your thoughts backways. Because your mother was a Cherb, you got to thinking that the Cherb part was the bad part, Danny the Spy. Because that's the way they think about Cherbs at your school. But it was your dad was the hard one. Your mum's the better part of you. She made sure you'd be looked out for when they were gone."

"How?"

"Your mum picked the people to look after you. Your dad set up a devilish web such as you've never seen, so that no one would ever find you. He was a devious one and no mistake."

"I thought . . ."

"It started to go awry in the last years. There were a lot of grim, smart folk trying to get to you. Pearl and

154

Stone didn't help. They started poking around trying to find out about you and they brought the whole shooting match running after them, blew their cover."

"So who . . . who was in charge of me—the government or something?"

"Lord, no," Nana laughed, her voice sounding strange in the echoing cavern. "There was no government or nothing looking after you."

"Who was it, then?" Danny cried.

"It was me, Danny," Nana said. "It was me."

Danny looked at her in wonder. He had thought that some shadowy secret service had been in charge of his upbringing, and instead it was this elderly traveler lady!

"Little I had to do, Danny. Your mum chose your guardians and your dad organized all else. But I was there. You never noticed the caravan. Many's the time we camped at the bottom of the road near your house. People never pay any mind to the travelers. We come and we go and none to care."

"Why did they go?" Danny thought that for a moment the whispering on the other side of the river got louder."

"They were ill, hunted, dying. The folks in charge didn't want to see humans and Cherbs in love, but they wanted you, Danny. They wanted the power of the Fifth."

"Two reasons. You said there were two reasons for bringing me here," Danny reminded her.

Nana looked troubled. "For those who know the river is a thing to cross over from one side to the other. But it is a river. It flows around where we are and who we are all

155

the time, son, and more than you think. This river will carry you to Wilsons. There is danger, hauntings, but if the need is there you will take the river."

A question hung in the air. It was Beth, standing to one side, almost forgotten, who spoke it out loud.

"If he doesn't make it down the river, if he has to go to the other side, will he see them there, his mum and dad?"

"Will he?" Nana's voice was stern. "Your mother and father are dead. Will you see them when you cross? My ma and da are dead these many long years. Will I see them when I cross? I know not, pet. It is not my business, nor is it yours. Leave that to the whisperers in the shadows."

"Then it is time to leave this place," Beth said firmly. "There's work to be done in the world we have, Nana."

The old woman bowed her head, accepting the rebuke. Beth took Danny's hand. They turned their back on the whispering of the dead and made their way out of the shadows until they stood in the open under the stars, the myriad constellations that set the night alight with white fire.

"This is where you belong, Danny," Beth said. "In the open, away from the shadows."

The next morning they drove through fields stiff with frost. No one spoke. They stopped in a meadow. Beth cooked bacon and eggs, and they ate in companionable silence, washing it down with hot coffee. Danny suddenly realized what Nana had been doing, surrounding him with warmth. He reached across and squeezed her hand. She bowed her head.

"Nothing I've done for you or yours comes to anything," she murmured.

"You can't say that, Nana," Beth said. "You do what you can, and you never know what the world will turn it into."

"You're right," Nana said, straightening. "And it's time we were on the move. You and Danny take the dishes down to that well over there and wash them. I've got things to do."

Nana watched Danny and Beth as they ran to the well. They are the teachers in this world, not me, she thought. She remembered Danny's mother and father and how she had left them to fetch water. When she'd returned, they breathed no more, but between them on the dry earth was written a single "S" and a single "G," and between those, a heart.

13

A FAINT ODOR OF CORRUPTION

Nana halted the van at an old wrought-iron fence and motioned to Danny to step down. He saw that the van had stopped at a graveyard. Ancient yew trees and ivy overran the place, but he could see crumbling headstones and mausoleums. Nana motioned to him to enter. Beth watched with a somber expression.

"What is this place?" Danny asked.

"A portal, a gateway into the world. On the other side lie dangers and enemies. You do not have to leave the ghost paths, Danny. You can go back."

"I have to finish. Too much depends on me."

"Well then." Nana moved closer to him, her sharp eyes like berries in her wrinkled brown face. "Well then. Be wise like the owl. Be cunning like the fox. Be kind like the dove. Be ruthless like the hawk. Forgive the weak their cruelty. Reward the brave. Remember that courage does not draw attention to itself and asks for no reward. Go with my blessing."

Flanked by Nana and Beth, Danny walked slowly through the graveyard. The far gate was closed, but he knew what lay beyond it. Ten feet from the gate, Nana and Beth halted. Beth kissed him on the cheek. It was a light kiss, but its imprint lingered. Without looking back, Danny approached the gate, opened it and stepped out.

The roar of traffic. Office workers walking briskly along worn pavement. High buildings towering over him. Danny felt as if he had traveled through centuries in a few steps. He flinched as a bus passed close to him, diesel fumes blowing in his face. He moved uncertainly along the pavement and turned to look at the graveyard, a gray wall with a tiny gate in it, dwarfed by the buildings around it, and almost invisible now.

He began to take in the streetscape around him, and he soon realized how much the world he had come from had changed. For a start, every third or fourth vehicle was a jeep or a military truck. The streets were full of men and women in uniform, and important public buildings like police stations had sandbags around their entrances. This city was on a war footing, he realized. People looked up nervously as a military jet passed overhead.

Danny's head soon started to ache from the thunder of the traffic and the fumes so soon after the peace of the ghost roads. He put his hand into one of the inside pockets of his coat and felt a wad of cash. Down a side street he spotted a small café. He slipped in and took a table in the corner.

The place was busy with workmen and taxi drivers sipping giant mugs of tea and eating sandwiches, and no one paid him any attention. The waitress brought him a cup of tea and he tried to gather his thoughts. One of the taxi drivers left, leaving a newspaper on the table. Danny picked it up. There were references to failed peace talks and the buildup of troops. There were photographs of warships, and there was talk of tense standoffs on the high seas.

"We ain't going to attack first," he heard a taxi driver say as he came in.

"They say they won't either," another replied.

"Something's got to give. It can't go on like this."

"At least they caught one of the little rat-spies they been sending in. Like that other who attacked the military base. Wouldn't mind getting my hands on him for five minutes. Always check the fares getting into the cab, make sure they don't have them different-colored eyes. Dead giveaway, that."

Danny ducked his head, hiding it behind the newspaper. Still half in the dreamworld of the ghost roads, he had forgotten about his eyes! Glancing quickly over the top of the paper, he saw the driver who had spoken. He was small and weaselly-looking, and his eyes darted about suspiciously. How was Danny going to get out of this place past him? Desperately, he fished about in his raincoat pockets, and yet again, the marvelous coat did not let him down. He pulled out a pair of sunglasses. They were very large and dark and would probably make him look like a film star trying to avoid the press, but he slipped them on, grateful to be shielded from the world.

He quickly paid for the tea and slipped out into the street. He had forgotten what it was like to be hunted, but now the full realization of it hit him. He had forgotten about the security cameras covering almost every inch of the city too, and he was lucky to pass through one street when he did: seconds later, a squad of police, backed by soldiers, blocked the pavements and started to check everyone's identification.

Now that he had gotten out of the café, he started to think. The taxi driver had talked about another person with eyes like Danny's being caught. Danny had a sinking feeling that Nala had been snared in Longford's web. If he had, would Longford use him as bait to bring Danny in again? Probably not. It wouldn't enter Longford's mind that Danny would have become fond of Nala. But that wouldn't stop them from interrogating Nala to find out how he had gotten to the Upper World and what he was doing there. Nala wouldn't crack easily; they would have to use harsh methods to force him to tell them what they wanted to know. After that he would be dispensable.

Danny's spy training was starting to kick in. He got on a bus and got off at the next stop in case he was being tailed. He doubled back on his own tracks. He had to find a base. He couldn't book into a hotel—he had no credit card—but he couldn't stay on the street and run the risk of encountering another checkpoint. He went into a newsagent and picked up a free advertising magazine. He found what he wanted on page three. He bought a mobile down the street, made a call and agreed on a price, saying he wanted delivery.

Half an hour later a red camper van pulled up down the street. Danny paid the puzzled-looking owner in cash and took the keys. He couldn't drive, but he didn't have to. He could leave the camper parked on the street and sleep in the back. It wasn't much, but it was a headquarters safe from prying eyes.

Safety was something Nala had forgotten about. He had not gotten far from the shelter in the woods. He had intended to find Longford, because he knew Danny would seek him out. But Nala had no spy training and was not familiar with the Upper World. It wasn't long before he attracted suspicion, crossing the road against the traffic lights, bumping into people as he walked through the shopping district of a nearby town. The police were called when he went into a café and started to help himself to food. Nala was used to dormitories and soldiers' canteens. He had never had to pay for food and didn't understand the idea of a restaurant. He was gone by the time the police arrived, but an alert was sent out, and it was picked up by a government department recently formed by Longford: the Department of Information Security, the DIS. Within an hour the department's discreet blue vans were cruising the town.

It was the train system that finished Nala. The trains

in his Westwald home were free to military personnel. Nala wasn't stupid. He knew that people were looking at him in a funny way and that it was time to get out of town. He found a train station and headed for the platforms. When he saw a barrier in his way, he jumped over it, the way soldiers did in Westwald, where no one would dare challenge him.

"Hey, you!" A cross-looking inspector came up behind Nala and put his hand on his arm. Nala upended him easily and strode on. Behind him a police radio crackled. He had found a seat on a train, not knowing where it was going, when the DIS agents descended. Nala got to his feet, but the DIS men were prepared. Three Tasers flashed. Writhing in pain, Nala fell to the floor.

He woke up on the floor of a DIS van, bound hand and foot. Since then he had been held in a secret detention center of the kind the DIS had established all over the country. The head warder was a calm, cold man called Smith.

"You're to be kept for Minister Longford himself," Smith said drily. "You should be honored. But he asked for you to be softened up."

Nala didn't know what "softened up" meant, but he found out later that night when his door burst open and he was drenched in freezing water. By the time his cell door opened in the morning, he was blue with cold. The following night loud, featureless noise was piped into his cell. It went on for a night and a day. The lights were never turned off.

But his captors had never dealt with a Cherb before.

Each time the door was flung open and another torment dealt out, he retreated into a corner of his mind where he could not be reached. Even so, he remembered the face of each of his tormentors.

Occasionally there were lulls, quiet periods at night that were almost worse than the torture itself as Nala lay awake wondering what was going to happen next. He had lost track of the days and nights he had spent there. He had lost track of the last time he had spoken to anyone but a jeering DIS operative. But one night there was something different, a noise he had not heard before. A tapping. Where was it coming from? He felt around the back of the hard little bunk and realized it was coming from the heating pipes. The tapping had a rhythm—three short, three long, three short. Nala had studied Morse code in military school and recognized it: *SOS*. Quickly he tapped back *Hello.* The answer came:

Who are you?

Nala. Who are you?

A friend, the response came. He heard the crash of boots outside his cell and vaulted back onto the top of his bunk as the door opened. Let them do what they will, he thought. He was not alone.

Danny set about planning his approach to Longford. He studied the newspapers and television to find out where Longford might be. He improved his disguise— the weather worked in his favor, the cold nights and sunny cold days meaning he could keep his sunglasses and coat on all the time. He walked the streets around the prime minister's residence, noting security checkpoints and cameras, trying to find a weak point. He remembered the words of Duddy, his Camouflage and Concealment teacher.

"There's always a weakness. But remember, it's the sneak thief who gets caught. The spy who walks in with his head held high is the one who succeeds. Hidden in plain view, hidden in plain view!"

But still he could not find a weak point, and according to the news, tensions were growing with more sightings of winged figures, thought now to be some kind of foreign spy drone. There were encounters between warships and border incursions, but there was still no excuse for war. Reading the papers, Danny felt that deep in their hearts, neither side wanted war, but they'd gotten themselves into a situation where there was no alternative.

Longford felt the same thing. For weeks now he had been trying to manufacture a provocation, some kind of incident that would bring about war, but there was resistance in his generals' hearts. He needed to find Danny. Power was within Longford's grasp, and he was impatient for it.

Conal had flown to Westwald and met with Rufus Ness in the fortress of Grist. Now the gaunt winged figure stood in Longford's study. It was midnight, and the desk light cast an evil shadow against the wall behind the Seraphim. A faint odor of corruption hung in the air.

"Ness is furious," Conal said. "He paces the floor calling for executions. The remnants of his army are dying on the bridge and he refuses to rescue them."

"Have you informed him that I've had the entire crew of the weather station hanged on their own antennae?"

"Yes, but he wants to know what has happened to Nurse Flanagan."

"Nurse Flanagan is a traitor," Longford said, "but she was close to Ness. There's no point in upsetting him more with that information."

Conal looked uncertain. Longford got up from behind the desk and put his arm around the Seraphim's shoulders.

"Sometimes, my dear friend, it is necessary to deceive one's allies—for their own good, I might add!"

Conal nodded, the movement releasing more musty smells from his feathers.

"All right. What do you want me to do now?"

"We must find the Fifth, Conal. All of our plans now rest on his shoulders."

Longford fell silent, his mind searching for Danny's. He could feel Ness in the distance, furious and incoherent. And Nurse Flanagan, fragrant and scheming. He shut them out and tried to clear his head of Conal's presence, which felt as though the odor of slightly rancid meat had filled his head. For a tantalizing moment Danny was almost there, but then he was gone.

It was enough. Danny lived, and he was somewhere close.

"Get in the air. The Fifth is nearby."

➤ 14 ➤

SLUGS OF SOMNOLENCE

Everything had changed in Wilsons. There were checkpoints everywhere. You were required to give your name and destination twenty times a day. Surveillance cameras had appeared on the outside paths and in the corridors. Smyck complained personally to Brunholm when Dixie once disappeared at one side of a checkpoint and reappeared at the other.

"All you wanted was to check my identity, isn't that right?" Dixie said, when she was summoned to Brunholm and Smyck. Smyck nodded.

"Well, do you know anyone else who can do what I just did?" Dixie demanded. Smyck shook his head, furious. It didn't stop Brunholm from giving Dixie a Third Regulation offense, but at least she got the satisfaction of seeing the look on Smyck's face.

"We can't do anything," Dixie complained later to Vandra, Les and Toxique. "You can't even go to the toilet without Smyck's permission." The cadets had managed to keep their summerhouse secret—it was the only place they could talk now. There was a gap in camera coverage in the shrubberies. If they ducked beneath the big laurel and climbed through the branches of the yew, they couldn't be seen.

"Whatever Brunholm's scared of, the security isn't doing him any good," Vandra said. Toxique nodded in agreement. They had both run a professional eye over Brunholm: he was pale, losing weight, his hair not brushed and his clothing disheveled. Something was definitely wrong.

"What's this?" Les said. He touched the doorframe. Someone had carefully carved initials in it—S & G.

"Same as on Danny's ring," Dixie said.

"But why is it written here?" Vandra asked.

"Somebody's trying to tell us something," Dixie said.

Toxique examined the doorframe. "We need to find them."

"But we can't if we're being followed everywhere," Les said. "At least Smyck has to sleep sometime. The cameras are worst of all. They're always on."

"Where are they controlled from?"

"Brunholm has a control room in the Pinnacle of the Leaning Buttress. There's only one way in or out. We'd never get there."

"We could ask Gabriel," Vandra said.

"I'm not sure that's such a good idea at the moment. Gabriel is acting pretty strange since Daisy got killed."

"What's that?" Dixie cried. They sat up. An eerie howling noise was coming from the direction of Wilsons. The sky exploded into light.

"Come on," Les said. "Run!"

They raced back to the shrubbery, Toxique, surprisingly, keeping his cool and insisting that they climb back the proper way, out of sight. As they scrambled out of the yew, a small figure, keeping to the shadows, ran fast toward the woods.

Wilsons was lit up by floodlights and hazard flashers. The howling noise was caused by a large siren mounted on the roof.

"Where did all that come from?" Dixie said in wonder.

"And what's going on there?" Les said, his eyes narrowing. On the very edge of the pool of light, a winged figure was taking to the air, and perched on its back was the small figure they had seen running through the shrubbery.

"A Cherb," Les almost snarled. "Gabriel's got a Cherb on his back."

"You sure?" Toxique asked.

"I can smell it from here."

"What's Gabriel doing helping a Cherb?" Vandra said.

"And what was that Cherb up to?" Les said.

They ran across the gardens, around the front and

into the entrance hall, where an excited crowd had gathered. Brunholm was slumped in a chair and Duddy was feeding him brandy from a flask. Les muttered to himself and ran off. Behind Brunholm a slender throwing knife protruded from the wooden paneling.

"Didn't even see the little devil coming at me," Brunholm said, gasping for breath. "I told you so. I told you, you can't drop your guard for a moment around here."

Devoy appeared and strode across the hall. He plucked the knife from the paneling, examined the hilt carefully, then handed it to Toxique. Toxique sniffed the tip. His nose wrinkled.

"Attar of black orchid. Deadly and evil. It works by stimulating dreams of such horror that the body can't tolerate the fear. Usually the heart fails, long after the mind has been destroyed."

"A Cherb weapon, then!" Brunholm declared.

"I don't know . . . ," Toxique began.

"Of course it is!" Brunholm roared. Detective McGuinness appeared in the doorway. He looked tired, and there was mud on his raincoat. He took the knife from Toxique, frowning.

"No one should have touched this. Any evidence is ruined now." He stared at the knife for a long time, then took a bag from his pocket and carefully slipped the weapon in.

"But why?" Vandra said, trying to piece something together in her mind. Everyone in the hallway was trying to talk at once, and Dixie was the only person to hear her.

"What do you mean?"

170

"Why set out to kill Brunholm in the most public of places? Why not ambush him somewhere quiet, or ambush any of us, for that matter?"

"They . . . they were trying to create a diversion . . . ," Dixie said slowly.

"A diversion so they could do what, though?" Vandra said. The answer came to both of them at once. Scattering cadets, they ran like the wind, out of the entrance hall, down the corridor, past the ballroom and past the Gallery of Whispers, Les and Toxique straining to keep up with them. As they mounted the stairs they heard a fusillade of shots from the apothecary.

"Too late!" Vandra gasped as they ran into the apothecary. The light was dim, and they didn't see the body on the floor. It was just as well, for as the two of them tripped over the form and went flying headlong, another fusillade rang out, the shots whistling over their heads and hitting a row of bedpans with a series of dull clangs.

"Stop!" Les's muffled voice could be heard from the floor. "Mr. Jamshid, it's me and Vandra and Dixie."

"Come out very slowly with your hands in the air," Jamshid said. The friends stepped out. Jamshid was training an old-fashioned tommy gun on them. His face glistened with sweat.

"Someone was here," he said hoarsely.

"Is she hurt?" Vandra asked in alarm. Before Jamshid could answer, a figure stepped out of the shadows behind him.

"Hurt? No. At least, not by whoever or whatever was here tonight." Pearl was pale and ghastly, her long

171

white nightgown making her look like a phantom that had emerged from the darkness behind her. The bruises had faded, although there were bandages on her hands. The memory of what had happened to her had not disappeared—her eyes were haunted by torment and by loss—but her voice was calm and measured.

"I thought they might come for me. When I heard the commotion I warned Mr. Jamshid. He protected me."

Jamshid gave her a gallant, if shaky, bow.

"But why would they come for you?" Vandra asked.

They all looked at each other. Even the skeleton of the Messenger hanging above them seemed to be waiting for an answer.

"Danny," Pearl said. "The only reason they want to harm me is to get at Danny."

"Then we'd better make sure nothing happens to you," Jamshid said, straightening up and running a hand through his hair.

"It seems that we know nothing," Pearl said, "that everything is a mystery."

"You may be right," Jamshid said, "but my advice as your physick is to get yourself back into bed. I know that much."

Jamshid gave his assurance that Pearl would be guarded, but it wasn't enough for Vandra.

"I'm going to stay here tonight," she said. "Have you noticed something? No cameras around the apothecary. Somebody didn't want the attacker to be seen."

Vandra accompanied Les, Dixie and Toxique downstairs. As they passed the ballroom, a camera swiveled to follow them. Dixie stuck out her tongue at it.

"How did you know, Dixie?" Vandra asked. Dixie shrugged.

"Just felt like a diversion is all. If they'd wanted to kill Brunholm, they would have killed him. Cherbs don't miss."

"So what do we say about what we saw?" Vandra said.

"About Gabriel and the Cherb? We need to tell someone," Dixie said.

"Tell who, though?" Les said. "Not Brunholm."

"Devoy?" Vandra said.

"We tell no one until we talk to Gabriel himself," Toxique said firmly. "We're forgetting everything he's done. If it comes out that he brought a Cherb into Wilsons, he'll lose everything, maybe even his life. Of all our friends here, Gabriel has proved himself most honest and brave. He deserves a little trust from us."

"Okay," Dixie said, "we'll talk first."

Vandra watched them go. It would be difficult to talk to Gabriel, she thought. The only time they'd seen him, he'd been flying high, almost a speck in the distance. Vandra wondered if he ever touched down. She thought he had gone from being an earthbound Messenger to a creature who lived on the wing. She wondered which Gabriel she liked best: the cold, remote one or the shabby one.

Les, Dixie and Toxique gathered on the balcony outside the Roosts. There were two cameras trained on the balcony—"for your own safety," as Smyck put it—making sure that the male and female cadets could not talk without being overheard. Les looked at the cameras, then took a notebook out of his pocket.

WE NEED TO FIND OUT WHO S & G ARE, he wrote. Dixie nodded but spread her hands, looking up at the camera. How would they do it without being under surveillance? As Dixie's gaze rested on the camera, a raven appeared from nowhere and landed on the device. It stood on the top of the lens for a second, then took off and landed on a branch a foot away.

"Look!" Dixie breathed. The lens of the camera was streaked with white. The raven opened its beak and cawed loudly. It sounded remarkably like laughter. Les scribbled quickly on his notebook and held it up.

TOMORROW NIGHT?

The raven nodded its head rapidly; then the branch shook and the bird was gone into the night.

Les checked his bed for listening devices before he got under the sheets. Vandra had warned him to do so, as she had found one on the back of her headboard the night before. Les felt carefully along the bed and was rewarded when he felt a small disc on the metal frame. He reached into his locker and fumbled around until he found an old referee's whistle. He got into bed and wrapped the blankets around him to muffle the noise as much as possible, then blew a sharp toot into the bug. He was rewarded with a gasp of pain from Smyck's bed.

*   *   *

When Vandra got back to Pearl's bed, the agent was awake.

"Do you want something to help you sleep?" Vandra said.

"Something you could inject into me?" Pearl asked.

"That's only for really serious things," Vandra said. "But I can get a pill from Jamshid."

"No, it's okay, I feel like talking. There's a phrase that keeps going through my head. They kept asking about it when they were interrogating me, whether Agent Stone had found any references. When I said no, they didn't believe me and they kept on hurting me."

Pearl shuddered and fell silent. Vandra took her hand where it lay on the covers.

"What was the phrase?"

"Kind of an odd thing: 'The Lost Boys.' 'What do you know about the Lost Boys. Tell us about the Lost Boys.' I told them I'd never heard of them, do you hear me, I've never heard of them!"

"It's okay," Vandra said, "it's okay."

There was no pill or injection to heal such fear. Instead, Vandra held Pearl tight, afraid to move as the woman clung to her. Late into the night, Vandra realized that Pearl was asleep, but she dared not move.

The Lost Boys. The phrase ran through Vandra's mind, gathering mystery to itself. Who were they? How would she find out? In the end she fell asleep lying across the bed, still holding Pearl.

The following evening the ravens gathered in the trees at the front of the school, silhouetted against the reddening sky as the sun went down. Les had puzzled all day as to what they should do. In the end he wrote ASK THE GALLERY OF WHISPERS on a sheet of paper and held it up to the others. They all nodded.

That evening each one pleaded tiredness and went to bed early (although Les thought Dixie overdid the elaborate yawning and stretching). They would use the time-honored method of putting pillows in their beds to imitate their sleeping forms so they could visit the gallery. Vandra produced four little boxes and gave them one each.

"They're Slugs of Somnolence," she said. "They're quite vicious and hate being enclosed in the boxes, so they growl all the time. The thing is, their growls sound exactly like people breathing. But whatever you do, don't open the box. They've got teeth."

When the time came, the cadets placed the Slugs of Somnolence under their pillows and sneaked out.

"Ravens got the message, then," Les said, looking up at the white-coated lenses of the surveillance cameras. The cadets were all wearing dark clothing, and Dixie produced a tin of camouflage blacking. They were barely visible as they made their way toward the front of the school.

"What's going to happen when Brunholm notices that all the cameras are going out? He'll smell a rat."

But the ravens had thought of that as well. Les picked the lock of the front door and they went into the hallway. Brunholm had insisted that two cameras would do the work of the porter, Valant, so despite his protests, he had been given duties in the archive. The way would be clear if the cameras were dealt with. Vandra nudged Les. Each camera had a raven sitting on top of it. They had folded their wings downward so that the lens of the camera was covered. The cadets hurried through, and the minute they were clear the ravens lifted their wings and flew ahead of them. If Brunholm even noticed what had happened, he would have thought it a temporary glitch with the cameras. The same thing took place with the cameras along the corridor and the ones outside the darkened ballroom.

The Gallery of Whispers was in shadows. Moonlight through the windows at the top of the gallery cast long shadows on the marble floors.

"What do we ask?" Dixie said. "We can't just say 'What's going on.'"

"I know," Les said, putting his cheek against the wall. "Who is trying to kill Pearl?"

They listened as the whispers traveled around the gallery, rising and falling, until in the end, Les's voice, low and distorted, emerged from the other side.

"Still he waits."

"'Still he waits,'" Dixie said, almost crossly. "What's that supposed to mean?"

"I haven't a clue," Les said, looking glum. "Doesn't get us very far."

"It does get us someplace," Toxique said. "It tells us that someone *is* trying to harm Pearl. We were only guessing beforehand."

"I suppose," Les said, not sounding convinced. "Come on, we'd better get back."

"Wait," Vandra said. "I have one more question. Something Pearl said."

She put her face close to the wall and whispered, "Who are the Lost Boys?" The sound traveled around the gallery, the whispering rising and falling, but this time the whispering sounded agitated. The cadets exchanged glances. The whispers reached the center of the gallery but would not travel any farther. The voices became more and more discordant, distressed. Les put his hand against the wall and could feel the stone itself vibrate. The sound became louder and louder now, less a murmur of voices than a roar. A few chips of masonry fell from the ceiling and the cadets backed away. They could feel the vibration through their feet now, a resonant shuddering force. The walls were vibrating so hard they were making a singing noise. A raven flew across the room in alarm. One of the great high windows cracked and then shattered. Broken glass rained down on the stone floor. The cadets cowered against the wall, holding their ears. It felt as if the whole building was going to collapse. Then, suddenly, the sound stopped.

There was a long silence, made all the more eerie by the noise that had come before. Into the silence came an exhausted voice, not even a whisper, but a gasp.

"Brothers."

The cadets looked at each other, shocked. It felt as if what had just happened in the gallery should have ended in words of clarity and wisdom.

Then the alarms went off.

The cadets took to their heels, the ravens flying in

front of them and covering the cameras. As they ran down the ballroom corridor, they could see piles of dry plaster on the floor and cracks in the walls.

They'd made it as far as the entrance hall when they heard running feet.

"Quick," Les said. They ducked behind a statue of a man hiding his face with a cloak. Smyck, Exspectre and others ran into the hallway. Once they had all passed, Les, Vandra, Dixie and Toxique ran out behind them. Exspectre looked around, surprised.

"Don't look at me, dozy," Les said. "We were behind you all the way from the Roosts!"

"Yeah, eyes front!" Dixie said. "Could be twenty Cherbs waiting around the corner."

"Armed to the teeth!" Vandra grinned. Smyck and Exspectre slowed down considerably at the prospect of running into a band of Cherbs. When they got to the Gallery of Whispers, Brunholm was already there.

"Vandalism!" Brunholm cried. "One of the most precious rooms in the entire Lower World, destroyed by wanton violence."

"It's only a broken window, sir," Les said.

"Silence, boy. I wouldn't expect the likes of you to understand . . . the perfection, the integrity . . ."

They were joined by Duddy and Spitfire, who stared at the destruction, aghast.

"The vandals seemed to move accompanied by a black mist," Brunholm said. "The cameras were shielded in order, thus permitting them to move unobserved." The cadets exchanged glances.

"If he looks at the cameras outside the Roosts, he'll see a white mist," Les whispered.

"This doesn't look as if it was vandalism," Spitfire said thoughtfully. "Look at the cracks in the wall—you'd think there was some kind of vibration."

"Yes, dear," Duddy said, "but vibration from what?"

"If the voices were somehow blocked," Spitfire went on thoughtfully, "it might set up a resonance in the stone. . . ."

Brunholm exploded. "Stuff and nonsense! We'll have none of that fanciful rubbish here. Spread out! The enemy is about somewhere!"

As Brunholm organized squads to search the grounds, Les, Toxique, Vandra and Dixie slipped back to the Roosts. The cameras outside were still obscured, and most of the cadets were up and engaged in the search, so they were able to have a quick cup of hot chocolate in front of the stove in the girls' Roost. After a quick check for listening devices they talked about the night's events.

"Spitfire had a point," Dixie said. "It felt like the Gallery of Whispers had been blocked somehow."

"Which makes the Lost Boys important, doesn't it?" Vandra said. "I mean that if somebody goes to all the trouble of blocking the gallery—I don't know how you would do it—they have to be important, don't they?"

"Funny," Les said. "All they did was draw attention to themselves."

"Not funny at all," Vandra objected. "Somebody went to a lot of trouble to cover a possibility that might never happen. I mean, what were the chances of anyone asking the gallery about the Lost Boys, particularly when we've only just heard of them? Somebody is playing a high-stakes game here."

Yawning, the boys went back to their Roost. They were ready for bed, but there was one last surprise waiting for them: Les's bed had been attacked. The pillows had been slashed and the blankets shredded.

"Bleeding Smyck," Les said crossly. But Toxique examined the blankets.

"Smyck doesn't own a blade as sharp as this one," he said.

"Hello," Les said, "looks like someone got themselves an unexpected surprise."

"What?"

"They opened the box with the slug in it and got themselves bit in the process."

It was true. The box that had held the Slug of Somnolence lay empty on the floor, and there was a pool of blood beside it.

"We'll see tomorrow who's got a chunk out of them," Les said, lying down and trying to pull the ragged pieces of the blankets around him.

"I wonder," Toxique said, "I really wonder."

The next day they scrutinized everyone for teeth marks, but no one showed any sign of the painful bite. It was another mystery in a night and day of mysteries.

15

THE PHONEMAKER

It was done under cover of night, as such things are best done. The gypsy Sye emerged from the shadowy canal bank and was almost on the sentry before the man saw him. The sentry's rifle came up instantly.

"Halt, or I'll fire!"

Sye stopped dead, an odd wheedling expression on his face.

"Sure don't be shooting at me, and me only here to give you a bit of information. Do my bit for the public, like."

"What information?" the guard asked suspiciously.

"Ah, it would be better for the two of us if I didn't give it to you, sure the head might crack on you with the importance of it. I'll be talking to the boss man, if you don't mind."

"If you don't mind, I'll crack your skull with this here rifle if you don't stop prattling."

"I know where he went," Sye said, the wheedling mannerisms suddenly gone. "The creature who blew up the base. I'll give him to you and you can do what you will."

The sentry eyed Sye. The boss was never happy to be disturbed for nothing. On the other hand, if this raggedy man was genuine and the information didn't get through . . .

"All right," he said, "come this way."

Sye followed the sentry. It wasn't the first time he had sold information, but he had a feeling that the payout tonight would be the biggest yet. He had seen the size of the manhunt that had been organized to find Danny.

But the night didn't go as he had expected. He was brought to a dark building in the far corner of a disused airfield. The sentry's boss—an officer, by appearance, but he wore a uniform with no insignia—had walked into the room, glanced at Sye and then walked out again without comment. Since then Sye had been sitting there on his own, awaiting he knew not what.

After he had been there for two or more hours he heard a scratching sound on the roof, followed by heavy bumps. He shifted nervously in his seat. It sounded like a bird landing on the roof of his caravan, except louder, much louder. The bumps were followed by a noise like something heavy being dragged over the roof. The palms of his hands were damp. He was starting to wonder if this had been such a good idea after all. Then there was the smell. A subtle odor of decay permeated the building.

Sye got to his feet. He could tell them he was mistaken, that he wanted to go back to the camp and get more information, that he would come back in the morning. No harm done. He turned toward the door. He froze. He hadn't heard the door open. For a moment he thought a piece of the night had become detached and filled the doorway. The odor was stronger now. The shape in the doorway was a man—no, not a man; it was too tall, and those things on its back . . . were they wings? They couldn't be. . . .

The figure moved farther into the room. Sye backed away, blinking, his mind unable to process what he was seeing. Old tales told around campfires when he was a child raced through his mind, stories about the creatures of the night that lurked in the darkness outside the firelight. A gaunt, evil face and burning eyes, a tall man, stooped and bony. And wings. Real feathered wings. Sye felt his insides turn to water. His legs gave way under him and he collapsed back onto a chair.

"The boy," the creature said. His voice sounded like he looked: ancient, without mercy. "Tell me where the boy is."

Sye tried to speak but his mouth was too dry. The creature loomed over him. Sye whimpered.

Danny had started to sleep during the day and go out at night. People didn't notice his eyes at night. He quickly learned where the police set up their identification checks in the neighborhood. In fact, he learned a valuable lesson

184

from watching them through the back window of his van. Like all organizations, they had their routine. Attempts were made to vary it, but the whole thing still revolved around meals and shift changes. If he wanted to move, the best time to do it was during one of these openings. The police clocking off were tired, and the ones coming on weren't up to speed.

He bought a television and a DVD player. He recorded many different camera shots of the prime minister and his bigwig friends arriving at the official residence, noting who was on security at the time. He bought a gray suit and had his hair cut short.

His height was a problem, although he had grown quite a bit in the previous year. He bought shoe inserts to make himself look taller. By the time he was finished he looked the part of a secret service agent. It was time to try the whole thing out.

He waited until the mayor was visiting a local flower show. There was no security, only a few policemen. Danny mingled with the crowd, then put on his dark glasses and started talking into an imaginary microphone in his lapel. People started moving respectfully out of his way. A policeman came up to him after twenty minutes and asked him if he had "seen the suspicious-looking character manning the cake stall." Danny assured him that the man had been vetted already.

It was childishly simple, though Danny knew that it wouldn't be as easy to infiltrate the prime minister's entourage. Apart from anything else, it was getting harder to move anywhere without being stopped by the police.

He needed some form of identification. He remembered Brunholm's voice.

"The law of supply and demand," Brunholm had said, *"always applies. If the Ring needs slaves, there will always be someone to sell them. If you need something when you're on the run, there will be a supplier—of guns, knives, passports, whatever you want, as long as you've got the money."*

So Danny went into the city at night. He sought out the poorer areas, where the shops stayed open long after midnight and men hissed at you from alleyways, trying to sell things that were stolen or illegal, or simply in an attempt to lure a passerby in and rob them. There were checkpoints on these streets as well, but the people were good at avoiding them. Danny got to know a few of the street sellers, working his way into their confidence by buying stolen car stereos from them or tipping them off when the police were coming.

In truth, Danny didn't have to do much to convince them that he wasn't an undercover policeman or any kind of threat. They had an instinct for their own kind. Everyone in these streets was on the run or hiding out in some shape or form, and no one asked any questions. If Danny wanted to wear sunglasses when it was already dark or keep the bill of his baseball cap pulled down over his eyes, then it was none of their business.

Duddy had once said that you could be taught a lot of things in the classroom, but it was no substitute for being out there, pursuit on your tail. Danny honed his spy instincts in these nights, learning from those around him, the pickpockets and fences and street people. If you didn't want to give your name, then nobody asked. If you wanted an alibi, or something that had fallen off a truck, or a gun, you got it with no questions. Danny learned that it was easy to get a fake college ID or a driver's license, but he looked too young for either. He needed a passport, and that was more difficult and more expensive.

After a week a young street seller, Pad Burden, sidled up to him.

"Got a smoke?" Danny shook his head. Pad moved closer and spoke rapidly.

"There's a man in a cellar on Elm Street. The sign outside says *Mobile Phones, Sales and Repair*. Go to the back of the shop."

Danny nodded thanks and slipped Pad a ten-pound note, knowing it would buy his food for the week. Pad slipped the note into his pocket, then spoke again. "Be careful. There's a lot of people looking for a kid about your age, your height."

"There's plenty of kids my age around here."

"There's not many looking for a fake passport, mate."

Ambrose Longford considered the information that Conal had extracted from the gypsy. Danny had embarked on the ghost roads. Which meant that he was now in the city. He had been accompanied by some foul old gypsy woman and her granddaughter.

"Do you want them?" Conal asked.

"What would I do with some raggedy old dear and

her snot-nosed granddaughter? They're only a distraction," Longford said.

"Perhaps we could use them as bait."

"No. The only leverage we have is on her sickbed in Wilsons. I want our efforts redoubled in that direction."

"And the Cherb boy?"

"Keep him where he is. He may come in useful sometime."

"The jailers are reporting some difficulties with Nurse Flanagan. She's making unreasonable requests for cosmetics and things like that."

"Let her have them," Longford chuckled, "I'm feeling generous today."

"If you insist," Conal said stiffly.

"What about our gypsy friend?"

"He did not survive the interrogation, unfortunately."

"Did not survive it, or did you finish him off when you had wrung all the information you could get out of him? Honestly, Conal, I do wonder what happens to all those people who die by accident in your custody. There never does seem to be a body to bury."

Conal's eyes glinted but he said nothing.

"Go now," Longford said, gesturing toward the open window. Conal took two steps, then hopped up onto the windowsill. He spread his wings and was gone, leaving behind a smell of rotting flesh.

Longford picked up the phone and dialed the number of air force headquarters, but he hung up before anyone answered. Conal was still of use. Then he called the chief of the metropolitan police.

"Our suspect is within the city boundaries," Longford said. "I suggest you look for his nest, his sleeping place. We are all at our most vulnerable when we are asleep, are we not?"

Longford replaced the receiver and reflected on his own words. The great game was on. Its conclusion neared. Danny was the wild card, but Longford was confident. Still, why had the words "Lost Boys" sprung to mind a week ago as he slept, and why did they keep returning? Things buried should be left buried. He had warned Steff Pilkington about that. But Steff had kept on digging. Steff believed in shedding light on matters. That was his downfall. There were secrets so great, so terrible, that you had to forget you knew them, had to lock them away in the back of your mind. Longford had held such a secret himself for many long years, and he wearied of it, as, he thought, must the other holder. Never mind; time moves on, he thought, and the end nears.

Danny waited for a dark, rainy night. As he made his way across the city, he knew it would be his last trip if he could not find some identification. Public transport was out of the question. Every last passenger was checked. Nine or ten times he had to double back or around to avoid a checkpoint. By the time he reached the North End, he was exhausted and drenched to the skin. He *had* to get that passport.

He found the mobile phone shop Pad Burden had told him about and let himself in. He was in a long, narrow, dimly lit shop. Dust lay heavy on every surface, though if you looked closely in the smeared glass cabinets, there was every kind of phone imaginable, from the ones with winders you saw in old films to futuristic instruments that might have come from downed spaceships. Danny threaded his way through cardboard boxes, heaps of old circuit boards, mouthpieces and other phone paraphernalia, until he saw a little kiosk at the very end, surmounted with an ancient sign saying DO NOT ASK FOR CREDIT FOR REFUSAL OFTEN OFFENDS. The glass of the kiosk was covered with yellowing laminated cards carrying warning about terms of payment and warranties.

In the middle of the kiosk sat a small bald man wearing a red polo, with several pairs of glasses pushed back on his forehead. He reminded Danny of a small vulture.

"I'm . . . er . . . looking for a passport," Danny said, deciding to plunge right in. His left hand was resting on the hilt of his knife in his pocket.

"Of course you are," the man said in a surprisingly deep bass voice. "Otherwise you wouldn't be here."

"Pad sent me . . . ," Danny began, but the man held up a hand to stop him.

"No! No names, no pack drill. Your passport. You of course want it for tonight, because you can't move about the city without it. That will cost five thousand pounds cash on delivery, that is now, on the nail, no discount, no haggling, no Christmas clubs . . ."

"I have it," Danny said.

"Good, good, now let me see. . . ." The man lifted the

glass top from the case in front of him. "Here, hold that for a second." Danny took the glass. "Now," the man said, fishing out handfuls of passports, "what do we have here? Ghana? No. Hong Kong? No. France . . . perhaps. Ah, here, Australia. That will do."

He replaced the other passports and put the top back.

"Go away and come back in an hour. With the cash, mind."

"What about a photograph?"

"Sorted. You were photographed as you came through the door." The Phonemaker gestured to a tiny camera mounted above the doorway.

Danny made his way back out onto the street. The Phonemaker set the Australian passport to one side. It would only take minutes to finish. He lifted the glass top from the case in front of him and smiled grimly. They fell for it every time. He took a small box of powder and a brush from his pocket and dusted the glass. When Danny had held the top of the glass case, he had left his fingerprints on it. The Phonemaker placed the piece of glass on a small scanner. He pressed a button and waited for a result as the scanner whirred. When it came, he sat very still for a minute, then let out a low whistle.

"Got you," he said to himself. "After all this time, I got you."

It was pouring outside. Danny huddled miserably in a shop doorway. A police patrol car drove slowly down the street, and he had to duck behind some dustbins that stank of old fish. He was itching to get hold of the passport and get back to his mobile home.

After half an hour he trudged back to the shop. The door scraped open and the bell rattled. The shop was darker than it had been, and he had trouble negotiating the piles of junk on the floor. He was halfway to the counter when he heard the click of the door closing behind him, followed by the sound of a bolt being slid across. He spun around, his hand on his knife. A deep voice spoke.

"Take your hand out of your pocket. You'd be shot down like a dog before you got your knife out."

Danny slowly withdrew his hand.

"Kneel down on the floor and put your hands on your head." Danny did as he was told. The Phonemaker stepped out of the shadows, an ugly, stubby Uzi in his hand.

"That's better." The Phonemaker stepped behind Danny, and he felt handcuffs being expertly clicked onto his wrists. For the first time since Danny had gotten the mobile home, he felt the power of the Fifth rise in him, but he suppressed it.

"Now," the Phonemaker said, coming around and squatting at eye level. He lifted Danny's chin and examined his eyes with interest. "That's better. Before the others get here we'll have a little chat."

"I've got nothing to chat about."

"Everybody has something to chat about. Especially those who want to change their identity. Especially when that person is the Fifth."

* * *

Nala wondered if he'd been forgotten. His meals were slipped through the door, but otherwise he was left alone. Every night a short message was tapped out on the pipes to him in Morse and he tapped back. One night he heard shouting and raucous laughter in the corridor. He listened carefully at the door. He gathered that the guards' commander had a regimental dinner every Friday, and that when he was gone, the guards smuggled in beer and spirits. He stored away the fact that it was Friday, so he could now keep track of which day it was; then he went to the pipes and started tapping. It was the first time he had started the conversation, and there was a long lull before an answer came.

"Sorry took so long."

"Okay. Guards drunk," Nala tapped.

"Can you help me?"

"Help?"

"Escape?"

"Who are you?"

"Flanagan."

A guard walked down the corridor, singing a drunken song. Nala waited for him to go before replying.

"How?"

"I can get key of cell. No way out after that."

"I can pick other locks."

"Next Friday."

"Okay."

Nala sat back in the darkness. Escape was possible.

Then he had to find Danny. He had no home. Danny was all he had.

The Phonemaker led Danny to the rear of the shop and opened the back door, which led into a dusty storeroom.

"What are you going to do with me?" Danny asked. He could feel the power surge in him again, and again he repressed it.

"Do with you?" The Phonemaker turned to look at him. "I don't want to do anything with you." He put his shoulder against a rickety cupboard at the back of the storeroom. It swung open smoothly, and a light came on, revealing a battered metal staircase leading down.

"Go on," the Phonemaker said, pushing Danny in front of him. It was a spiral staircase, so Danny couldn't see what was at the bottom. Some of the bulbs along the way were broken, and a feeling of foreboding grew in him.

Finally he stumbled out into a dark tunnel with rounded walls.

"Where am I?" he asked. The Phonemaker tapped an enameled sign directly in front of him. It said SKREEN JUNCTION. The man touched a switch and a light came on. Danny gasped. They were in an underground train station, but one that had not been used for a long time. The rails were covered with dirt and debris and the walls were dusty. The platforms, however, were lined with computers and other technical equipment. In one corner guns were piled against the wall, gleaming with oil.

"What's going on?" Danny said, then stopped as his

eye fell on a plaque mounted on the far wall. It showed an intertwined *S & G* exactly the same as the one on his ring!

"Wh-what . . . ," he stammered, turning to the Phonemaker, "what is this place? Who are you?"

"They call me the Phonemaker, and this place is the center of resistance set up by Steff Pilkington many years ago to protect the world against the catastrophe that is now almost on us."

"Steff Pilkington, my da . . . ," Danny blurted out.

"Yes," the Phonemaker said with a smile, reaching out to undo Danny's handcuffs, "and his raincoat looks very well on his son, I have to say!"

"I don't understand," Danny said, sitting down on a bench.

"Your dad knew the treaty would be broken eventually. He knew the Upper World needed an underground. Wilsons was very much against it, and he defied them."

"How did you meet him?"

"I was a student of history and I came across some very odd documents that spoke about the existence of another world, and how what we thought of as angels were in fact the emissaries of that world. I published several papers on it. Many people laughed at me, but others approached me who had made the same discovery. Your father read one of my papers and then contacted me. We set up a network. There aren't many of us, but we will be here to support you."

As Danny watched, people started to emerge from side tunnels. Ordinary people, but harried-looking, as if they were under surveillance by a ruthless enemy. Danny's only thought till now had been to get close to Longford and to punish him, but when he saw these people, he realized that he couldn't just think about himself. Shuffling forward on the dark, dusty platform, they looked at him as if hope had suddenly entered their hearts.

A small man in a dark coat approached the Phonemaker with a slip of paper.

"This is just in," the man read. "Professor Longford has brought the armed forces under his direct control."

"He'll watch us fight until we're on our knees, and then he'll take over," the Phonemaker murmured.

"Over here," a gray-haired woman called. She was sitting in front of a monitor, wearing headphones.

"Special forces activity in the north of the city," she said. The Phonemaker went to a young woman in a knitted cap.

"Can you get the traffic camera up?"

"Working on it." The girl's computer screen flickered and came to life. A gray streetscape came into view. Danny stared. He recognized the street, and the mobile home parked on it.

"That's mine," he said, watching as half a dozen black cars pulled up quickly at either end of the street. Armed men poured out. Suddenly the street was full of them, taking up positions. Danny's throat tightened. If he hadn't come to the Phonemaker he would have been asleep in the caravan. One of the men stood up and signaled.

"They're going to storm it now," the Phonemaker

said. But that wasn't what the signal meant. As one, the men trained their weapons on the caravan and opened fire. The heavy bullets ripped through the flimsy shell of the mobile home, which rocked and shuddered, metal and glass debris flying through the air. The withering fire did not slacken. The caravan seemed to collapse on itself, and bright orange flame flickered in what was left of the interior.

"Good," the Phonemaker said with satisfaction.

"Good?" Danny looked at him suspiciously. "What do you mean by 'good'?"

"Look." The flames were spreading quickly. "If they had taken the caravan intact, they might have found clues to lead to you, or at least to your intentions. Now they have nothing. Longford will be furious. You can stay here now, if you want. You'll be safe."

Danny nodded, but he scanned the faces in front of him. He knew that Longford's first act when he got into power would be to recruit as many spies as he could, and that he would take delight in infiltrating an opposition movement. But it was hard to believe that among the faces there could be a traitor. An image flashed into his head of these people being led out of the underground station, handcuffed, betrayed and defeated. Spy Danny felt a warm glow of malicious pleasure. But then his eye landed on the intertwined *S & G*, and he felt Spy Danny rebuked, a flood of shame washing over him.

"We're here to help you," the Phonemaker said. "We have experts in many fields. Just tell us what to do."

Danny looked at him. He was used to working on his

own. He had planned his approach to Longford, and his plans hadn't included anyone else. The Phonemaker's shrewd eyes watched, as if he sensed Danny's difficulty.

"We can create diversions. We can shut down street cameras, computer systems, even security systems. Just tell us what to do and when to do it. You don't have to give us a reason for it. That's your business."

The Phonemaker led him to a small office to the side of the platform—a stationmaster's office, perhaps. There was a small bunk in the corner.

"You can sleep here. Your passport is ready, by the way, but what about your eyes? Every policeman and security agent in the country knows about them and is checking everyone. I don't know how you've gotten this far."

"Don't worry," Danny said gruffly, "I'll look after that. I've got ways of keeping out of the way." In truth, he didn't want to change his eyes again with a temporary membrane as he had on past missions. They were part of who he was. His mother was a Cherb! He felt a flash of pride. The Phonemaker turned to look out a little window that opened onto the platform.

"They come here in the evening after work, or at night after the children are put to bed. Sometimes they work all night through and have to go to their jobs the following morning. Because they believe in S and G. They know what's at stake. People like Longford would destroy the world and stand over the rubble, a lord of ruin."

"And do they know that I could bring that ruin on them as well?" Danny asked.

"They're not stupid. They may not know the power of the Fifth, but they know that you are a risk they must take. I thought that showing you the hope in their faces, their belief in you, might strengthen your mind. Perhaps I was wrong. But whatever you plan to do, time is short. The fact that Longford has brought the army under his control means war is not far away. You must act soon, Danny."

Danny couldn't believe he was in the heart of an organization founded by his parents. It should have made him feel closer to them, but part of him felt that they could have put a little time aside to look after him while they were busy making plans to save the world. The Phone-maker left and Danny slept, falling into uneasy dreams of ghost trains in the underground and caravans bursting into flames.

Longford was incandescent with rage. The CIS officers had taken it upon themselves to destroy Danny's caravan. All evidence was gone. He had arranged for the officer in charge of the raid to be debriefed by Conal. No one had seen the man since. Thankfully, the boy's remains had not been found. He was still out there, but he had to be used soon. Longford had taken control of the army, but the generals were suspicious. There was a growing anti-war movement that had to be curbed. He had thought the trial of Nurse Flanagan as a spy would help things along, but now he had other plans for her. He lifted the phone and called the jail.

                              *   *   *

Danny woke early, the power stirring in him. He was
always aware of it now, and knew that he had to be alert.
He looked out at the railway platform and saw that it
was busy, the people looking agitated. He pulled on his
clothes and went out, stopping a black-haired girl with
earbuds gripped forgotten in her hand as she hurried
down the tunnel.

"What's happening?" he said. She looked at him in
confusion, then backed away from him, turned and ran.
He got other strange looks from other operatives, mostly
ones he hadn't seen the previous evening.

At the end of the platform he saw the Phonemaker
and hurried to join him.

"What is it?"

"This," the Phonemaker said grimly, and brought up
a news network on the computer screen. The screen filled
with a photograph of Nurse Flanagan. She was splayed on
the floor, her eyes wide open, indisputably dead.

"The trial of terrorist suspect Flanagan is in turmoil,"
a grim-faced newsreader said, "after she was murdered
during an apparent escape attempt. Professor Longford
sees it as an attempt to stop material incriminating the
foreign power from coming to light during her trial."

"Who murdered her?" Danny said, a feeling of foreboding coming over him. The question was answered
by another photograph flashing up on the screen. Nala.
Reported to be armed and dangerous. Danny's eyes
narrowed.

"What is it?"

"Of course," Danny said. "Longford was never going to let Nurse Flanagan go on trial in an open court. The first thing she would do is dish the dirt on the Ring of Five, and Longford in particular. She was always going to be bumped off, and it was handy having Nala there to be blamed for it."

But where was Nala now? Once again the newsreader answered Danny's question.

"The murderer is at large in the city. Police say he may be part of the gang that detonated a bomb at a key government base. Once more, the public are warned not to approach the suspects."

"The peace is stretched to breaking point," the Phonemaker said. "Whatever you plan to do, you'd better do it soon."

"I'll do it today, if I can," Danny said. "I need you to find out what the prime minister's engagements are today."

The Phonemaker called a male operative over and issued instructions.

"Is that all you want?"

"That's it," Danny said. He trusted the Phonemaker, but his organization could be riddled with spies.

Ten minutes later the man came back with the information. The prime minister would address Parliament that afternoon and would return to his residence at four p.m.

"That'll do," Danny said, "but I never did get that passport off you."

"Here." The Phonemaker handed over the passport. "But you might not need it. There are tunnels from here all over the city."

"Okay," Danny said, "but only you know where I'm going, is that clear?"

The Phonemaker nodded, looking at Danny in a strange way.

"What is it?" Danny demanded.

"Nothing," the Phonemaker said. "It was just that for a minute, you sounded exactly like your father."

They were ready to go at three o'clock. Danny spent the morning studying maps, working out his plan. The Phonemaker led him to a service tunnel. Only when they were out of sight of the underground station did Danny put on a suit borrowed from the Phonemaker but quickly started to regret having put it on so soon. The tunnels were filthy and hot, and he had a lot of trouble keeping it clean.

After forty minutes the Phonemaker turned into another side tunnel. After a few more minutes he pointed to a little metal door.

"Here we are," he said. Danny took his map out and the Phonemaker showed him exactly where he was emerging.

"Good luck," the Phonemaker said. "And if you need us, here." He handed a small phone to Danny. "All you have to do is hit Send. I'll answer it."

"Okay."

A shadow passed over the Phonemaker's face.

"Your mother and father were fine people. Very strong-willed, both of them. It grieved me to hear that they are gone." He bowed his head in sorrow.

How can you listen to someone talking like that about your parents when you didn't even know them? a wearily familiar voice snarled in Danny's head. *You'd be better off without him and his friends.* An image of the S & Gs being led out in handcuffs came back into his mind. He pushed it back. He had to be at his sharpest. Betrayal, no matter about its dark attractions, was not for now; perhaps it could be savored later.

The Phonemaker took a key from his belt and opened the door. "Good luck," he whispered.

Danny slipped past him and into the crowd outside a busy Underground station. The door closed behind him, one of those nondescript service doors that no one ever pays any attention to. Danny was lost in the crowd in seconds. The tube station was busy. There was even the odd tourist, despite the threat of war. The scene was exactly as he had studied it on the map, and he slipped quickly down the avenue toward the entrance to the street where the prime minister's residence was situated. A stand of trees that hadn't been shown on the map confused him momentarily, and he felt panic rising; then, beyond the trees, he saw the large stone arch through which all traffic had to go. He moved quickly. If the prime minister was punctual, then there was no time to spare. Danny preferred it that way. The longer he hung around, the better his chances of getting caught.

Keeping an eye on surveillance cameras, he moved toward the arch in the distance, but he could hear sirens approaching rapidly. He slowed down. He was twenty yards from the arch, fifteen yards, ten . . . The prime minister's motorcade appeared at the top of the street, officers on motorcycles clearing the traffic. Danny took ten quick strides forward and stepped into the cover of the arch, where the cameras could not see him. He slipped his dark glasses on and opened his raincoat to reveal the gray suit. The motorcycles entered the archway, the sound almost unbearable as the sirens reverberated off the walls. The first of the security detail running alongside appeared, one of four on each side. The careful observer would have noticed that when the motorcade emerged from the arch, there were five runners on the right-hand side. The motorcade sped toward the security gates, which swung open at the last minute. Cameras flashed, and some onlookers cheered. Then the gates swung closed again. Danny was in.

He fought to keep his head; he didn't have long. The sudden heat and blare and noise of the cars had disoriented him momentarily, and he had run through the gates in a blur. He took stock quickly. The security had relaxed now that they were out of the public thoroughfare. The prime minister's car pulled up at the entrance to his residence. The door opened, and with a shock that felt like a physical blow, Danny saw a man standing there. Longford!

Longford descended the steps grinning broadly, as though *he* were the prime minister, not the red-faced man getting out of the car.

"Any news of the killer?" the prime minister asked anxiously.

"Nothing. We've expelled their ambassador, and they've thrown ours out. It means war."

"It means nothing of the sort." The prime minister snorted. "We won't take any more provocation, but war would be a disaster."

"Of course, of course," Longford said, taking the prime minister by the elbow and steering him up the stairs. The security men glanced quickly around and then relaxed, one of them even taking out a packet of cigarettes and lighting one. A young man appeared with a cardboard tray of coffees. Danny smelled danger. The security men's eyes would track the tray, would realize that there was one too many in their company. Danny wandered behind a catering truck. *Hide in plain view!* He could hear Duddy's words ringing in his ears. He opened the cab door.

"You," he said to the driver, "where's your ID?"

"I already got checked," the young man said, looking frightened.

"This is an in-depth check," Danny said, "double-lock security. What's your clearance?"

"I don't know," the youth almost pleaded.

"What meals are you serving?"

"Er, snacks for a Ghanaian delegation, soup and sandwiches for war cabinet staff and, er, afternoon tea for Professor Longford."

"Okay," Danny said, "we're going to do a security drill. I'm going to try to breach security by pretending to be one of your staff. I want you to take me through it, teach me what to do, dress me in the right clothes. It'll be a real test of security."

"Are you sure?"

"We do these drills all the time. You want me to call your boss?"

"No, no, that's fine." The young man sat up, looking pleased with himself. "I bet I can get you all the way in there."

"You think so?" Danny said. "My money's on the security."

Twenty minutes later, Danny was serving drinks to a delegation of Ghanaian civil servants. He had become expert at standing in profile to the person he was talking to so that they saw only a brown eye or a blue eye, depending on which side they were standing on. But when he saw Longford at the other side of the room, his composure deserted him. As his gaze fell on the head of the Ring of Five, Longford stopped. Danny could feel the man's mind eagerly probing. He knew Danny was nearby.

For a second Danny was joined to Longford and the others. He could feel the brooding anger of Rufus Ness and the presence of Conal, hard and cold as it always was, but accompanied by something else, not a physical odor, but something sickening that made Danny turn away and cut off his mind. He ducked his head and turned his back to Longford. A new batch of delegates arrived in the room, putting bodies between Danny and Longford. He was shielded, but he was under no illusions. Longford knew he was close. From being the hunter, Danny had turned into the hunted.

He started to make his way toward the servants' exit, his mind clearing. He realized that the fragrant presence of Nurse Flanagan had been missing from the joining of minds. Had that presence masked the foulness of Conal's mind in the past? He risked a glance back and saw Longford talking urgently to a serious-faced man wearing a suit, but with an unmistakable military bearing. Danny could see the eagerness in Longford's face and, almost without thinking about it, joined himself with Longford's mind. Longford was caught unawares.

Instantly Danny could feel the man's triumph—he *wanted* Danny to be here! Had perhaps organized the whole thing! Danny cut off his contact with Longford's mind before the man could react. He ducked through the kitchen, looking for the youth who had led him in. But when he saw him, he no longer looked like the easygoing lad who had been sitting in the catering van. Now he was hard-faced and carrying a gun. It had all been a setup!

Danny looked up and saw a camera swivel toward him. He ducked and made his way toward the rear door of the kitchen, but two security guards now stood there. He moved toward another internal corridor. At least it wasn't guarded. The power welled up in him and he forced it down again. He tried to think what Longford might expect. He would want Danny to head down, to try to escape. So Danny would head upward. He found a service stairwell and made his way up with no other thought than to buy some time. There were no cameras here, but Danny knew his reprieve was only temporary.

He forced himself to sit down on a step and tried to work through his choices, quickly realizing that he had none. If cornered, he could surrender, or he could use his power. There was nothing else. The power was strong within him. He could use it sparingly, perhaps, control it. . . . No, that was a lie. He didn't have the strength to control it.

Suddenly a speaker burst into life above his head.

"Good afternoon, Danny," a voice said, its tone warm, almost amused.

Longford.

Nala was bewildered. He looked down at his clothes. They were covered in blood. But he hadn't hurt anyone, or had he? He could remember the elegant woman coming to his cell and waking him. Still half asleep, they had made their way out into the corridor. There was no sign of any guard. She had smiled at him, encouraged him, been kindly. And he had done well, picking lock after lock with one of her hairpins. They had almost made it. At the last door he could smell the fresh night air outside. But then what had happened? Lights, noise, men shouting, the sound of a gunshot. He had woken on the ground, blood on his shirt, a gun in his hand.

After that, there had been running. But a strange thing had happened. He had arrived at a metal fence on the edge of the prison compound. It was tall, but the strands weren't very thick, and Nala thought he could squeeze through. There were signs on it like lightning bolts, but Nala didn't know what they meant. He was about to lift the first strand, but as he did so, a raven flew into his face, its sharp claws drawing blood. Nala reeled back in pain and confusion. Suddenly there was a flock of ravens about him. They were carrying a piece of wire underneath them. As if at a prearranged signal, they dropped it onto the fence. There was a bright blue flash and a burning smell. When Nala climbed through the wire the ravens did not try to impede him, but the wire was hot in his hands.

Now he was on his own, moving blindly across country, pursued by soldiers and dogs. The ravens harassed him all the way, or so he thought. He had stopped by a stream to take a drink. He had taken off his socks and shoes to bathe his feet and a raven swooped from nowhere, grabbing one of his socks. He had thrown a stone at it, but it was no good. The sock was gone, and now he limped along, one foot blistered and bleeding.

Nala could not know what had happened to his sock. There was a dog team on his trail: German shepherds, moving fast and silent across the country. The raven had landed five hundred yards in front of them, just where Nala had crossed a stream. In what looked like a strange, raggedy dance, the raven had started to sweep the sock across the ground with its beak, moving backward. It covered a few hundred yards; then another raven took over, and so on in relays. When the dogs got to the river, they found a false scent trail leading along the banks. They followed the trail for miles up into the mountains. The ravens were nothing if not thorough.

So Nala made his weary way across country, guided in a thousand small ways by the ravens. One night he made his way toward a train station. He saw a freight wagon with its door standing open (although he hadn't seen the ravens slip the holding pins away from the door). He climbed in, and when the train lurched to life, he fell into a deep sleep on a pile of cardboard boxes in the corner of the boxcar.

Deep in the night the engine driver saw a shadow in the engine headlights. A man! He slammed on the brakes, cursing. Nala was thrown against the bulkhead violently. Instantly he was on his feet. The train driver strained against the brakes, but the man stood on the track without moving. The train would not stop in time. Sparks flew from the protesting wheels. It was no good. The train bore down on the figure, but just before it struck, to the driver's amazement, the figure flew apart, black shapes disappearing into the darkness.

The shapes converged on Nala's carriage, filling it with the beating of their wings, crowding about him and pushing him toward the door as he cursed and flailed at them. Only after he had jumped from the carriage and the train had creaked into motion did they leave him alone. Exhausted and dazed, he climbed over the high wall beside the track and found himself in a graveyard.

The dead held no fears for Nala. He found an empty crypt, crawled into it and fell back to sleep.

Danny tried to shut out the voices. Whatever Longford was going to say, it wasn't going to be good news.

"Danny," Longford went on, "you have my congratulations. You showed great resourcefulness in getting this far. But I know your heart, my boy. I knew you would long for revenge. I have always held that you were bad at heart, although poor Nurse Flanagan disagreed with me. But there is too much Cherb in you. And once a Cherb, always a Cherb."

Danny listened. He heard murmuring in the stairwell below him. He had to move, but Longford's voice held him. He stood up, but then stopped stock-still.

"It's about time for a short history lesson, my young friend. Your parents. Everyone is a little coy about what happened to them, but I know, my dear Danny, and I will share the information with you. Your father was a worthy adversary, and your mother, well, she was bright for a Cherb, and brave as a lion."

Danny's heart was beating like a hammer. To hear Longford speak about his parents made the rage rise in him.

"Your father was a brilliant spy, but he died screaming like a baby. I saw it."

Danny felt as though the sea were roaring in his ears. His teeth were clenched, the stairwell charged with electricity.

"So did your mother, for that matter. Never mentioned your name, either of them."

Danny felt the power surge to his fingertips. A vision formed in his mind of the building around him crumbled to dust. Flames shooting into the sky. People screaming. . . . He remembered the *S & G* ring being placed in his jacket. It was the cold, dead hand of his father or mother that had placed it there as he and his friends had roamed the Butts endlessly.

Now there were shouts in the stairwell below him, but around him, the paint on the wall started to bubble, the fabric of the building to crumble. Longford would die, and then it would be Brunholm's turn. The murmurs below Danny turned to panicked shouts.

Then, just before he lost control, the voice that plagued him, the voice of Spy Danny, spoke in his head. It was cold and malicious and pierced the fog of destruction in his head.

Why did Longford contact you through the speakers? Everyone in the building will have heard. Think, Danny, what's he up to?

What was he talking about? *Everyone in the building will have heard.* . . . It meant that Longford did not intend anyone in the building to survive, so it didn't matter what they heard.

It's a great idea, Spy Danny sneered. *He gets rid of the prime minister and the government, blames it on you and gets to start his war.*

Longford had to have an escape plan—and Danny knew what it was. He started to run up the stairwell, clearing the stairs three at a time.

He burst out onto the roof just as Conal took off from the parapet, Longford on his back.

"Fly, Conal! Fly, you vulture!" Longford cried. Conal's great wings beat slowly with the added weight. Longford turned with a snarl on his face.

"Your parents," he goaded, "the terrible things that were done to them. Danny, remember?"

But Danny knew now what Longford intended him to do: destroy the government and start the war. He raced toward the parapet and, just before Conal flew out of reach, he grabbed the Seraphim's leg to pull him back.

"You'll come back here and roast with the others, Longford," Danny snarled in a voice he barely recognized as his own. Longford smiled thinly.

"I don't think so. Conal?" With two powerful beats of his wings, the foul creature pulled clear of the building. Danny was pulled off his feet and found himself dangling a hundred feet above the ground.

"What would the filth that spawned you think now?" Longford crowed. "I can see the power, Danny. I can feel the air shiver with it. Drop him, Conal. Let the power consume him!"

A jolt of knowledge ran through Danny's body like electricity. There was a tone in Longford's voice that he had heard before. All was revealed to him, all made obvious. He looked up. The power roared until he was aware of nothing else. The sky had turned black. The Lost Boys, he thought, and let go.

16

SEE. SEE. SEE!

Les couldn't explain it except to say that everything about Wilsons felt *wrong*. It was as if something had been holding the place together all along, and that something had weakened, if not disappeared altogether. He started to notice how shabby the place had become. It had never been particularly spick-and-span, but now there was rubbish blowing across the lawns at the back of the school, and broken guttering spilled water down the side of the building. The damage to the Gallery of Whispers had not been repaired, and there was green mold on the walls where the damp had gotten in. Even Ravensdale, the mysterious village that functioned as a canteen for the cadets, seemed unkempt, with weeds growing in the streets and ivy crawling up the walls.

"Is it me, or are there fewer cadets here every day?" Dixie asked one afternoon in the Roosts.

"It's not you," Vandra said. "Parents are taking their children out of the place. They're all saying that Wilsons's days are over, that it stood for something once, but the world has moved on."

"What do you think?" Les stared moodily out a window.

"I think we need to find out what's going on," Vandra said firmly, "and for that we need to know what happened the last time there was no treaty."

"I've tried to talk to Master Devoy," Toxique said, "but every time I get close, Brunholm or one of his crew of telltales stops me."

"I know," Vandra said. "I asked Duddy and Spitfire about him, but they just said they never get to see Devoy either."

"It's up to us," Dixie said. "If we can't get answers from the living, we'll get them from the dead!"

They all turned to look at her, and she moved rapidly from one part of the room to another in an annoying, fidgety manner.

"What do you mean?" Vandra asked.

"If we're going to find out who the Lost Boys are, who else are we going to ask?"

"Er, we could ask Devoy, or Brunholm, or McGuinness. Or we could go to the library and look it up. That might work." Les had no desire to go among the dead again.

"Did I hear someone mention the Lost Boys?" an unexpected voice said. It was Miss Duddy.

"Why, do you know something about them, Miss Duddy?" Les said eagerly.

"The Lost Boys was a game when I was a girl," Duddy said. Les looked at her, disappointed. They weren't going to find out anything from a girls' playground game.

"How did you play it?" Dixie asked. Duddy stepped into the light. She had always looked a bit eccentric, but today she just looked shabby. Her long graying hair needed brushing and her spectacles were askew.

"Oh dear," Duddy said, "can I remember? Yes. . . . *Dum de dum de dum.* . . . Hold up your hands, Dixie. It's a clapping game, very complicated. . . . *Dum de dum.* . . . Put up your hands like this." Duddy started playing the game with Dixie, showing her the moves. It was a schoolyard game such as children everywhere play, and Dixie was good at it, picking it up fast, Duddy *dum-dum*ming at top speed. It was the end that took Dixie by surprise. The game got faster and faster, and when they got to the last part, instead of clapping Dixie's hands smartly the way she had done before, Duddy swung, right, left, right again, each time a stinging blow to Dixie's face.

"Ouch, ouch, ouch!" Dixie gasped. "What was that?"

"Fun, wasn't it?" Duddy grinned.

"Great fun." Les looked amused.

"Fun, but it doesn't get us anywhere," Vandra said.

"Hang on a moment," Toxique said, "where's the rhyme?"

216

"What rhyme?" Vandra said crossly.

"These games always have a little rhyme that goes with them.

"He's right, you know," Duddy said. "Let me think how it goes. . . . I got it."

She put her hands up again, but Dixie looked at her askance.

"Please, Dixie," Toxique said, "for me."

"What does your gift say?" Dixie looked at him.

"It anticipates you're going to get whacked in the puss," Les said, waiting for the entertainment to begin. Dixie gave him a sour look but gamely put up her hands.

Duddy began to sing:

> *"Two lost boys*
> *Two lost boys*
> *Want all the toys*
> *Want all the toys*
> *Spies are we*
> *Hate is all we feel*
> *Tap, tap, tap,*
> *Who are we?*
> *Tap, tap, tap*
> *See, see, see!"*

On the "see, see, see," Duddy dealt Dixie three fast hard slaps again. Dixie turned away, her cheeks burning.

"Sorry, dear," Duddy said, "but you did ask. It always struck me as rather a cruel game."

217

"Well, that was helpful," Les said sarcastically. Vandra said nothing, but Toxique was playing the game as if against an invisible opponent and muttering to himself.

"Come on, Toxique, let's go," Les said. "The dead have got the kettle on for us."

"Don't joke," Vandra said with a shudder.

From the main building, cold eyes watched the group. The endgame was at hand, let the chips fall as they may.

The cadets made their way to Ravensdale, where leaves blew down the main street.

"I don't ever remember *weather* in Ravensdale before," Les said. A cloud of leaves fluttered past, and from the middle came a solitary caw. The cadets walked on, but Vandra hesitated. Something had caught her healer's ear.

"Wait," she said.

"It's only one of the ravens," Dixie said. "Come on, I'm starving."

"No," Vandra said, "you go on. I want to find it."

"Give it a break," Les said, but Toxique was looking at Vandra.

"I'll help you look," he said. "I'm not all that hungry." Les threw his eyes to heaven, but he turned back to help.

It didn't take long. They spotted a pile of leaves against one side of the building, and from it, a raven emerged, dragging one wing behind it. It staggered as though drunk and fell back as the wind caught it.

"Oh, the poor thing!" Dixie exclaimed. Les caught Vandra's eye. The ravens were subtle, intelligent and sometimes cruel in pursuit of their own ends. None of the cadets had ever heard one referred to as "poor thing."

218

Nevertheless, the bird was in trouble, tumbling backward as though it had to contend with invisible winds as well as the gusts blowing through Ravensdale.

"Looks like poison to me," Toxique said. No one argued. Les took his coat off to throw it over the bird, but Vandra shook her head.

"Careful, Vandra," Toxique warned. A blow from a raven's beak was severe at the best of times, but if that beak carried toxins, contact could be fatal. But Vandra didn't flinch. She knelt down and stretched her hands out. The stricken bird fought to move toward her, its legs barely able to carry it. And when she gathered it up, it lay still and trusting in her arms. Vandra stroked its feathers. There were tears in her eyes.

"I cannot heal you," she said. "I can only give to humans." She was aware of Dixie standing beside her.

"Let me have a look," Toxique said.

"In a moment. She's a mother, I reckon," Dixie said. The raven cawed faintly. "Give her to me."

Vandra hesitated, then handed the bird to Dixie. Dixie looked down at the raven, closed her eyes and disappeared.

The others waited for Dixie to reappear—her Quality of Indeterminate Location never took her far.

This time was different.

"We need to go looking for her," Les said after many long moments. Vandra shook her head.

"She'll come back to this place. What if we're not here?" So they waited.

In the end Dixie did reappear by the gable wall of the

Consiglio dei Diece, the cadets' dining house. She was breathing hard.

"What is it?" Vandra said.

"Whatever it is, we need to move," Les said. There were voices coming up the road toward them, and among them he could hear Exspectre's reedy tones.

"Come with me," Dixie said. Her voice was sad and serious. They followed her up the road leading into the heart of the village, and soon the voices of the other cadets had faded into the darkness behind them.

They reached the gallows that stood at the crossroads in the middle of the village. Les kept his head down and would not look at it. Vandra realized that none of them had ever entered the dark streets beyond.

As soon as they left the dim light of the crossroads, they knew they were in a different place.

"How come we never came up here before?" Les whispered.

"Why are you whispering?" Toxique said.

Les shrugged. "Just don't feel like talking out loud." And in truth, none of them did. There was an ancient feel to the place. The houses were tall and gaunt, and through a window here and there they caught sight of beautiful silk drapes shot through with holes, covered in dust. There were gilded ceilings and great portraits, but none of the houses looked as if they had been lived in for many, many years.

"What happened to the people who lived here?" Vandra wondered. The empty houses provided no answer.

Dixie led them on, her white dress ghostly in the dim

light. Her silence was enough to make them a little bit uneasy. Normally she was full of chatter, but she had fallen under the spell of the place.

"This looks like the posh part of town," Les said. "Good thieving territory!"

"Shut up, Les," Vandra said.

They found themselves walking along a canal. Tall buildings leaned over the water and into each other, almost ready to topple into the dark waters. Mist drifted up from the water, wreathing them as they walked.

"I'd no idea any of this was here," Vandra whispered. They passed what had once been gaily colored canal boats, now sunk in the ooze. The path in front of them was blocked with debris, so they crossed an ornate little footbridge, Dixie moving with determination in front.

Finally they came to rusty wrought iron railings running down to the canal. Beyond the railings there were overgrown lawns leading up toward a gloomy, shuttered mansion. The gates of the mansion hung sagging on their hinges.

The cadets pushed through after Dixie.

"This is the place," she said. "When I disappeared earlier, I could feel the raven guiding me. Hurry!"

They followed her up the potholed driveway. The house loomed above them. As they neared, they could see that the paint was peeling and some of the glass panes were broken.

"Round the side," Dixie said. They followed her, walking past tumbledown coach houses and servants' quarters.

"There," Dixie said, pointing at a strange tower, a tall, tottering structure of stone that had no doors or windows. Instead, along its walls were hundreds of little nooks in rows. And somehow the group sensed that in each nook, there was something living, breathing.

"What is it?" Les whispered.

"I know," Toxique said. He was breathing hard. The ghost town they had passed through had spooked him, but he kept his emotions under control. "It's a dovecot," he said. "We have one at Toxique Towers. They used to keep pigeons in it—they'd use them to send messages."

Vandra approached the foot of the tower. There were a dozen ravens on the ground, all moving feebly, smaller than the ravens they normally saw. Faint caws came from the tower above.

Vandra lifted a small shape from the ground. It was a baby raven. It opened its beak, but no sound came out.

"They've all been poisoned," Toxique said.

"Could be a disease or something," Les said. Toxique shook his head. Scattered on the ground around the tower were many half-eaten potatoes. Taking out a handkerchief and covering his hand, he lifted one and smelled it.

"There's a yeasty smell. Birds are susceptible to molds and mildews. Someone has taken a naturally occurring mold that grows on potatoes and developed it into an avian neurotoxin."

"Pardon?" Les said.

"A bird poison. Something they might see, like a bit of mold on old potatoes, but wouldn't pay any attention to."

"These are all mothers and babies," Dixie cried. "We have to save them!"

"I can't do anything," Vandra said.

Toxique frowned. "I don't know bird poisons. I'm not familiar with the way a bird's system works."

"You have to do something," Dixie said. "Look at the poor little things!"

"If I can synthesize the poison from the potato, find out what it is, maybe I can find an antidote, but I need a lab."

"Where are all the males?" Vandra said. "The mothers and babies don't have any protection."

"I don't know. Gather up as many of those potatoes as you can, but don't touch them. The poison is meant for birds, but we better not take any chances."

"Where'd Les go?" Dixie asked.

"I don't know. Come on. These birds don't have all day."

For the next ten minutes they gathered as many of the potatoes as they could, noticing that they had an odd greenish hue.

"That looks promising," Toxique said, "but I really need a lab!"

"Would a kitchen do?" Les had reappeared, a little dusty.

"Where?"

"I broke into the big mansion. There's a massive kitchen in the basement. Hasn't been used for a long time, but there's a stove all set with logs and ready to go."

"It'll have to do," Toxique said.

They clambered through the back window where Les had forced the latch and found themselves in a big old-fashioned kitchen. There were Tilley lamps and lanterns hanging from hooks and Dixie soon had them all lit, flitting around the kitchen at speed. Les got the big black stove burning while Toxique collected glassware and Vandra gathered up all the young ravens she could find. She put them in wooden crates she found stacked at the back door and placed them around the stove. The heat, when it came, seemed to help the birds a little. Some of them moved their wings weakly.

Toxique moved so quickly that only Vandra was able to keep up with him. Dixie and Les watched for a while; then Les whispered, "Fancy exploring this place?" Dixie nodded.

"One condition, though," she said. "No stealing."

"Scout's honor," Les said, with an expression of such innocence that Dixie nearly burst out laughing.

They sneaked out of the room and went up a small servants' stairway. They took the first door they came to and found themselves in a great hall with oak paneling and portraits hung all around.

"This is pretty nobby," Les said. "Shall we dance, my lady?" He turned the handle of an old-fashioned record player and the strains of a waltz sounded through the hallway. Dixie frowned.

"Too spooky," she said. It made her think of long-forgotten balls, carriages pulling up on the gravel, beautiful ladies and handsome men, all now gone and turned to dust. She could practically hear the laughter, the clink of glasses, the whirr of fans, the brush of crinolines on polished wood. . . .

There was silence. Les had lifted the needle off the record.

"That was weird," he said. "I felt as if I was really at a ball or something."

"Me too," Dixie said. "Really strange."

Les picked up a tennis racket from a rack beside the great door. Suddenly he could smell cut grass, hear the pock of tennis balls being struck. Meanwhile, Dixie had lifted a silver candlestick from the sideboard and heard the clink of knife and fork on plate, the murmur of diners' conversations.

"What is this place?" Dixie said. Les picked up a dance card and once again heard music, a waltz this time. The heading on the dance card read *The Hall of Memories Annual Ball.*

"The Hall of Memories." Les gazed around. "I wonder if they built it deliberately, or did the walls start to absorb memories?"

"Goodness knows," Dixie said. Then, in a tremulous voice, she called, "Mum?"

Les heard a soft musical voice: *"Tidy up your toys, dear, it's time for bed."*

The voice faded away. Dixie looked stunned. Les put his hand on her arm.

"Maybe you shouldn't think of things like that, Dixie." Her face glistened with tears.

"It was her, Les. It was really her. I remember that night."

"Then remember this, Dixie: we've got to make sure that no other children lose their mums and dads like we did." He drew her gently out of the great, sad hall. "Come on," he said, leading her up a great staircase. "Let's explore a bit more. Did your mum and dad do that disappearing thing you do? I bet it must have been really funny in your house. . . ." Les prattled on in a kindly way, trying to distract Dixie from her sorrow, leading her farther into the depths of the strange old house.

In the mansion's kitchen, Toxique was frowning. He had tried every compound he could make in the primitive lab he had built, but none worked. The boxes of fledgling ravens around the stove made him desperately aware of the urgency of the situation.

"You have to do something," Vandra said.

"There is something . . . ," Toxique said slowly, "but it isn't guaranteed, and the price is high."

"What?" Vandra demanded.

"I need to examine the body of a dead raven, carry out an autopsy, see which organs are affected."

"But I haven't seen any dead ravens yet," Vandra said.

"And by the time they start to die, it will be too late," Toxique said. Vandra absorbed what her friend had said, her eyes wide.

"You can't mean . . . But it's the ravens, Toxique. You wouldn't dare . . . I mean . . ."

"Not even if it would save them?" Toxique's face was somber.

"You couldn't," Vandra said. Toxique laughed mirthlessly.

"I am an assassin, remember?"

"You are and you are not," Vandra said. "To do such a thing would haunt you for the rest of your days." She bowed her head. "It will be me. They will never forgive me, but there is no choice."

"No," Toxique said. "You are a healer."

Neither of them had seen the mother raven who had summoned them. She had dragged herself into the kitchen and painfully climbed through the shadows onto one of the rafters. She cocked her head to one side as she listened to Vandra and Toxique. If she hadn't been looking down on a box containing her own chicks, drawn up by the stove, you would have thought she was laughing.

Toxique stifled a squeal as a black object hurtled passed him and struck the corner of the stove with great force. Vandra froze.

"What is it?" Toxique said. Vandra bent to the floor and picked up the limp body of the bird.

"It's the raven that fetched us," Vandra said. "Her neck's broken. She's dead."

Toxique took the raven from Vandra.

"You can't, Toxique—her babies are there!" Vandra was appalled.

"Why do you think she flew against the stove and broke her own neck?" Toxique said furiously. "She heard what we were saying. I needed a body and she gave it to me. And I'm still not sure I'll be able to find the answers I need!"

"She didn't ask you to be perfect," Vandra said. "She just asked you to do your best."

Les didn't know how they had found their way onto this landing. It seemed even older than the Hall of Memories. There were suits of armor, and great swords hung on the walls, notched with the signs of battle. Les touched a great dented helmet and lifted the visor, then dropped it quickly. Had he seen the gleam of eyes inside? Surely not.

"Maybe we should make our way back down-stairs . . . ," he said. But Dixie was in a strange mood.

"We'll just take a little look around," she said.

"Seems to be mostly bedrooms up here," Les said, peering through a doorway at a massive four-poster bed hung with moldering drapes. Dixie opened doors and restlessly flickered here and there, as though looking for something.

Les was uneasy. "Maybe we should—"

"Wait," Dixie interrupted. She went into the large room at the end of the landing. Les waited a moment, then followed. Dixie held up her lantern.

It was a child's room, or rather a children's room. There were identical beds on either side, both with dusty blue counterpanes. There were pajamas on each pillow, and toy boxes beside the beds. And on each side there was a clothes rack filled with old-fashioned suits. Les lifted down one of the suits.

"Somebody about fourteen or fifteen, I'd say, by the size of this."

"Look here," Dixie said. She had opened the big wardrobe at the back of the room.

"Wow," Les said, "great stuff!" The wardrobe was a spy's dream. There were disguises, gun pens, poison-tipped umbrellas, devices for listening through walls, dozens of invisible inks, and cipher books.

"Cool," Dixie said, "our two boys were spies!" They looked at each other, the thought hitting them both at the same time.

"Two boys. *The Lost Boys!* It couldn't be!"

"Hang on a second," Les said. "If these boys were proper spies, then this can't be all there is to it." He climbed into the wardrobe and started tapping the sides and back of it. He reached down and twisted an innocent-looking wooden support. There was a click, and then, in well-oiled silence, the back of the wardrobe slid open.

"Spooky," Les said.

"More than spooky," Dixie said with a shudder. "You go first."

Les clambered in and gave a low whistle. The little room beyond the back of the wardrobe was covered in dust and cobwebs, but there was no mistaking that this was spying of a different order.

Les looked along one side of the room. "Poisons, darts, knives . . ."

"Torture instruments," Dixie said. "Thumbscrews, pincers, electric shock machines, hot irons . . . Ugh! This is horrible!"

"Seems our boys had a secret life," Les said.

"Look at this," Dixie breathed. At the rear of the

room was a tailor's dummy—or at least, that was what it looked like; it was hard to tell, for it was slashed, stabbed and burned with acid.

"Pretty vicious, our two Lost Boys," Les said.

"If that's who they were," Dixie said with another shiver. "Les, I want to get out of here. . . . Les . . ."

Les heard the tone of alarm in Dixie's voice and spun around. The secret door they had come through was sliding shut.

"Dixie, go!" Les knew he wouldn't reach it, but Dixie could flicker to the door and get through easily. When she hesitated, he shoved her. One minute she was there, and the next she was gone. Les watched as the narrow opening closed.

What now? He recoiled at the thought of gas flooding the room, or perhaps water, for he had no doubt that this was a defense mechanism and that the two boys hadn't finished with him yet. He caught a flash out of the corner of his eye and jumped. A steel blade almost ten feet long protruded from the floor where he had been standing. Another movement. Les jumped behind the stuffed dummy and a blade pierced it. Then another, and another, bright, quivering blades, razor sharp, at first seeming random . . . but Les soon realized that his escape routes were being cut off one by one.

A blade shot across his face, followed by another as he spun out of the way of the first, and he felt a sharp pain in his thigh. When he put his hand down, it came away wet with blood. Why not just kill me? he thought. But part of him knew why: whoever had designed this didn't want to just kill an intruder, he wanted to toy with him first.

And Les was tiring. His right leg where he had been wounded now barely supported him. Sometimes the blades shot at him three or four in quick succession; then there might be a lull of a minute or two. The attacks came from the floor, from the walls, from the ceiling. The entire room was now a latticework of steel. He knew had to find corners and gaps, keeping in mind that any gap might have been left deliberately so as to lure him into it. The feathers of his wings had been parted several times, but all at once a blade passed through a thick clump of feathers, pinning him against the wall. He watched weakly as the bright blades cleaved the air. It was only a matter of time, but he felt detached, almost peaceful. So much so that he quite resented the loud explosion that came next, the flame and smoke filling the air, the dust and debris.

"Come on!" Dixie shouted, grabbing him. She seized a stiletto and slashed at the feathers that held Les to the wall. Limping, half blinded with smoke, his lungs burning from acrid fumes, he took Dixie's arm and stumbled back into the bedroom.

"What . . . ?" he gasped.

"They had a bomb kit in the wardrobe. Took me a few minutes to work it out. I might have overdone it a bit. . . ." Dixie spat out a piece of plaster. The bedroom was devastated. Both beds had been upended and blown against the wall, and the ceiling had collapsed in places.

"You did a job on this gaff," Les said shakily as he

clambered over the rubble. His injured leg gave way beneath him and he pitched forward onto his face.

"You okay?" Dixie said anxiously. "You know, I don't like this house very much."

"I know what you mean," Les groaned. Then his eyes fell on something in the rubble: a leather satchel, the front of it badly burned from the explosion.

"What is it?" Dixie asked as he lifted the satchel.

"Look," he said. Most of the name had been burned away, but five letters remained: *ARCUS*.

"Arcus . . . Marcus! At least now we know who one of the evil boys is," Les said grimly. "Marcus Brunholm!"

"Hang on," Dixie said, "I can smell burning."

Les limped over to the place where the bomb had gone off. The floor had been shattered, and smoldering debris had fallen into a bedroom downstairs, landing on a huge four-poster bed. As Les looked, flames licked at it; then, with a *whoosh*, the whole thing burst into flames. Les fell back.

"We need to get out of here," he said.

In the kitchen below, Toxique bent over a homemade filter system. Vandra had gathered up as many of the chicks as she could, but she realized that the birds high above in the dovecot were out of reach, too ill to fly down.

"Anything?" she asked anxiously.

"It's hard," Toxique said. "If this substance had been made by an expert in poisons it would be easier. This one has been put together by someone who has only a little knowledge but is very, very clever. I think I've got it, but I need to test it out."

"Please don't start experimenting on the babies, Toxique."

"Babies, mothers, it doesn't matter. I have to try it on one of them."

"Does the poison work on people?"

"I'm starting to suspect it's even more toxic for humans." Vandra came over to the table where Toxique was working. Before he could stop her, she picked up a piece of the poisoned potato and swallowed it.

"Now," she said calmly as Toxique looked on, aghast, "your antidote better work."

"Why did you do that?" Toxique asked.

"Because I'm a healer. It's part of my job. I can't sit here and watch you experiment with mothers and babies, even if they are ravens. So. How long does the poison take to act?"

"You should start showing signs within ten minutes. But I haven't made enough of the antidote for a human, Vandra! I was only going to test a little on the birds!"

"Well, you'd better get moving, haven't you? Ouch. I can feel it already. My stomach's a bit queasy."

Toxique stared at her, beads of sweat breaking out on his forehead.

"It's all right, Toxique," she said, "I trust you."

Toxique turned back to his equipment, but there was a tremor in his hands where there had been none before.

"I wonder where Les and Dixie are," Vandra said. "I wish they hadn't wandered off. . . ."

* * *

Les and Dixie were still in the Lost Boys' bedroom, and they were in trouble. If Vandra had left the kitchen and looked outside, she would have seen flames starting to leap from the fifth-floor windows. The fire had spread rapidly, faster than Les and Dixie had expected. Dixie had spent several minutes trying to staunch the blood flow from Les's injured leg. When they had tried to leave the room, it was too late. Dixie put her hand on the doorknob and snatched it away.

"What is it?" Les said.

"The handle is red hot." Dixie wrapped her hand in a towel and reached for the doorknob again.

"Stop!" Les said. "Don't. The fire is on the other side of the door. That's why the handle is hot. The flames will consume you." Dixie looked at Les's frightened face and took her hand away.

"The Cherbs," Les said, "they burned our house. . . . I remember. . . ."

Dixie took his hand.

"We'll find another way out."

"At least you can," Les said. "You can disappear and reappear somewhere else." Dixie shook her head.

"I can only do it for short distances. And I have to know where the fire is. I could reappear right in the middle of it. Better not to chance it."

"I wish I could fly, but I can't," Les said. "This wing won't hold."

"Well, if we can't go downstairs, we can go up," Dixie

234

said. "I don't know if you noticed, but it's getting a bit hot and smoky in here."

"Up?" Les raised his eyebrows. He knew that the farther they got from the ground, the less hope there would be. But there was smoke coming through the floorboards. At least on the roof there would be air. Les went to the window again and looked down. As he did so, one of the great windows of the Hall of Memories was blown out by a jet of flame. A thousand voices rose, the sounds melting together until all he could hear was a great sigh that swelled, then faded away, an infinity of memories lost to the night air.

"Right," Les said, relieved that the murmurings were gone, for he had dreaded hearing the voice of a loved one, the way Dixie had. "Let's hit the back stairs."

They ran up the servants' stairs, passing the garret bedrooms where the maids would have slept. The stairwell was starting to fill with smoke—another minute or two and they would have been too late—and they choked as they ran. The air cleared a little when they reached the top floor. Les spotted a small attic door and they ran through it, out into the starlit night. They paused, coughing, on the rooftop.

"Strange," Dixie said.

"What?"

"The roof's flat. You wouldn't expect that in an old house. And there's another building on it. A little hut."

"Never mind that," Les said, "look!" He pointed toward Wilsons. The village of Ravensdale was hidden in mist, but they could see the front of Wilsons clearly, and the view was disturbing. A motley collection of vehicles was pulled up at the front of the school—cars, vans, motorcycles with sidecars, even an old-school charabanc. Pupils were streaming out the front door as the porter, Valant, tried to organize the flow.

"They're evacuating the school!" Dixie cried.

"We need to be thinking about evacuating this roof," Les said. He tried to flex his injured wing and winced.

"What's going on?" Dixie stared toward Wilsons until a gout of black smoke erupted from the floor below them and hid the view.

"Maybe there's something we could make a parachute out of," Dixie said.

"Kind of a long shot," Les said, "but we'll take a look in that hut. There might be something there."

Les sounded bright and brave, but they both knew it was a long way down, and there was no other way off. They made their way across the slippery roof. Les felt Dixie take his arm, and when she said it was because she didn't want to fall, he knew she wasn't telling the truth.

Vandra wondered if she had misjudged everything. Her stomach was taut as a drum and her forehead was bathed in sweat. Toxique did not look in control of the situation, and he had begun to mutter his old oaths of "blood and entrails," or "pain and death." He had knocked over his equipment several times and spilled the compound, each time starting again from scratch. The ill ravens were restless, and to add to matters, there was a strange, smoky atmosphere in the kitchen.

"Got it!" Toxique cried. He handed a glass to Vandra with shaking hands. Vandra gulped down the foul-tasting liquid. They waited. Nothing. Toxique watched nervously. Vandra's system was different from those of ordinary mortals. Perhaps the poison would react differently. She slipped off her chair and fell to the floor, but when she lifted her head and spoke, her voice was clear.

"It's all right, make more. It's working!"

Toxique turned back to his instruments. Vandra got to her feet shakily. Something was wrong. The smoke and smell of burning was getting stronger. She stepped outside, and looked up, appalled. Flames leapt from the top windows of the house, and heavy black smoke rolled from the lower floors.

"Les, Dixie," she whispered. She ran back into the kitchen.

"Toxique, the place is on fire!"

"Then we'd better work fast," Toxique said.

"What about Les and Dixie?"

"They can look after themselves. They'll have to."

As Toxique worked, Vandra used a spoon to drip the antidote into the birds' beaks. As soon as she had finished, she brought them outside and carried them as far away from the house as possible, then turned to look at the dovecot in despair. Those birds were too high up and too sick to help. She started to work on the ones on the ground, trying to ignore the steady roar of the fire and the heat on her back.

*   *   *

Les and Dixie had reached the long, low structure in the middle of the roof. Although the rest of the building was old, this looked new, and the heavy lock on the door was bright and oiled. It took Les precious minutes to pick it. They pushed it open.

There was nothing old about the contents of the building either. There were several high-powered telescopes set in alcoves along one wall. There was listening and recording equipment, banks of it, with rows of dials and switches. There were directional microphones and infrared body heat detectors.

Dixie opened a cupboard. It was lined with tapes, each one with a date and a record of its contents written in bold letters on its cover. She opened another cupboard—the same.

"Whoever uses this place has been spying on Wilsons for decades," she said. "Look, here are photos of Danny arriving at the place. Here's us sneaking into the Butts. And this is the time we went to Tarnstone."

"Wait a second," she said, picking up a tape from the windowsill. "This one says it shows us coming up through Ravensdale and finding the sick ravens. That's only about an hour ago!"

"Which means that whoever was recording from here has only just left," Les said. He stroked his chin. "Dixie, when you looked out the window did you notice anything strange?"

"Like what?"

"Well, the Hall of Memory was on fire, but there was still only smoke coming from the floor below us."

"So?"

"The fire started in the room below us. It should have spread slowly downward. There were two fires. Somebody started one in the Hall of Memories. Someone wanted to get rid of us by setting the building on fire."

Dixie looked about, alarmed.

"They're not here, Dixie, they had to be below us. Whoever it was set the fire and ran."

"Les, have you noticed? The floor is starting to get warm. And there's a bit of smoke coming up through it. . . ." Dixie's voice was tremulous. Les put his arm around her.

"There's nothing in here we can make a parachute out of, is there?" she said. Les shook his head.

"Maybe we should go outside," he said gently.

"Okay."

Holding hands, Les and Dixie walked out onto the roof. Flame had burst through here and there. The air was full of smoke, and under their feet they could feel the very fabric of the building trembling as the fire devoured it.

"We should go to the edge of the roof," Les said. "I think there's a bit more air there."

"We're not going to get off this roof, Les, are we?" Dixie said.

"Maybe you can try disappearing," Les said.

"It's too far to the ground. I'd fall and kill myself. Besides, that would leave you on your own, and I'm not going to do that."

Still holding hands, they walked to the edge of the roof. From below came the sound of crashing timber, and a great fountain of sparks burst from the front of the building, cascading down into the night.

"It's beautiful, isn't it, Les," Dixie said. "I mean, not just the sparks, but the whole world."

"It is, Dixie," Les agreed. "We'll just sit down here for a while, will we? There's a little bit of a breeze."

"It is getting hot," Dixie said. They sat down. Below them the fire roared like a great ravening beast. Someone looking from the ground would have seen them sitting on the parapet, holding hands and chatting, before a huge billow of smoke blew across the roof and they were seen no more.

17

THE BOATMAN

The ravens knew what was happening at the dovecot, but they flew fast and true in the opposite direction. The wild birds had brought them information of troops massing at the ports, and migratory fowl had reported armies on the move. Even more disturbingly, there were reports of activity at remote nuclear bases in the Arctic. Squadrons of Seraphim were in the air, staying high, it was true, but making no real attempt to conceal themselves.

Nothing about the ravens' flight showed their agony at heading directly away from their dying wives and children. They flew straight and true, converging on a single point, that point being the prime minister's doomed residence. What was more, they contrived to arrive at exactly the right time to catch Danny when Conal dropped him, surmising that in Danny's last moments despair would cause him to unleash his power. Stunned, Danny looked up. He had fallen into a complex web of ropes woven from straw, the end of each rope held in the beak of a raven. There were hundreds of them, but they struggled to hold his weight. Conal and Longford, on seeing Danny fall, had taken off at great speed to avoid the power, but on seeing what had happened, Conal had made a great banking turn and was now speeding toward the net. The ravens and their straw ropes would never resist his awful strength. But as he bore down on them, another crowd of ravens flew into his face. With a cry of rage, he tried to drive through them. Once, twice, three times he tried, but they would not yield. They flew at him, driving him away. With a screech of rage and frustration, he turned and fled.

Danny could feel the power pulsing like electricity in every cell of his being. He longed to yield and yet he could not. He looked down. The prime minister stood on the pavement outside his residence, gazing skyward and resisting the attempts of his security men to bring him inside under cover. He could not tear his eyes away from the sight of his chief advisor being borne away on the back of a screeching, winged creature. A television camera was tilted upward. The ravens moved sideways so they wouldn't be seen. Danny could feel that they were at the limits of their strength but that something drove them to hang on, something that was not lust for power or the urge to betray. Down the woven straw ropes he felt their love and despair. With a terrible effort he forced the power to subside. Now was not the time.

As if he no longer weighed as much, the ravens lifted

him higher into the air. The city was laid out beneath him, a place of air-raid shelters and guns, ready for war. The ravens bore him over it, and after ten minutes he found himself drifting slowly down. At first he didn't recognize the destination—he hadn't seen it from the sky before—but as the ground approached he saw graves, mausoleums and a little gate, barely visible, letting onto a busy road. The ground sped toward him now, an urgency communicating with him through the straw ropes. With a thump he landed. The ravens had brought him to the entrance to the ghost roads. He looked to the sky, thinking to somehow thank them, but they were already black specks in the distance.

Danny stood up, trying to get his bearings. He had to get back to Wilsons—the answer lay there. And it had to be soon. He had traveled the ghost roads with Beth and Nana, but they had driven, and even then it had taken days, or was it weeks? Time was different when you were on the ghost roads. He had to move faster than that.

He concentrated, gathering his thoughts. The power had subsided a little in him during the flight, but it was still there. The slightest thing could push him over the edge.

Wait a second, the voice in his mind counseled. *Why are you leaving this whole world to Longford? It could be yours. You could rule it wisely.*

Danny tried to shut out the sly voice of Danny the Spy. In the end, he had to negotiate with it. I have to deal with Wilsons one way or another, he thought. When I've finished there, I'll be back to my spy ways.

The voice fell silent, and as it did, something hit Danny hard from behind. The air was driven from his lungs and he fell to the ground. He twisted around violently and felt fingers like steel hawsers at his throat. He fought for breath and raised his hand to strike his attacker, feeling the power rise in him again. But the fingers loosened, the red mist faded, and he found himself staring into a pair of eyes, one blue and one brown.

"Nala!" He gasped. The Cherb boy released him and hauled him to his feet. Danny rubbed his throat as Nala watched him warily, not knowing what to expect, but Danny looked up and smiled.

"You know," he said, "there's something about seeing a friendly face. I never thought I'd say it to a Cherb, but I'm glad you're here."

Nala didn't say anything, but Danny thought he was pleased. He grabbed Danny's arm and pulled him to a nearby crypt. One wall had fallen in, and Danny hesitated in front of the dark maw, but Nala pulled him inside. The Cherb had obviously made his way out onto the street to look for food, and he had found it. Danny examined the cartons and boxes on the ground. There were prepacked sandwiches just in date, Swiss rolls and biscuits just out.

"Where did you find this?" Danny asked.

"Big steel case," Nala said, and Danny guessed he had found them in a Dumpster behind a supermarket. But they were none the worse for that. Danny grabbed a BLT and wolfed it, washing it down with a bottle of lemonade. Nala watched him approvingly as he followed it with a large chunk of Swiss roll.

"Thanks, Nala," Danny said when he had finished. "I needed that. I can think better on a full stomach."

The little graveyard was peaceful, the noise of the city beyond the walls almost inaudible. The picture of Longford soaring over the rooftops came into his head. Longford had wanted Danny to destroy the prime minister's residence to provide a reason to go to war. But his plan had been foiled. Worse, he had been seen on the back of one of the winged creatures. His relationship with the government was damaged, probably irreparably. But men like Longford didn't make do with just one plan. They had backups, maybe three or four of them. What would Longford do? If he couldn't trick or provoke Danny into using his power, what else would he do?

Coldly Danny allowed himself to enter the evil part of his mind and unleashed the spy, the schemer. *If it were me, I would capture someone you loved and hold them until you did what I asked. What's more,* the voice sneered, *you would do as I commanded, for you fear being abandoned more than you fear death itself!*

Angrily Danny pushed the voice away. Nala was watching him with concern. The voice was right. The only person who mattered to him was in the apothecary.

Not the only person, he reminded himself. Les and Dixie and the rest of his friends were still at Wilsons. And feeling Nala's eyes on him, he knew that he counted Nala among his friends as well.

Any veneer of civilization had dropped from Longford. He would do anything to get his way. And Wilsons had been infiltrated at the very highest level. Danny knew that.

"What's wrong?" Nala asked.

"I need to get back to Wilsons," Danny said, "but the ghost roads could take weeks and I don't have weeks!"

"There is other way," Nala said quietly.

"What?" Danny demanded. "What other way?"

"The way of the dead," Nala said, "the dark stream."

"But don't you have to be . . . dead?"

"No," Nala said with a strange look. "Not dead to travel dark stream. Maybe dead at end."

"Why? Is it dangerous?"

"Dangerous? Not like gun or knife dangerous."

"What is it, then?"

"You ever see someone killed with fear?" Nala said. "You can die of fear."

Vandra and Toxique had dealt with all the sick birds they could reach. Vandra turned again and again to the burning building.

"Where *are* Les and Dixie?" she said in despair.

"They can look after themselves," Toxique said, but there was no conviction in his voice.

"And *they* can't," Vandra said, looking up at the rows of sick birds.

Suddenly there was a great whirring and the air was thick with birds. "What's that?" Toxique said.

"More ravens," Vandra said, "but there's no way they're big enough to carry the sick ones out of here."

"No, they're not," Toxique agreed, "but *those* are!"

The ravens had gathered a battalion of birds, all big and strong. There were pelicans and geese, swans and golden eagles. Vandra could have sworn afterward that she saw an albatross among them. Without waiting for direction, each of the great birds took a sick raven in its beak and flew to the ground with it, as far from the flames as possible. The other ravens flew above the mass of birds, directing operations, it appeared.

"Come on," Toxique said, "we've got work to do." Not trusting Toxique's shaking hands, Vandra grabbed the bucket full of antidote and they started on the first birds.

There were many of them, and they looked sicker than the ones that had already been treated. Vandra prayed the antidote would bring them all around. The scene would have looked hellish to an onlooker, a ghastly light cast over it by the burning building while sick birds cawed feebly and the air whirred with wings. Vandra heard a shrieking noise and looked up fearfully. A great owl, a handsome male she had noticed earlier, had flown too close to the flames. His feathers had caught fire and he plunged, his plumage ablaze, to the ground.

Vandra shuddered. She looked to the roof of the mansion, but it was consumed in flame. Les and Dixie! She felt a sharp peck on her hand and flinched in pain. One of the ravens stared up at her, then plunged its beak into her hand again. She looked down. There were four fledgling ravens on the ground in front of her, barely moving. She took up her teaspoon and started to feed the antidote to the first one. Tears ran from her eyes onto the baby raven's plumage. It opened its beak and uttered a single soft caw.

"Tell me everything you know about the dark stream, Nala," Danny said. Fear or no fear, he had to get to Wilsons.

"Not much," Nala said. "Boat comes when you want it. Don't touch other bank of river, whatever you do."

"Okay," Danny said, "we better get moving, then." He stood up and suddenly felt that someone was prodding him with a stiletto: Longford was trying to get into his mind! He swayed and almost fell to the ground. Nala put out a steadying hand and looked at him with real concern as Danny pushed Longford away.

"I'm fine," Danny said gruffly. "An unwelcome guest is all." Nala shrugged, not understanding. Danny started to walk, but Nala pushed in front of him.

"You need to learn to walk in ghost road," Nala said.

And there was much to be learned. Danny hadn't realized the whole time he was with Nana and Beth that Nana was traveling a complex path that required much thought and concentration, particularly in a vehicle. For a start, you always had to be on the left-hand side of the road; otherwise, the ghost traffic, invisible and unfelt, traveling on the right would slow you to an eventual standstill, leaving you too exhausted to move and not knowing why. There were sayings and invocations for crossing bridges and cresting hills. Passing through forests at dawn or dusk (Danny realized that Nana had avoided this), you had to turn your jacket inside out so that evil spirits would not recognize you. There were patches of ground to be avoided because to cross them was to be assailed by terrible hunger. There were Pools of Regret, where swimmers were overcome by sadness and sank unprotesting beneath the surface. Danny realized that when he had been learning maths and history in school, Nala had been learning about the ghost roads. Cherb education was all about learning what you needed to know to stay alive in a hostile world.

It took two days to reach the entrance to the dark stream. Nala found food. He hunted and killed without mercy. They ate rabbit and partridge. But Nala could also find wild garlic, and tiny strawberries growing under hedges. He gathered fragrant mushrooms in the dawn cool, and berries deep in the woods. Danny could feel health and strength flowing back into him, and a sense that the Danny he had left far behind, before he had been sent to Wilsons, was back. Nana and Beth had looked after him in a gentle way, but Nala expected him to gut rabbits and to make snares. He was being given the weapons to fight the forces struggling within him.

On the evening of the second day they reached the dark stream. Nala, always quiet, had said less and less as they approached the glen.

"What's wrong, Nala?" Danny asked. But Nala wouldn't speak. He had produced a set of wooden beads from somewhere and ran them through his fingers continuously, his lips moving.

"You sure you want to do this?" Danny prodded. Nala nodded brusquely and put the beads in his pocket. They descended the stone steps leading to the little door. Danny touched it and it swung open silently. Downward they went, the dark enfolding them, warm and intimate. Danny could feel Nala's shoulder against his, could sense his fear. He felt Longford's mind probe for his and recoil instantly—was it the proximity to death that scared Longford?

They heard the water before they saw it, a rushing sound that echoed gently in the cavern around them. They forged on toward the river and arrived at last at the landing stage, the water flowing dark and velvety in front of them, the rushing now overlaid with whispering voices, millions of voices, perhaps.

"Look!" Nala said in a hoarse whisper. Moving toward them on the water, riding easily and smoothly, though no hand guided it, was a boat. It was long and narrow and was made of a smooth black wood with no ornament save for simple silver mooring rings at either side of the bow. The mooring rings looked too much like coffin handles to Danny's eyes, but he didn't share the thought with Nala.

The boat glided to a halt at the little dock. There were two simple wooden benches inside, but no oars or any other means of steering. Nala muttered something.

"What was that?" Danny asked.

"What if . . . what if it take us to the other side? Nothing to stop it. Maybe Nala not get on board."

"You're coming with me," Danny said. "I'm not getting into that thing on my own. Come on!"

Without thinking, Danny stepped down into the little boat and stretched his hand up. Nala hesitated, then took it and stepped into the bow. Danny could see the whites of his eyes in the gloom. With a tiny jolt, the boat moved away from the slip. Nala was caught off balance and stumbled backward, the seat behind him catching him in the back of the knees. He would have fallen overboard if Danny had not steadied him. Nala quickly sat down, grabbing the thwarts with both hands. Danny looked down into the water, if water it was, and wondered what would happen to someone who fell in. Were there living, swimming things in the water? Danny tried not to let his mind dwell on what kind of fish might inhabit the river of the dead.

The boat floated midstream and caught a faster current. No air moved around them to indicate how fast they might be going, but Danny could see a tiny wave at the bow and a swirl of turbulence behind the boat. He tried to give Nala a reassuring smile, but it felt more like a grimace.

For an hour they moved on the river, their surroundings unchanging, the whispering of the throng on the far bank constant, the voices of the multitudes lulling Danny into a strange state between consciousness and sleep. He was aware of Nala's eyes on him, but nothing else, unless it was voices calling to him, voices of memory rising out of his past. . . .

"Look out!" Nala shouted. Danny came to. The hull of the boat grated on shingle. Danny was remotely aware of water lapping on a dark shore, of hands reaching out, of voices calling, but as he awakened, the boat swung away from the shore, the voices faded, and the grasping hands turned to mist and disappeared.

"You must stay awake." Nala's voice was low. "You can't let them call you to the dark shore."

Danny was shaken. He thought he'd heard some voices he recognized—Stone, perhaps; even his parents—or was it a fancy that his mind had constructed? He didn't have time to think about it. The surface of the river was starting to change. If he had been on a real river in a real boat, he would have said they had hit rapids. The boat tossed and plunged. He held on tight to the thwart. There was terror in Nala's eyes.

"What is it, Nala?" Danny said.

"Beast, beast!" Nala cried. Danny looked down. What he had taken for waves were glistening black coils covered in scales, as if the water was full of a thousand snakes. The boat was being tossed from side to side, but there was a rhythm to it, as though they were being toyed with in a terrible game. Then the movement ceased and the boat stopped dead in the water. Danny did not know what force commanded the boat, but it would take great power to stop it.

There was absolute silence. Nala moaned. The Cherb, brave and stoic in the face of most danger, was now paralyzed with fear. His eyes widened.

"Easy, Nala, easy," Danny said, trying to soothe him.

Then he realized that Nala was looking not at him but at a point over his shoulder. Danny felt as if someone had placed an icy hand on the nape of his neck. He turned slowly and found himself face to face with the most hideous thing he had ever seen. A creature with a head like that of a horse, a dead horse, with flesh hanging in gobbets from its skull. Two great nostrils flared above a mouth in which jets of greenish flame replaced teeth. And above the nostrils: empty sockets for eyes, a darkness in which eons of evil knowledge lurked.

The creature breathed out and Danny gagged. He felt as if he had been submerged in a pond of foul slime and rot. He reeled back and saw that the head was attached to the great coils that had tossed their boat about so playfully. The creature moved closer to him. He scrambled back and fell into the bottom of the boat. He felt the power of the Fifth rise in him but instinctively knew that he was faced by a much older and deeper power.

The creature seemed to be sniffing him, but it wasn't looking for scent. Danny felt as if something was tugging at his actual mind, sucking in the essence of who he was, taking his thoughts, everything. . . . With a moan of pure fear Nala threw himself between Danny and the beast. The beast reared back, then bent his great neck forward again, and anger and malice swept the little boat as if the gates of hell themselves had been opened. Danny felt himself enveloped in terror, blinded to all else. He was aware of Nala holding his own face with desperate hands, as though he could stop the beast from sucking his mind out. Danny's head filled with a cold howling and he knew that the beast was speaking words of infinite loneliness and hatred to him, though he did not know its language.

There was a great surge in the water. He was dimly aware of the beast's tail rearing above the boat, then slapping the water. He tried to duck but a great sheet of water swept over him. For a moment he felt as though part of him was dissolving in it, and he feared that his soul was stolen. There was a great ache of fear, and then, somehow, a calm. And through the calm he heard a whistle. That sounds just like a referee's whistle, he thought, and through all the noise and cold commotion and hatred a laugh bubbled up inside him, a tiny chuckle at the absurdity of the thought that somewhere in this zone of the dead there would be someone to referee one of the games he had played long ago in the playground.

It wasn't much of a laugh, but it was enough to make the beast turn aside, puzzled by this strange emotion coursing through the mind of its prey.

There it is again! Danny thought, the whistle shriller this time. The boat rocked and was almost upended as a judder ran through the creature's coils. Danny grabbed the gunwale with one hand and got hold of Nala with the other. The whistle sounded again, but this time it was loud and long like a silvery trumpet and the creature reacted even more violently, thrashing around and throwing masses of water—if it was water—high into the air, where it hung in great sheets before falling slowly back to the surface. The boat bucked and shuddered but somehow did not capsize. From the same direction as the whistle came a loud voice.

"Begone, foul serpent! Crawl back into your vile lair! Return to the stench pit prepared for you and await the coming of doom. Await your extinction there or meet it here, it matters not to me!"

The serpent gave another great shudder. The surface of the water boiled, and then, as if the beast had never been, it was gone, the water was restored to velvety stillness, and Danny felt the current catch the boat and turn it back to its proper path. Behind them a light glowed, and as it neared, Danny saw a lantern hung on a pole over the bow of another boat a little like their own, but dented and patched in places. It had a mast, oars and a sail that was filled with something that could not be wind, for there was none in the cavern through which the dark stream flowed; nevertheless, the boat was catching up with them, its captain standing in the stern.

"Ahoy," a voice rang out. "Hold on there, you two."

"I don't know how to stop it," Danny said.

"Just tell the darn thing to stop."

"Er, stop, boat," Danny said. He reached out and pulled Nala to his feet as the boat slowed and halted. The other boat drew alongside and Danny got a good look at its skipper. He was a bright-eyed man with white hair and a beard. He wore a captain's hat with an anchor on it, a frock coat with brass buttons and polished knee boots. He reached out and grasped the gunwale of their boat with one gnarled hand.

"Don't know what you two did," he said, "but that old serpent hasn't been seen this many long year. He used to snatch the travelers as they crossed over. He'd drag them

255

down to his lair and feed off their souls for millennia."
Nala let out a low moan.

"It's all right, my young Cherb, he was never that
partial to you lot. He had a big interest in your half-Cherb
pal, though, whatever was going on. He would have had
him if I hadn't called foul on him. Get it? Foul? See,
it's a referee's whistle, adapted for his ears. Foul? Referee? Never mind. Just because you're in the underworld
doesn't mean you can't have a sense of humor."

He looked moodily at the dark water flowing by.

"I'm sorry if we're being rude," Danny said, "but
we were so scared by the . . . the creature . . . the whole
place is a bit strange to us." Then, thinking he had gone
too far, he added hastily, "I'm sure you get to like it when
you've been here for a while."

The man threw his head back and laughed uproari-
ously.

"Here for a while? You could say that. But thank you,
young fella, that was well spoken. It's a bad joke, I know."

"Thanks for rescuing us," Danny said sincerely. Nala
clambered out of the bottom of the boat. He squeezed
himself between Danny and the bearded man.

"Who are you?" Nala growled suspiciously.

"I'm known as the Boatman," the man chuckled, "but
do you know, I always think that sounds a bit dark and
grim. I once was called Taylor, and I think of myself as
that."

"Dark and grim?" Danny said, looking around him.

"I know," Taylor said with a laugh, "it could hardly
be described as the most cheerful place you've ever seen.

But it's what people expect. I think they'd be kind of disappointed to reach the underworld and find it all sweetness and light. They'd think they weren't being taken seriously. I mean, imagine arriving at this place and being given a slice of pizza or a hot dog and being told to have a nice day. Just wouldn't work. You need to give them the old Boatman routine." Here he pulled his hat over his eyes and set his mouth in a hard expression.

"Do ye wish to pass to the place from which none return? Step on board and no more set eyes on mortal shore!"

The Boatman threw his head back and laughed with such good humor that Danny had to grin.

"You see—they're dead impressed by all that malarkey. But enough of me. What are you doing down here?"

Danny drew a deep breath. Despite the urgings from the dark part of his mind, he knew that a lie would not cut any ice with Taylor, that for all the man's good humor, he wasn't to be messed with.

"The treaty is broken and Longford's trying to start a war and then he's going to take over so we're going back to Wilsons to stop him."

Danny realized he had said it all in one breath, the way a child recites an answer in class, but Taylor was regarding him seriously.

"So you think you can stop him? Or perhaps you want to be him?"

Danny turned his face away into the darkness so he wouldn't betray the shadows in his mind.

"It's all right, young'un," Taylor said with a weary

smile. "You can't hide anything here. As far as I'm concerned, you're ready to *try* to do the right thing, and that's all that any of us can say. I'll put it to the vote. Who votes to help this pair?" He stuck his hand in the air. "Carried with acclaim. Apart from anything else, there'll be a lot of work down here for me if you fail . . . so don't fail." And this time there was no smile in his eyes.

"Right, you need to get to Wilsons. Let's go."

Asked afterward to relate the story of their journey, Danny would always drift into something like a trance. The river valley was full of wonders, of dreams, almost. They passed though vast caverns with crystals glittering in the roof like a million stars. They were caught in great storms where black rain fell in sheets and wet nothing. They passed vast cities where the inhabitants moved and yet were still, where they breathed and yet lacked life. Shadowy birds flew overhead as the boat passed under canopies of black-leaved trees like none Danny had ever seen. And once, as they passed close to the shore from which no one returned, Danny heard hooves and thought he saw prancing manes and tossing heads, as of great horses running silently by the riverbank.

But all journeys must end, and at the end of this one they came to a small landing stage. There was no sign to say where they were, but Danny knew they were back at Wilsons. Taylor examined the landing stage with a frown.

"What is it?" Danny said.

"It is the job of the dead of Wilsons, the faithless ones, to keep this in good repair. They've been working on it recently. They think it's going to be used soon, and used heavily, by the way they've reinforced it."

"I could send a few more this way." The words escaped Danny as though they had not passed through his mind first, or rather had forced their way out without his permission. Nala looked at him approvingly, but Taylor gave him a shrewd, penetrating glare that he didn't like.

"I'd keep an eye on that if I were you" was all he said. Nala and Danny clambered out onto the dock. Danny looked down and saw a tiny *S & G* carved into the railing.

"Good luck," the Boatman said, shaking both of their hands, adding with a meaningful look at Danny, "Make sure you succeed by fair means rather than foul. Foul—you get it?" Chuckling to himself, Taylor pushed off from the dock. "Hope I see you later rather than sooner," he shouted. The sail above his head filled, and in a few minutes he disappeared into the darkness.

"Let's go," Danny said, his heart filling with dread at what he might find.

18

THE DEAD

The fire had raged while Vandra and Toxique and the ravens had toiled all night, giving antidotes, carrying the sick birds away from the flames and falling debris. Both cadets were covered in ashes and grime, burned here and there by hot cinders, their hands pecked by ravens striking out blindly in their pain and distress. When dawn broke there was a scene of devastation. The flames had died down, but smoke still poured from the ruined mansion. The canal bank was littered with ravens. Many of them were struggling to eat food brought by the adult males, and some of the mothers had managed to fly for a few feet, though they were still weak.

"Dixie and Les," Toxique said, echoing Vandra's thoughts.

"Don't worry," she said, "they got out somehow. Maybe one of the Messengers lifted them off the roof."

"Maybe," Toxique said, not sounding convinced. "You know what's strange, though?"

"What?"

"Nobody from Wilsons came. The fire must have been visible for miles."

"We'd better get back. I reckon Les and Dixie must be there."

Wearily the two cadets made their way to the streets of Ravensdale. It was breakfast time, and normally the street would have been teeming with cadets, but this morning there was no one. The doors of the dining cubicles were lying open, swinging in a mournful breeze. Then they saw two figures approaching them. Vandra's heart sank: it was Exspectre and Smyck. Smyck was scowling and carrying a huge cudgel.

"Ravensdale is out of bounds," he snarled. "Don't you read notices? You lot should be gone home out of here."

"What happened to you two, anyway?" Exspectre said. "You look like you got dragged down a chimney."

"Don't suppose either of you saw Les and Dixie?" Vandra said.

"I don't know," Smyck said. "Did you notice a flying rat and a simpleminded jumping bean, Exspectre?"

Vandra grabbed Toxique's arm as he stepped forward, fury on his face.

"Death and entrails," he muttered, spittle running from his mouth.

"Scared, we are," Exspectre mocked.

"Terrified," Smyck joined in.

Toxique paused. He bent his head to wipe his mouth on his sleeve, gathering himself, and when he straightened again, the two sneering cadets took a step back. Toxique's eyes were steady and full of ice, his voice cold and urbane.

"So you think you can mock one of the Toxiques? If I were you, I would find a better weapon than a cudgel. I would lock my door at night. I would touch no food or drink for fear of poison. I would put my affairs in order, for when you mock death, it may mock you back."

Exspectre looked as if he was about to burst into tears.

"You threatened us," said Smyck. "I heard you."

"Yes, I did," Toxique said.

"I'll tell Professor Brunholm about this," Smyck warned.

"Do tell him," Toxique said, his tone soft and full of menace, "and tell him I will be waiting for him when he comes to visit. In the meantime, direct me to Professor Devoy."

Smyck backed away with a snarl on his lips, but Exspectre, scared stiff, blurted out an answer.

"No one's seen him. They don't know where he is." His voice rose to a squeak at the end of the sentence, and he turned and took to his heels. Smyck hesitated, then followed.

"That was impressive," Vandra said. "Not sure I liked the new you, but it was definitely impressive."

"Now I think I know what's happening around here," Toxique said. "What has Brunholm done with Devoy?"

They went to the bottom of the Ravensdale street, passed through the curtain and stepped into Wilsons. They looked at each other uncertainly.

Wilsons had always looked a little bit shabby, but now it had a derelict feel to it. For a long time there had been windows that were cracked and patched, but now whole panes were missing. There had been miles of dusty carpets in the place, but now dead leaves blew along the corridors.

"Let's find Valant," Vandra said. Her eyes were grainy and tired, and her brain wasn't working. The school porter was solid and reliable. He would know what was happening. But when they got to the entrance hall, the porter's desk was unattended.

"What's going on?" Vandra whispered.

"We'll go to the Roosts," Toxique said. "Maybe we'll find out something there."

But the Roosts were empty, beds unmade, lockers emptied in a hurry, the stoves cold to the touch.

"What do we do?" Vandra said, sinking onto a bed, despair in her voice. They had only left Wilsons the previous evening, but it felt as if had been months ago.

"You need to sleep," Toxique said.

"I can't," Vandra said, but Toxique insisted. She had been up all night and had taken poison into her system.

"I can't risk you becoming a liability," he said.

"Liability," she snorted, giving him a cross look. But she relented and put her head down. In a few seconds she

263

was asleep. Toxique got up and walked to the window. Although it was daylight, lights burned in the upper floors of the main Wilsons building. He turned to look at Vandra, how deeply she slept, two red patches burning on her pale cheeks. He would not leave her. The jeopardy of the Two Worlds rested in this place, instinct told him, the same instinct that let him know that you didn't leave your friends alone.

It had been a long flight for Conal and Longford. They had been forced to fly below radar to avoid the air force planes looking for them. Longford's mind was working quickly. He could pass off his flight with Conal as a kidnapping by one of the mysterious winged creatures. That shouldn't be a problem. And he could see now that it had been a mistake to try to get Danny to use his power to spark off war. It didn't really matter, anyway. The atmosphere was so tense that war was almost inevitable. The only focus for opposition to war was Wilsons. The job should already have been done, but Wilsons had a way of defying his will. He had to make sure that any uprising there was ruthlessly suppressed. He joined his mind to Rufus Ness. He could feel the fury and impotence of Ness but cut him short. *Get to Wilsons, bring as much force as you can muster.*

Valant was one of the few inhabitants who realized just how much the ravens did in Wilsons. They patrolled the building at night. They picked up litter in the corridors. They carried out small acts of maintenance, often warning him about burst pipes and the like. But there were other, more important things that few people were aware of. The building itself was strange and old and sometimes treacherous. A young cadet could find himself or herself in a wing of the place where the floor was rotten, liable to give way at any time. An open manhole might appear where none had been before. The ravens kept the building in check, Valant was sure of it.

But he hadn't thought about their role in dealing with the dead, keeping an eye on them in the Butts. The dead there were, after all, the most treacherous band in history, the spies and the traitors, and would do mischief if they were allowed. Now it appeared that, with the ravens absent, the strongest of the dead had started to cause mischief in Wilsons. There were terrible smells at night. Fresh food turned rancid in front of your eyes. And the noise—that was what had scared most of the cadets away. The sounds drifting up through the school were not the cartoon moans and chain-rattling of most ghost stories. These were eerie cries full of loss and hatred and desolation, unbearable to listen to.

Then there came the poisonings. First the Messengers were struck down. Already demoralized by the death of Daisy and the virtual disappearance of Gabriel, they fell prey to violent cramps, weakness and evil dreams. The sickest of the Messengers were moved to the apothecary, while the others took to roosting on a roof that was inaccessible by foot. Jamshid the apothecary

265

worked out that the poison had been placed in their evening cocoa.

"They were lucky," he said to Valant. "The poison was made for humans, but the Messengers have a lot of bird in their makeup. That protected them. If we could find that dratted Toxique boy, he could do more for us."

The teachers were uneasy. Duddy in particular was unnerved by the wailings of the dead.

"I can't sleep," she complained, her hands shaking.

"Don't be such a fusspot, Dorothy," Spitfire snapped. In the end a decision was made to move all the teachers to the apothecary. It was then that they discovered that Devoy was missing.

"I was talking to him just yester—well, maybe the day before . . . ," Blackpitt, who had also moved to the apothecary, began. Then they realized that no one had seen Devoy for days on end. Brunholm was vague and dismissive when asked where he was.

"Master Devoy has better things to be doing in these hard times than mollycoddling you lot," he growled, before shooting off, waving a dismissive hand.

The staff often forgot about the very existence of the Storeman, who kept to his Stores, but McGuinness kept an eye on him, and it was McGuinness who found a devastated Storeman wandering on the parade ground in the morning light. Someone had opened a valve to the school water pumping station and the Stores had flooded.

"Forty years of work lost," the Storeman moaned.

"More than that," McGuinness told Spitfire, after he had brought the Storeman to the apothecary. "Nearly all of our guns and ammunition were in the Stores. The water has destroyed them."

The Messengers were not easy patients, and Jamshid was often exasperated with them. He could not have coped had it not been for Agent Pearl, who moved uncomplainingly among the Messengers, dispensing food and medicine. Even when Smyck and his sidekicks forced their way into the apothecary "for reasons of security" and attempted to search the Messengers' beds, Pearl urged patience.

"Can you not see that they are frightened, and lost as well?" she said as Spitfire, with Jamshid's backing, threatened to "bust open a few skulls."

Docterow, the maths teacher, and Bartley, the Inks and Ciphers instructor, sat together beside the fire, playing bezique and twenty-five. Bartley, who was given to cryptic comments, muttered things like "The owl is in the November sky, but who will feed the offspring of the moon?"

Everyone was waiting without being sure what they were waiting for, and a growing sense of dread filled the apothecary. Only Pearl did not allow fear to dominate her, dispensing soothing words and smiles to all as night fell over the strange old building.

Danny had not realized how deep the Butts were, or how complex. For hours he and Nala tried to find their way out, moving through dark corridors and chambers, catching glimpses of the dead from time to time, knowing they were being watched. Nala jumped at shadows. Danny knew that the dead would not challenge him, that they would feel the power, but neither would they help him. He and Nala could wander for days in the Butts. They could wander for the rest of their lives.

"Help us get out of here!" Danny shouted into the dark spaces in front of him. He sat down heavily on a carved wooden bench. He was tired, hungry and thirsty. He had not dared to drink from the dark stream, and although there was water running down the walls of the Butts in places, there was an unwholesome look to it. Nala stopped and stayed very still.

"Sit down, Nala," Danny said crossly. "Even you must be getting tired." But Nala didn't move.

"Listen."

"What?"

"Quiet." Danny strained, but at first all he could make out was the steady drip of water and his own heartbeat. Then he heard it: a distant voice.

"Danny! Danny!"

"Les!" Danny shouted back. "Les, we're down here!"

"Keep shouting!" he heard Dixie yell. "We'll find you."

It was ten minutes before he and Nala saw a light approaching, bobbing along an unlit corridor Danny hadn't spotted before.

"Dixie!" Danny exclaimed as the girl flickered and appeared right beside him.

"Danny! Oh, Danny—you're all right! And you too, Nala!" she said, smiling brightly at the Cherb, the smile made even whiter by the fact that her face was covered in soot and there were singe marks on her dress.

"What . . . How . . . Oh, never mind. You can tell me later," Danny said as Les came into view, a broad smile on his sooty face. "I can see there are more stories than mine!"

"There are indeed," Les said, "but we have to hurry. Wilsons is falling to bits and we don't understand what's happening." He looked around furtively and lowered his voice. "Even the lot down here are getting pretty uppity. I think the ravens were keeping them in check, but now there's no sign of the ravens."

"Right," Danny said. "Do you know the way out?"

"Follow us," Dixie said. Les seemed to notice Nala for the first time. He frowned.

"Let it go, Les," Danny said. "He's saved my bacon more than once."

"Still . . . ," Les said.

"Stop it," Dixie said. "Wilsons is more important. We've got friends up there, if you haven't forgotten."

"I suppose," Les said, glaring at Nala.

"We're a long way from the surface," Dixie said to Danny. "You can tell us what happened as we go."

Danny told them everything about the ghost roads, about Longford and how the armies of the Upper World were poised to destroy each other.

"Longford was trying to get me to use the power of the Fifth. It would start the war. When the two sides had fought each other to exhaustion, he'd be able to move in and take over."

"If the Treaty Stone hadn't been broken . . . ," Dixie began, but trailed off with a look at Danny. "I'm sorry, Danny, I don't mean to blame you."

"I blamed myself enough," Danny said, "but it might have been a good thing. We couldn't stay the way we were. If we can win this fight, then the future might be better for the Upper and the Lower Worlds."

They were climbing an old spiral staircase, and they soon had no breath for talking, the stale air rasping their lungs. When the staircase leveled out, they were able to speak again. Les quickly told Danny about the mansion and the Lost Boys, and the fire that had been set.

"We found letters spelling 'arcus' on a satchel in the bedroom," Les said. "We reckon it's part of Marcus Brunholm's name. It figures, with Devoy missing and the school falling apart around us."

"Devoy's missing, all right." A gravelly voice spoke from the darkness. There was a shuffling sound and then they saw the hideous features of the dead spy Hinault. Dixie gaped at him.

"It's all right, little miss," Hinault said. "I was never any oil painting to begin with."

"What do you know about Devoy?" Danny said warily, remembering his last encounter with the dead man.

"Word down here is that Brunholm has Devoy locked up in the teachers' quarters, and he's plotting with Longford to bring down Wilsons. Things are getting a bit out of hand down here and all. Without the ravens, some of this lot . . . well, they're just plain wicked."

If anybody had been watching Danny, they would have seen him shake his head slowly, but they were all too intent on Hinault's words.

"The ravens should be back soon," Dixie said, "as long as Toxique's antidote worked."

"There's more," Hinault said rapidly. "Word is that Rufus Ness has gathered up a ragtag gang of Cherbs. The only fighting men left alive were the prisoners in the dungeons of Grist—they're a pretty dangerous lot. The last I heard was that they'd gotten a boat to bring them across the sound."

"We have to move quickly," Danny said.

"The school is wide open," Les said, "but if they're expecting an attack they can defend themselves."

"Them that's left are holed up in the apothecary," Hinault said. "That's where you need to get to. Follow that staircase there." He pointed. "It'll take you to the rooms underneath the apothecary. Run!"

Hinault's mouth opened and a blast of rancid air struck them. They didn't need to be told again. The staircase was narrow and steep, and they climbed in single file. Les and Dixie led, moving faster than Danny, sometimes almost getting out of sight so that he could see them only faintly in the distance, their bodies lit by a phosphorescent glow from the walls. Nala could have run faster, but he had insisted on taking up the rear; Danny guessed that the Cherb wanted to keep as much distance as possible between himself and Les.

At last the staircase opened out into a broad balcony carved with ravens. At the end of the balcony was a small wooden door. Dixie and Les were standing by it. Danny reached them, Nala following, but staying a little behind. Danny grabbed the door handle and threw it open, revealing an old sitting room with suits of armor around it.

"Okay," he said, "Les, you and Dixie lead—you'll know the way better. Nala can watch the rear."

"We can't, Danny," Dixie said.

"Why not?" Danny looked at her in surprise.

"It's not allowed," Les said.

"What are you talking about?" Danny said. "This is no time for silly rules."

"Really, Danny," Les said, "we aren't allowed."

"I don't understand," Danny said.

"He does." Les nodded toward Nala, who was standing warily several yards away.

"Danny," Dixie said gently, "we didn't make it out of the fire."

"You mean . . . No . . ."

"They dead, Danny," Nala said, fear in his voice. "They both dead."

19

BESIEGED

Danny slumped back against the wall, staring at Dixie and Les.

"We were trapped, Danny. There was no way out of the fire, the smoke . . ." Dixie looked almost apologetic.

"It can't be true," Danny said. "It *can't* be."

"Afraid it is, old mate," Les said. "It's taking a bit of getting used to, I can tell you that. At the same time, it's not too bad. The crowd in the Butts—well, you've met old Hinault, but most of them aren't too bad."

"No!" Danny said angrily. "They can't take you away!"

"We haven't gone nowhere, Danny," Les said. "We're still here. And will be for the foreseeable future, as far as I can tell. But there are rules, and one of them is that we've got to stay in the Butts."

"The ferryman put us down in his book as Faithless, even though we aren't really, so that we could stay. Said you probably needed all the help you could get."

"You're so . . . I don't know . . . normal about it or something," Danny said. "I want you to stop it."

"Stop what?" Les said, a gruff tone to his voice. "Being dead? Can't do that, I'm afraid, Danny."

But Dixie had seen the tears in Danny's eyes. She took his hands in her own now quite cool hands.

"Danny, we didn't choose to be here. But we are, and we have to make the best of it. We're still your friends, and we can still do some things together and talk all the time. I know you're hurting, and you feel that every time you get close to someone they leave you, but that's not an excuse for not getting close to people."

"Sorry, Danny," Les said. "I didn't mean to get cross with you. Should be glad that you feel a bit sad. Be worse if you didn't care."

"Course I care," Danny said, pulling a sleeve across his eyes. He looked down at Dixie's pale hands. "It's just not fair."

"It's *not* fair," Les said, his tone changing. "Someone put a match to that mansion, and we want you to find out who it was, Danny. My money's on Brunholm. He and Longford have to be the Lost Boys."

Danny opened his mouth to speak, but as he did so, an explosion rocked the ground beneath their feet.

"Go, Danny!" Les said. "Quick!" Still, Danny hesitated.

"We'll still be here when you get back," Dixie said. "Go on, you twit!"

Nala grabbed Danny by the elbow and pushed him roughly forward.

"Go!" he said.

"Hate to say it, but he's right," Les said. "You don't want any more of your friends ending up in the Butts."

Danny allowed Nala to push him away. When he looked back he could barely see his friends, not because they had faded, but because his eyes had filled, and tears were streaming down his face.

"Not cry," Nala said fiercely, "revenge!"

Vandra saw Pearl's face light up on their entry. The agent almost ran over to her.

"Have you heard anything of Danny?" she asked, her face falling when she saw Vandra's expression.

"Nothing," Vandra said, "but that might be a good thing."

"She means that we probably would have heard if he had used his power," Toxique said. He looked tired. He had decided not to cross from the Roosts to the school until Vandra woke up, but it was dark by the time she stirred. He made her a cup of tea, and then watched over her when she went back to sleep. He had spent the night guarding the Roosts, barricading the door. He had dreaded the return of Smyck and Exspectre and their gang, but they had not come. All they had to keep them company was the distant glow of the apothecary and a single light burning in the teachers' quarters.

Toxique had woken Vandra in the dawn light and they had crept across the empty lawns and into Wilsons, which had sunk into dereliction with a speed that astonished them. Plaster was falling from the ceilings. Water pipes had burst, flooding corridors. There were molds and ferns sprouting from the walls, and a wind that seemed to have no origin blew unchecked through the building.

"What's going on?" Vandra whispered.

"Wilsons is more than a building," Toxique said. "It needs the will of the ravens and perhaps the will of the staff and students to hold it together. That's what I think. But there's an evil will working on it as well, somebody speeding up the decline."

Ahead of them they saw a small shape skipping along the corridor.

"Vicky!" Vandra said. "What's she up to?"

"Nothing good, at any rate."

The siren was pausing at each window and putting a telescope to her eye, looking toward the Sound of the Lower World, where any enemy might be expected to first appear. Then she became aware of Vandra and Toxique, turned the telescope on them, emitted a shrill burst of laughter and skipped off into the gloom up ahead.

"Mad as a hatter," Vandra said.

"Yes, but she can still do harm," Toxique said.

They reached the apothecary without incident. The rooms of the healer looked like the aftermath of a battle:

groaning and complaining Messengers lay everywhere, and tired men and women of the teaching staff sat silently in corners. Once Vandra and Toxique had spoken to Pearl, McGuinness drew them aside. They told him what had happened to the ravens.

"Thank goodness they're healing," McGuinness said. "I don't think any of us realized how much they did for this place."

"But what's happening?" Vandra said. "I mean, the way the place is falling apart . . ."

"There is a guiding intelligence at work here," McGuinness said, "and the feeling of a game long-played coming to a conclusion. We must be alert and ready to fight for our lives."

"I had better go to Jamshid," Vandra said. "He'll need me for the Messengers."

"No!" McGuinness said sharply. "The Messengers are getting better without you. Save your strength. If only we could contact Master Devoy. Agent Starling is out in the field; she may be able to bring us some news of him."

But the news Starling brought two hours later was not of Master Devoy. Vandra wheeled around as Starling crashed through the door. Her clothes were torn and there was a streak of fresh blood on her temple.

"Cherbs," she said hoarsely. "Rufus Ness is in the building with a gang of Cherbs. We need to get defenses up around here."

"Perhaps we could negotiate," Duddy said nervously.

"Negotiate?" Starling said, staring at her. "The Cherbs call themselves the blood drinkers. They've already been in Tarnstone, and blood drinkers isn't just a name."

"Block the staircase," McGuinness said. "They can't get at us from above."

"We're very low on weaponry," the Storeman said, "very low indeed. I did an inventory, typed in triplicate, indeed according to caliber and lethal capacity—"

"What have we got?" McGuinness cut him short.

"Two rifles, three sidearms, six boxes of ammunition, three swords, two cudgels and a crossbow."

"Against a gang of bloodsucking Cherbs!" Duddy moaned. Spitfire lifted a sword and swung it through the air with a thoughtful look on her face.

"Move!" McGuinness said. "What can we use for a barricade?" The teachers joined him in dragging tables and cupboards to the top of the stairs.

"Come with me, Vandra," Toxique said. "We've got work to do."

"Where are we going?" Vandra asked. Toxique pushed open the door of Jamshid's stores. There were rows of glass chemicals in jars, barrels of powders and tables covered with mortars and glass tubing.

"Let's get to work," Toxique said. Vandra didn't question him. Toxique had changed.

"What's happened to you?" Vandra asked. "You're not, well, frightened of everything anymore."

"The closer you are to death, the less you fear it."

"What do you mean . . . the gift?" She had forgotten about Toxique's Gift of Anticipation.

"I feel it," Toxique said simply.

"No, please . . ."

"Stop it, Vandra. If I don't fear it, then neither should you. As a healer, you live in the shadow of death. You know better. Now, our friends need us."

The first attack came at nightfall. The Cherbs had tasted blood and were eager for more. These soldiers seemed to be larger than most Cherbs, howling and cursing as they charged the barricade without thought. A fusillade of shots from the defenders was enough to break the charge and send them back down the stairs, carrying their wounded. A few Messengers came forward to fight, but most huddled in their beds, moaning.

"I wring their necks," Jamshid said fiercely, forgetting his status as a healer, "like chicken!"

"They're just frightened," McGuinness said. "The Messengers are brave if they are led."

The defenders settled down behind the makeshift barrier. Jamshid had rigged up one of his autopsy lights so that it shone down the stairs, blinding attackers. Every so often a Cherb crossbow bolt would strike the barrier, "just to remind us that they're out there," Master Exshaw, the most ancient of the teachers, said as he drew a cleaning rag through his revolver.

The next crossbow bolt that struck the barricade carried a burning rag. The defenders extinguished it quickly, but soon the burning bolts were coming thick and fast, the air filling with smoke as the defenders struggled to carry enough water to the barricade to put the flames out. After half an hour they were exhausted, but still the bolts came, with the smoke making it harder to see where the flames had gotten a grip. Each time a defender rose to throw a bucket of water over the piled-up furniture, another crossbow bolt would whizz close to their head. It was only a matter of time before someone was hit. The defenders knew they couldn't hold out indefinitely, and by the sound of the jeering and whistling coming from below, the Cherbs knew it too.

Once more the Cherbs charged, crashing into the barrier and scrambling over. McGuinness fired calmly into the smoke, picking his targets carefully. The Storeman and Spitfire stood shoulder to shoulder, waiting for the first Cherb to get over the wall. Docterow and Bartley attempted to load the crossbow but looked more likely to lose a finger in the powerful mechanism. Suddenly a huge Cherb appeared on top of the barricade, a knife between its teeth. With a howl of triumph it flung itself down onto Bartley. McGuinness froze. He couldn't get a free shot. The Cherb whipped the knife from its mouth and raised it. Bartley raised his hands. The Cherb's eyes flickered. A barrel of amputated finger bones crashed down on its head. With a groan it slumped sideways and fell to the ground. Blackpitt looked down on him with satisfaction.

"The ale flows from the barrel, but when it is dry, the bones weigh more," Bartley said shakily, easing himself out from under the Cherb's body, the finger bones crunching under his feet.

And still the attackers came, the air full of cries, muzzle flashes and woodsmoke. Time and again the defenders repulsed the attack, but each time a little more wearily. It wouldn't be long before an arrow or spear hit home. The

Cherbs wore no uniforms, merely a mixture of prison rags and clothes they had stolen in the town of Westwald.

McGuinness reeled back, temporarily blinded from a handful of dust flung by a Cherb. Pearl stepped into the breach and fired at a grizzled old Cherb wearing a stolen bus conductor's uniform and a woman's flowery hat. The barricade could not hold under the weight of the attackers. Behind them the face of Rufus Ness appeared, threatening, bullying, driving them forward. Spitfire slipped and fell. Duddy, wielding a cutlass, parried a spear thrust and got her to her feet again.

"This is where Wilsons falls, after all the centuries," Jamshid said, blood from a cut running down his face.

"Not if I can help it," Spitfire said, fighting bravely.

"There are too many!" Duddy cried.

"Get out of the way!" a voice called from behind. "Move!"

The defenders scattered. The Cherbs howled in triumph and surged forward. Vandra dashed out of the apothecary storeroom and swiftly laid two planks against the barricade. Toxique, wearing a handkerchief over his mouth, came behind her, rolling a small barrel that hissed and fumed. He propelled the barrel toward the ramp Vandra had created. As it picked up momentum, he let go.

"Get down!" he shouted. The barrel hit the ramp and flew upward. Every eye was on it as it hung in the air over the attacking Cherbs—and then it exploded.

The concussion of the explosion was enough to shatter the wooden staircase, sending those standing on it tumbling into the abyss that had opened below. But that was not all Toxique had planned. A jet of foul, choking gas shot down the stair opening. Those Cherbs left standing fled, tearing at each other in their panic, their screams echoing as they faded.

The defenders got shakily to their feet, coughing from the fumes in the air.

"That was just in time," McGuinness said.

"I had to make sure the fumes were directed down the tunnel," Toxique said. "It'll take them hours to recover."

"But they will recover," McGuinness said.

"They won't be able to get up the stairs," Duddy pointed out.

"They'll find a way," Starling said. "Rufus Ness is in charge. He won't care how many Cherbs he has to sacrifice to get control of Wilsons. They might be afraid of us after this, but they're more afraid of him. They'll be back."

"What's that? Someone's calling," Vandra said.

"Our nemesis and our saving," Toxique said.

"What does that mean?"

"I don't know—the gift . . . it just came to me."

"Quiet!" McGuinness said.

"Hello? Vandra? Jamshid? Is there anybody up there?"

"It's Danny!" Vandra's face shone. "Quick! Quick! We have to help him."

McGuinness lay on the floor and looked down. Danny and Nala were standing in the fallen debris on the next floor.

"Here," Jamshid said, handing McGuinness a rope. McGuinness lifted a coil, then took his hand away in distaste. The rope was covered in old blood.

"Er, I used a bit in an autopsy, forgot to cut it off."

McGuinness looped one end of the rope around the remaining post of the staircase and lowered it to Danny. Slipping and slithering on the greasy rope, Danny climbed up, Nala scrambling up after. Vandra grasped Danny's hands. Pearl stayed in the background, unsure of her welcome, but there were tears on her cheeks.

"You're back, then," McGuinness said, looking deeply into his eyes.

"Yes," Danny said.

"You look fine, Danny," Vandra said.

"Thanks, Vandra, but I don't feel it. What happened here?"

"Cherbs led by Rufus Ness," Starling said.

"Where's Brunholm?"

"We don't know. We think he's holding Devoy in the cell in the teachers' quarters."

"Danny, I've got some bad news," Vandra said. "We can't . . . can't find Les and Dixie."

"I found them," Danny said.

"Great!" Toxique said, but Vandra stared at him.

"Where—" she began, but before she could finish her sentence a flaming bolt shot over their heads and embedded itself in one of the roof beams.

"We need to build up the barrier," McGuinness said, "and we could do with more of those weapons."

"And we need them quickly," Spitfire said from the

283

window. Danny ran over. Three Seraphim were wheeling in the air above Wilsons. As Danny watched, a squadron of the vile creatures flew high and fast over the school, banked and landed on the roofs of the Roosts.

"They don't need a staircase," Danny said.

"Look!" Duddy said. A troop of Cherbs marched across the lawn toward the Roosts.

"We're not going to be able to hold them off," Starling said.

"It's hopeless," Duddy moaned.

"Not hopeless," McGuinness said. "There is one chance, if we can use it. Danny's power."

The power! Danny waited for the gnawing sensation to rise in him, the power welling up, demanding to be used. But it wasn't there!

"It's . . . it's gone!" he stammered.

"How can it be gone?" Spitfire said.

"Wait," Jamshid broke in, "how did you get here?"

"What do you mean?"

"From the Upper World to the Lower. How did you get here?"

"By the dark stream," Danny said. The others stared at him.

"Then the waters of the dark stream have absorbed your power, Danny. It is gone."

"Gone? How can it be gone?" Anger rose in Danny, but this time the anger was not accompanied by power. Part of him felt relief, but Spy Danny raged, a wordless shriek in his head.

"Danny?" There was concern in Vandra's voice.

She touched his arm and then snatched her hand away as though burned, the healer in her detecting the rage within.

Go away, he thought. Leave me alone!

The fury was driven from his mind as Spitfire shouted and dived away from the window. As if in slow motion, the glass exploded inward. A huge Seraphim landed lightly on the windowsill, a Cherb clinging to its back. As those inside ran for cover, the Cherb unleashed a hail of crossbow bolts. Spitfire rose from the debris and took her blackboard eraser from her handbag. With deadly accuracy she flung it across the room. The Seraphim staggered backward as the eraser ricocheted off its temple, and fell from the windowsill.

"Danny, get to the teachers' quarters and find out what's happening with Devoy and Brunholm," Vandra said.

"Go, Danny," Duddy said. "We can't hold out much longer. We need help. Take the . . . the young gentleman with you."

Danny got to his feet, and suddenly a voice filled his head. Longford! And Danny did not have to look out the window to know that Longford, on Conal's back, was circling overhead.

It's not too late, Danny, came the voice, seductive and reasonable. *Save your friends. I promise you Wilsons will be spared. . . .*

It seemed too much to bear. Danny's face creased in pain. A warm hand was laid on his arm. He looked up into Pearl's face.

"You can do it, Danny," she said. "Come home safe to me." He nodded dumbly, the sincerity in her voice making Longford's sound shrill and insincere. Nala looped the rope around him, and the others lowered him down into the aperture left by the shattered staircase. When he had reached the bottom, Nala quickly shinned down after him. Looking up, Danny saw a circle of faces, then heard another crash and a cry.

"Seraphim, Seraphim!"

Danny hesitated, but Nala took him by the arm and dragged him away.

20

THE GREATEST SPY

The two boys raced past the ballroom and into Valant's hallway. They went to the front door and looked out. The air was full of Seraphim, almost all of them carrying a Cherb, and more Cherbs were making their way across the front square in twos and threes. Nala singled out one on his own who was wearing a ragged coat and a battered top hat.

"Wait," Nala said. He walked out the door and called to the Cherb. For a moment Danny thought Nala was going to betray him. He watched as Nala took the Cherb by the arm and led him toward a small group of shrubs growing at the edge of the square. They entered the shrubs together, but when Nala emerged a minute later he was alone, carrying the Cherb's coat and top hat under his arm. He presented them to Danny.

287

Danny pulled the coat and hat on. Immediately he looked like one of the disreputable Cherbs. Together he and Nala slouched across the front of the Wilsons buildings. Seraphim were dropping Cherbs onto ledges and windowsills on the apothecary floor, and there was the sound of muffled shots. Rufus Ness stood on the gable of the boys' Roosts bellowing curses and threats at his troops. Danny and Nala made for the masters' entrance. Just as they reached it there was an explosion and a rumble of falling masonry.

"One of Toxique's bombs," Danny said excitedly. The apothecary window was obscured by smoke. The Seraphim scattered into the sky, but as the smoke cleared, Danny could see that the defenders had achieved their respite at a cost, for part of the wall had collapsed, exposing the interior to attack.

Nala pushed Danny through the masters' entrance. Inside they saw the same dereliction that had overtaken the rest of the school. Rubbish was piled in corners, and lights were either flickering or out altogether, which gave a nightmarish quality to the climb upward. Bluebottles buzzed in corridors, and there was a smell of decay. Danny could see the whites of Nala's eyes in the gloom.

As they approached the masters' quarters, Nala's nose began to twitch.

"Fresh coffee?" Danny said, puzzled. They entered the masters' quarters and crept along the bedroom corridor. The smell of coffee got stronger. Danny could even smell toasted muffins. Nala looked at him in wonder.

Wilsons was under deadly attack, but someone was having coffee and muffins.

"In case you're wondering," a familiar voice drawled, "there's hot chocolate as well, if you don't like coffee."

They stepped into the masters' sitting room. Marcus Brunholm was sitting at the fire, holding a toasting fork. He smiled unpleasantly at them.

"Well, well, look who it is. The Fifth, with his treacherous little pal in tow."

"Danny!" The second voice came from the barred window in the little cell on the right-hand wall of the sitting room.

"Master Devoy!" Danny said.

"Once again they have made me prisoner in this school," Devoy said. "Tell me what's happening."

"The Cherbs are attacking. Longford and Rufus Ness are here."

"Then I must get free!"

"You won't free him, Danny," Brunholm said, his eyes fixed on the boy. "I think you are now beginning to discover the complexities of our world, how things are never as they seem."

He's right! The voice of Spy Danny was a whiplash in his head. A revolver had appeared in Brunholm's right hand.

"Danny, please. Allow the better part of you to triumph. Wilsons hangs by a thread." Danny felt his feet move forward. He no longer knew which part of his mind was in control.

"You won't shoot me," he sneered at Brunholm in the voice of treacherous Spy Danny, but it appeared that his actions were his own as he moved jerkily to the door of the prison and reached for the key. Brunholm had an odd smile on his face.

"No," he said softly, "I will not. Indeed, I cannot. And one part of you knows that. But which part? I wonder."

The key clicked in the lock and the door swung open.

"Will you shoot me, Marcus?" Devoy asked as he stepped forward, his face as unknowable as it had been the first time Danny had seen him. Before Brunholm had a chance to react, Nala, who had been edging around behind him, snatched the gun from his hand. Devoy, moving with great speed, smashed the glass case on the wall and seized the blowpipe and the poison darts that hung there.

"Perhaps you would step into the cell, Marcus?" Devoy slipped a dart into the blowpipe and waved it vaguely in Brunholm's direction. Brunholm got to his feet, a grim smile on his face. He brushed past Danny.

"Which Danny are you?" He turned in the doorway and gave a mock salute to Devoy.

"It's over," Devoy said. "All over."

"Yes, it is, for better or for worse, Narcusus," Brunholm said.

"Don't close the door!" It didn't sound like Danny's voice. Everyone in the room froze. Devoy turned to Danny. For the first time since Danny had met him—for the first time in many decades—Devoy's face changed expression. His mouth widened, the corners turned up.

Devoy smiled.

There was a hissed intake of breath from Brunholm.

"What was it that gave it away?" Devoy said.

"It had to be the least likely person," Danny said. "Why is Wilsons no longer the power it once was? Why have Longford and the Cherbs known everything about what was happening here? You allowed me to go to the Ring of Five, thinking that they would turn me, make me one of them, and remove a danger to your plans. When you were ready, you could use me. Only you knew that I would try to rescue my moth—rescue Agent Pearl, and that I would use the power. There were too many things. And then Les told me what he found at the mansion."

"Ah, the late Mr. Knutt," Devoy said. "He could not have escaped the fire I set. It was fun watching them trying to find a way out. You must have met him in the Butts. Of course, he forced me to hide myself during these last days. The Slug of Somnolence he put in his bed bit me."

Devoy held up his hand. There was a nasty suppurating wound on it.

"But there was something else," Devoy said, "something just now."

"Your name," Danny said. "Les said he found letters spelling 'arcus' on a satchel in the boys' bedroom. He thought it was part of Marcus Brunholm's name."

"I see," Devoy said. "And then you heard Brunholm use my first name."

"Narcusus," Danny said. "The letters were part of *your* name."

"But why not Brunholm?"

"Because only a great spy could penetrate Wilsons, and a great spy would not be so obviously wicked as Mr. Brunholm."

"Flattered, I'm sure," Brunholm murmured. Devoy pointed the blowpipe toward Danny.

"Not so fast, Danny." Devoy's voice was soft, almost inaudible. "There's many a twist to your tale, and perhaps another. Why did Brunholm use my first name? In all our long acquaintance, he has never once spoken it. Unless . . . unless . . ."

Devoy turned to look at Brunholm. His mirthless smile broadened, giving him the look of a skull. "Unless the greatest spy of all is in our midst. Let me put my theory to the test."

Before anyone could move he put the blowpipe to his lips, but instead of aiming the dart at Brunholm, he turned and fired straight at Danny.

"No!" Brunholm shouted. Faster than Danny would have believed possible Brunholm flung himself across the room, diving in front of Danny. The dart, aimed for Danny's heart, struck Brunholm in the shoulder. With a groan he fell to the ground. Nala struck the blowpipe from Devoy's hand. Devoy snarled at him and cuffed him across the face, the blow sending the Cherb reeling across the room. Devoy ran to the window and flung it open. He crouched on the windowsill as Danny ran toward him, his face twisted in a hideous rictus, as though the stored hatred and bile of years had come to the surface. With a screech of triumph he flung himself from the window. Danny saw him fall through the darkness, falling without hope, until, from nowhere, Conal, still bearing Longford on his back, swept beneath him, catching him in his long, thin arms and carrying him to the ground.

Brothers! Danny thought as he wheeled around to Brunholm. The Lost Boys!

Nala had already reached Brunholm and was gently easing the dart out of the man's shoulder. He looked up at Danny and shrugged. Brunholm was very pale.

"Keep the dart," Danny said. He knelt down. Brunholm's face had changed. His cheeks were no longer puffed out arrogantly. His eyes didn't dart here and there as though seeking an advantage. Even the bushy mustache had drooped. His eyes met Danny's.

"My coat looked good on you," he whispered. The voice was even; Brunholm's sly, double-dealing tones had gone.

"Who . . . who are you?" Danny said, although with every fiber of his being he already knew.

"You know, don't you?"

"A great spy?" Danny said slowly. "Perhaps the greatest of all . . . Steff Pilkington . . ."

"Yes, my boy . . ." The man flinched in pain as the poison moved through his system. "Your father."

Things weren't going well for the Wilsons defenders. The next bomb made by Vandra and Toxique had been too powerful and had blown a large section of the wall away. The Seraphim were swooping in, trying to land Cherbs on the teetering floor of the apothecary. Several had fallen and lay motionless on the steps of the building, but Rufus Ness drove them on from the Roosts, heedless of the casualties. The skeleton of the Messenger fell from the ceiling and lay in a pile of bones, and when three Seraphim made a concerted attempt to land Cherbs, Valant seized a razor-sharp wing bone from the pile and bravely drove them back.

"We're running out of ammo," the Storeman said. Vandra raced out of the back room with a handful of homemade tear-gas bombs. The bombs were very effective in momentarily driving off the Seraphim, but within minutes the wind had changed, driving the gas back into the defenders' faces so that they coughed and choked.

"We can't hold it anymore," McGuinness said. "Back!" A falling piece of timber struck Starling on the temple and her knees buckled. McGuinness put his arm around his wife and backed toward the inner ward of the apothecary. The air was full of wings. The defenders stumbled and fell, wings beating around their faces, wings . . .

Black wings.

The air was alive with ravens. Furious, cawing, they flew with savage courage against the Seraphim and the Cherbs, clawing and pecking at faces. Groups of young ravens descended on a female Seraphim and in seconds stripped the feathers from her left wing. With a shriek, the Seraphim plunged toward the ground. Another male

Seraphim, in a desperate attempt to escape, flew straight into the wall of the building with a sickening fleshy thud. On the gable of the Roosts, Rufus Ness flailed savagely at the ravens, which flew at him by the dozens. Without Ness driving them on, the Cherbs faltered, and the Seraphim lost their appetite for battle. One by one they peeled off from the attack. In five minutes the sky was empty save for a circling and vengeful flock of ravens.

21

EYEBALL DYE

Danny had realized at once that his only hope of getting his father—his father!—to the apothecary, and to Vandra, was to go through the Butts. Through the window he could see the whole front square thronged with Cherbs and Seraphim. There was no way through there.

"Let's get him downstairs," he said to Nala. "We have to get into the Butts."

Nala, small though he was, scooped the semiconscious Steff Pilkington into his arms. They walked down the corridor toward the staircase. Nala stopped at one of the bedrooms and cocked his ear. He nodded toward the door. Danny flung it open. Vicky the siren, who appeared to have been listening at the door, sprawled back onto the floor.

"What are you up to?" Danny demanded.

"None of your business," Vicky snarled back. She looked around Danny at Brunholm. "What's wrong with *him?*"

"He's been poisoned," Danny said. "We have to get him to the apothecary."

"Good luck," Vicky said, studying her nails.

"We're going through the Butts," Danny said, "and you're guiding us." To his surprise Vicky got to her feet.

"All you had to do was ask," she said, and set off in front of them. Danny looked at Nala. Nala shrugged.

Danny's head was reeling. He had started suspecting Devoy a long time ago, though he hadn't admitted it to himself. It hadn't been any one thing—Devoy hadn't put a foot wrong—but as Danny became more experienced in the art of betrayal, he learned to recognize it in others, and Devoy's treachery had verged on genius. He had done everything he could to thwart the Ring while all the time making sure that the power of Wilsons decreased from year to year. . . .

And then there was Steff Pilkington. The man moaned in Nala's arms. Danny knew that he should feel pity for him, and love, but all he felt was a growing hatred, a turmoil raging within him that was worse than the power that had threatened to tear him apart.

Vicky led them into a dark cellar smelling of earth. Nala looked about suspiciously, fearing a trap, but Vicky took them straight to a small door in the wall. She opened it and stepped through. Danny heard a familiar, eerie sound—the rushing of the dark river.

"It's all right," he reassured Nala. The Cherb glanced

at him, then stepped across the threshold, still holding the now unmoving form of Steff Pilkington.

"We'd better get a move on," Vicky said, eyeing the man skeptically.

They entered not far from the bank of the dark stream, but soon they left its quiet rushing behind and found themselves in the damp and moldering tunnels of the Butts, moving always upward along narrow passageways and treacherous stairs. If the dead watched in the shadows, Danny was not aware of them.

"I reckon we must be nearly under the enemy," Danny whispered. Vicky stopped and held up her hand to silence them.

"They're . . . the dead . . . they're close," she said.

"Close?" Nala said quietly. "Dead are all around." Danny was suddenly in the grip of an icy chill that penetrated to his very bones. The light faded and a cold fleshy mass pressed against him, jostling and murmuring.

"Go away!" he heard Vicky exclaim. "Leave us alone, mad dead folk!"

The throng around Danny parted and he saw a familiar hideous face. Hinault!

"What are you doing down here, sport?" Hinault said.

"We must get him to the apothecary," Danny said, pointing to the prone form in Nala's arms.

"Looks like he'll be joining us fairly soon." Hinault peered at Pilkington.

"If you don't let us go . . . ," Vicky said.

"No can do," Hinault said. "Looks like Longford's

winning the fight up above. Me and the rest of this lot know which side our bread's buttered on. Longford'll make it hard on us down here when he takes over."

"He's not taking over," Danny said, with more confidence than he felt.

"Be that as it may," Hinault said, "you lot are staying with us." Danny took the Knife of Implacable Intention from his pocket. Hinault started to laugh.

"What are you going to do? Kill us?" His laugh was taken up by the dead surrounding him, a ghostly hooting noise that sent a chill through Danny and a look of pure terror across Nala's face. Danny could suddenly see the throng around him, men and women, some dressed in rags, others in splendid clothes, much stained and faded. There were ghastly injuries, severed arms, stitched-on heads, hideous disfiguring scars. A cold odor of decay rose from their clothes. Danny tried to move, but he was held in their chilly press.

"Let me go, let me go!" Vicky squirmed in their grasp, but they did not relent. Instead, the throng turned toward a dark staircase leading downward. Danny's feet were off the ground, his arms pinned to his side. Nala moaned in fear. They would be carried down into the underworld, perhaps never to return.

"Stop!" A familiar voice rang out. Danny's heart leapt. Les and Dixie stood at the top of the staircase. Les had a long sword in his hand, and Dixie was squinting over the sights of a crossbow, which wavered alarmingly.

"Ha!" Hinault said. "It'll take more than you two to stop us!"

"I know that," Les said, smiling. Behind him appeared a silent crowd of children and teenagers, wounded, half starved and ghostly, but carrying clubs and staves and chains. Hinault snarled and stepped forward. His mouth opened and the sound that had terrified Danny burst forth. Nala, still carrying Pilkington, fell to his knees. Even Vicky looked impressed. But Les stepped forward, swung the sword two-handed behind his back, and struck with all his force. The blow caught Hinault at waist level and cut him clean in two. His legs fell one way and his torso toppled the other. The torso rolled across the floor and fetched up against the wall. Hinault looked down at the place where his legs had been.

"That wasn't very friendly, sport," he said mournfully. "It'll take a bit of stitching to put me together again."

With a loud cheer Les and Dixie's army charged. There was a twang and a crossbow bolt whistled past Danny's head and went straight through a severe-looking duke, who stared down at himself in surprise. The children were in among the other dead, swinging at them with their weapons. Where they were too small to carry an implement, they ran among the feet of their foes, tripping them and stamping on their toes.

"Run, Danny!" Les shouted. Danny didn't need to be told twice. Pulling Nala to his feet, he ran, Vicky fleeing in front of them.

Upward they went, Vicky sure of her way, until they found themselves in a cellar under the floorboards of the front hall. Above them booted feet clumped and they heard shouting.

"What are they saying?" Danny said.

"They're going to attack again at nightfall," Nala said.

"That gives us a few hours," Danny said, "but how do we get up to the apothecary?"

"There's a hidden staircase," Vicky said. "Devoy used it sometimes."

Danny remembered the attack on Agent Stone when he was in the apothecary. . . . Devoy!

"Let's go," Danny said grimly. Vicky led the way up the staircase, moving so fast now that they could barely keep up. Nala was starting to wilt under the weight of the poisoned man. Danny stopped Nala to check on Pilkington. His color was bad and his breathing was labored.

"Hurry, hurry!" Vicky shouted.

"You can wait a few seconds for an ill man!" Danny shouted back. Nala gathered his strength and began to plod upward again. Danny tried to share the burden, but Nala shrugged him away. Vicky disappeared from view.

Three minutes later they stood at a battered wooden door. Vicky turned the handle, which opened easily. They stepped into a gloomy bathroom hung with cobwebs, unknown substances stuck to the wall. Danny turned his head away from the spectacularly stained toilet bowl and followed Vicky out into Jamshid's living quarters, which were scarcely any cleaner than the bathroom.

When they emerged into the lab, the defenders spun around, guns leveled at them. There was delight that they had got back—delight that turned to concern when they saw the injured Brunholm.

"Can you help him, Vandra?" Danny asked anxiously as she examined him.

"If I knew what the poison was . . . ," she answered. Danny took the dart from his pocket.

"Careful with that," Toxique said sharply. He took it from Danny and sniffed the point.

"An ancient neurotoxin. It's gone a bit stale, which might reduce the effect. I think you can bear it, Vandra. Question is, do you want to? You'll be helpless afterward."

"It's Brunholm, after all," Valant joined in. "He probably betrayed us all."

"There isn't time for argument," Danny said. "He's dying!" Vandra looked long and hard at Danny.

"Danny and Nala thought it worthwhile to carry him here . . . ," she pointed out.

Danny wanted to plead with her, but the treacherous part of his mind overrode the feeling part. *He let you down! Let him die!*

"Danny?" McGuinness said.

"Let me finish," Vandra said. "I am a healer. I have no choice but to save him."

Her two long incisors grew out onto her lower lip. She blushed as she always did when her teeth appeared, knowing how it made her look. Then she bent her head to the man's neck and bit.

Danny felt hot tears in his eyes. His friend had not

hesitated, but had chosen to save Pilkington, at grave risk to herself.

Fool! Danny the Spy sneered. *No,* Danny thought, *she isn't a fool. Leave me alone!* He knelt and took his father's arm in his left hand and Vandra's hand in his right, and in that moment, Danny the Spy was banished from his thoughts, to appear again now and then, perhaps, but his influence was gone, like that of the liar who is found out, the traitor who is unmasked.

McGuinness looked down at Danny's hand clasping the man's arm. Vandra made a choking sound and fell, her eyes rolling back in her head. Toxique knelt quickly beside Pilkington while Jamshid tended to Vandra.

"She hasn't gotten enough out," Toxique said. "The poison is still too strong. . . ."

"What do you mean?"

"He'll die, is what it means," Valant said. No one but McGuinness noticed the whimpering sound that had escaped from Vicky.

"There is nothing to be done, then?" Duddy said sadly.

"Nothing." McGuinness was watching Vicky closely. Tears welled in her big blue eyes—revealing tears, for as she cried, her left eye turned from the clearest blue to hazel. McGuinness nudged Duddy.

"Eyeball dye!" Duddy exclaimed. As mistress of disguise, Duddy knew how to change eye color with dyes, and also knew that if you were using one you must on no account weep, for tears would wash the dye away.

"She's a Cherb!" Spitfire exclaimed, leaping to her feet and grabbing a sword. "What have you done with the real siren!"

"There never was a real siren," the woman said, not lifting her eyes from Pilkington's face. "All is over now and the truth can be told. I am Grace Pilkington, your mother, Danny. For many years I toiled undercover with my husband working against the Ring, he as Brunholm and I as Vicky the siren. Our work is done now. Devoy is unmasked, and the cost has been . . . too much."

There was pandemonium, a dozen voices talking at once. Danny stared. It was too much to take in. He felt numb. Spitfire and Valant had started to argue. Starling and McGuinness were trying to calm people. Then a voice silenced them.

"Out of my way." Vandra had got to her feet. She looked ghastly, her skin gray, her cheeks sunken. "Out of my way. I haven't finished my work."

"No!" Danny said.

"It's not your decision," Toxique said. "Let her pass." Danny, his head reeling, stepped back. He stumbled as he did so, and a pair of hands steadied him. He looked up. It was Pearl.

Vandra bent once more to Steff Pilkington. This time when she finished she fainted dead away, and Pilkington groaned and opened his eyes. He groped for his wife's hand and found it. She stretched out her hand for Danny's. Danny hesitated, then stepped away from the sheltering arms of Pearl and took it.

"Very touching," a familiar voice said, sounding

amused. The defenders spun around. Longford stood behind them, surrounded by Cherbs, each with a crossbow leveled at the attackers. "So at last all our plotting and planning comes down to this."

"Where's your brother?" Pilkington's voice was weak.

"Here." Devoy stepped out from behind the Cherbs. "Brilliant, Marcus, or should I say Steff? To have kept up such a deception over so many years. Whose was the greater achievement in treachery, I wonder, mine or yours?"

"Or that of the lovely Grace, I might suggest," Longford added.

"Yes, of course," Devoy said. "Very gallant of you, Ambrose." The staff of Wilsons stared in horror.

"M-Master Devoy . . . ," Duddy stuttered.

"Silence!" Devoy said. "You were always naive to the point of stupidity, Duddy."

"All along," Valant whispered, his face pale, "all through the hard years. When I asked you for funds for repairs, for defenses, you said they were all gone. . . ."

"The coffers of Wilsons are full—positively groaning, in fact," Devoy said. "I'll enjoy spending it. And you all should enjoy having witnessed the greatest feat of undercover spying ever seen in the history of the world!"

Danny stood up.

"My . . . my father's undercover feat was the greatest because he did it to protect the world, not to take it over!"

"Yes," Longford said, "a great achievement as a spy, but as a father? To abandon his son? And all those times you were in danger? Not to step forward?"

"Verging on the unnatural," Devoy said. "But then, our own father was the same, was he not?"

"Yes," Longford said. "He did not abandon us but set us one against the other, always competing. . . ."

"For years we secretly plotted, one to control the Ring of Five, the other to control Wilsons. We succeeded beyond our wildest dreams."

"The Two Worlds teeter on the edge of ruin," Jamshid said, rising from his position beside Vandra, "all because two boys wanted to prove who was better." He spat on the rubble-strewn floor.

"Yes," Longford said.

"And what is the answer, Brother?" Devoy said.

"They will never get to know, anyway," Longford said. "It is time to say goodbye, my dear Danny. And goodbye to you, Steff and Grace."

Devoy gestured to the Cherbs. The bowmen stepped forward, slipped bolts into the crossbows and raised them. The defenders looked at each other in horror; the only sounds in the room were Vandra's labored breathing and the click of each bow being cocked. Danny's eyes met those of Agent Pearl and held them for what seemed like an eternity.

"Fire!" Longford said. Danny closed his eyes, waiting for the cold steel to plunge into his flesh. Nothing happened.

"Fire!" Longford said again. Danny opened his eyes. The Cherbs had lowered their bows. There was a rustling sound behind them, a sound as if someone with wings was passing through the throng of bowmen.

Gabriel.

The Cherbs parted to let Gabriel through. He smiled at Danny.

"What . . . what's going on?" Jamshid stammered.

"Sometimes you have to pay for the evil you do. Not always, but sometimes," Gabriel said. "When Daisy was killed I flew away to the lonely shore of the sound to mourn. But my tears were interrupted by the cries of the Cherbs abandoned by Rufus Ness on the ruins of the bridge. I flew out to them. At first they were suspicious and hostile. But they had no choice but to trust me. One by one, hour after weary hour, I flew them to the forest beyond the summerhouse. We set up camp there, and they gave their allegiance to Wilsons. I learned that the Cherbs are not the enemy. They wish to be led, and to belong. The Ring led them to evil. Wilsons will do better."

All eyes were on Gabriel. It was a mistake. With the swiftness of a snake striking, Devoy seized a long knife from a Cherb and put it to Pearl's neck. With his brother behind him he edged toward the door, dozens of crossbows trained on him.

"Don't let them get away!" Pearl cried. "Shoot!"

"Don't fire!" Gabriel ordered. The Cherbs kept discipline.

"Conal. Attack!" Longford screamed. He flung Pearl to the floor and he and his brother ducked through the door. Immediately crossbow darts embedded themselves in the wood. Simultaneously a squadron of Seraphim flew into the gaping hole in the wall, Cherbs leaping from their backs. Desperate hand-to-hand combat broke out. The

307

attackers were driven back, not expecting the ferocity of the defense. Danny could see ravens outside attacking the flights of Seraphim. Then another squadron of Seraphim appeared, carrying a huge gossamer net between them. Before the ravens could fly away, they were scooped up in the net. The Seraphim flew several times around a tall pine tree, securing the trapped ravens to it. Danny could see more enemy Cherbs mounting Seraphim far below them. He felt someone poking him. Nala.

"Longford! Devoy!" Nala said. He was right. They could not be allowed to get away. Nala ran a few steps and looked back at Danny. Danny followed just as a squadron of Seraphim landed a fresh platoon of Cherbs on the apothecary floor.

THE TREACHERY TROPHY

They went out onto the hidden staircase. Nala began to go down, but Danny shook his head. He knew that the two brothers would not be able to resist seeing their triumph unfold. He led Nala upward.

The rooftops of Wilsons were a kingdom to themselves, great gables and peaks rearing and falling, fire escapes and aerials dotted across them. It was starting to get dark. Danny and Nala moved quietly toward the front of the school. Nala pointed down. There were two sets of footprints in a bed of dead leaves. Fresh footprints.

On they went, until they reached the edge of the roof. They looked down. The air was full of wheeling Seraphim screeching in triumph. Danny longed to be back with his friends, to stand or fall with them. Nala nudged him.

Twenty yards away, in the shadow of a tall chimney, the two brothers stood. The last rays of failing light silhouetted them, casting long shadows that danced and gibbered as they bore witness to the fall of Wilsons.

"Around the back of the chimney," Danny whispered. They crept across the roof until they were behind the two men. They listened.

"I was always the best at inks and ciphers," one voice said, but Danny didn't know whose; he could no longer tell them apart.

"Perhaps, but I excelled at disguises."

"Father never did award one of us the trophy. I wonder where it is."

"I thought you might ask that. I have it here." There was a hissed intake of breath.

"Let me see, let me see!"

"I took it from the house before I had to torch it to get rid of Knutt and that featherbrain girl. It was still in the same place—on the sideboard where Father would polish it every morning and remind us how Grandfather had given it to him."

"Give it here!"

Danny risked a look around the chimney. Longford was holding a small silver trophy crowned with the figure of a prowling man wearing a hat, a dark coat, and a mask over his face. Longford was staring at it with longing.

"The Treachery Trophy," he breathed. "I should have it, for my mastery of the Ring."

"But what about me? I stayed in character for years as Devoy. I fooled them all, I sacrificed everything!"

"I was always the more treacherous. Remember when I made Father believe that Mother was after his money and he sent her away?"

"Yes, I remember," Devoy said wearily, "it is true. You were always more treacherous. You must take the prize. But perhaps I could hold it for a minute, here in the hour of our triumph."

"Yes, Brother, of course you may." Longford stepped forward till he was even with the roof parapet, his hand outstretched. Devoy, his face blank as stone, took it, then leaned forward and, almost delicately, pushed his brother in the chest. Longford teetered on the brink for what felt like an eternity; then, with a look of disbelief, he fell. His scream seemed to last forever.

"I *liked* Mother," Devoy said. "Who is the more treacherous now, dear Brother?"

Danny stared in disbelief as Devoy polished the trophy with his sleeve. He seemed in a trance, only shaken out of it when the tone of triumph from the shrieking Seraphim turned to rage. He peered over the edge of the roof.

Things had not gone well with the defenders in the apothecary. They had held the attacking Cherbs at the edge of the floor but had suffered many injuries. Toxique and Jamshid worked frantically. Spitfire was unconscious, Valant had taken a dart in the leg, and the Storeman was fighting with one arm dangling uselessly by his side. The bravery of the Cherbs meant that they had sustained most of the casualties, and several lay still on the floor. A sudden onslaught by Gabriel drove the remaining attackers into a huddle.

"Don't let them regroup," he shouted. Pearl grabbed a sword and swung at the first attacker to get to his feet. Gabriel ran to the ward containing the injured Messengers, who were cowering together at the far end.

"Get up!" He loomed over them and they cowered even more.

"Get up and fight!"

Uncertainly, they got to their feet.

"You can stay in here and die on the floor, or you can go out and fight with glory on the wing. Messengers of Wilsons, this is your hour!"

A tall, stooped Messenger named Fred Morton rubbed his face as though shaking off the effects of sleep, then straightened his back and flexed his wings.

"Damn it, Gabriel, you're right. What do I do?"

The sky around Wilsons belonged to the Seraphim. The air was dark with their wings while the trapped ravens struggled in vain. The end had come for the school, and the foul winged creatures wished to prolong their triumph. Conal, the great leader of the Seraphim, scanned the ground for carrion, but there would be time . . . and when Rufus Ness shouted "Savor your moment!" Conal licked his lips.

Conal looked up as he swept over the Roosts. Some commotion was apparent at the jagged entrance to the apothecary. Perhaps the Seraphim and the Cherbs were squabbling over spoils. He flew closer. There was a melee of Seraphim and Cherbs around the aperture in the wall, the Seraphim swarming like bees. Conal moved close so that he could witness the pillage of the defeated enemy. As he did so the knot of Seraphim parted, thrown outward, their Cherb riders tumbling through the air. Through the middle of the attackers flew a squadron of Messengers, led by the steely-eyed Gabriel, like a figure of vengeance from an old book. Each Messenger carried a Cherb with a crossbow on its back, and the crossbows twanged in unison. Conal squealed with rage.

"Attack, attack them!" he commanded his troops. They turned in the air, but the phalanx of Messengers flew through them like an arrow, and Seraphim and Cherbs fell from the air in their dozens.

Conal rallied his fighters in the time it took the squadron of Messengers to circle for another attack. As they closed, the Seraphim tried to attack their flanks, flying side by side with the Messengers while the Cherbs on their backs fought each other. The Messengers had lost their immediate advantage of surprise. Many were elderly, and they were up against a vicious and experienced enemy.

The Seraphim managed to separate Fred Morton from the squadron. His Cherb fought bravely, but they were surrounded by four of the enemy. Fred's left wing took a blow from an enemy knife, and gore dripped from both him and his Cherb defender, who was bleeding from a dozen cuts. He looked desperately for Gabriel, but his leader was not to be seen. Howling triumphantly, the Seraphim rained blows on him until he could take no more. He spiraled downward, landing spread-eagled in a tree, where he lay unmoving, his Cherb companion beside him.

The Messengers regrouped, but there were too many Seraphim surrounding them in the air like shrieking birds of prey, harrying them, trying to separate them from their group. The Seraphim sensed the Messengers' weariness and uncertainty and redoubled their attack. Tired blades attempted to parry. The watching Conal smiled thinly. The defenders were spent. It was only a matter of time. . . .

Conal heard the rushing wings before he saw them. The remaining Messengers had been roused, and Gabriel was at their head. Like a storm they fell upon the Seraphim, and this time there was no reprieve. Gabriel cut through the Seraphim like a knife, wielding a shining sword above his head, and none could withstand him. With one stroke he freed the ravens, and their fury knew no bounds. The Seraphim reeled. The Cherb attackers leapt from their backs to the ground rather than face the onslaught. The Seraphim fell back. Conal raged in vain until at last he came face to face with Gabriel.

"Draw your sword, vermin," Gabriel said. "The time of reckoning has come."

But Conal could not face him. He turned and fled. With a wail of terror the remaining Cherb attackers ran into the woods. The Seraphim took flight, the Messengers in pursuit, singing a battle song as they flew.

Danny couldn't see what was going on from his hiding place. He could only judge the battle from Devoy's behavior. At first the man danced up and down, kissing the Treachery Trophy and clutching it to himself. His mood darkened, then rose again, and he skipped along the parapet. Then he stopped skipping and stood stock-still. Danny could hear a song of victory from below, and knew it was not the Seraphim who were singing. Devoy placed the Treachery Trophy on the parapet beside him. In the fading light Danny could see the Seraphim fleeing, pursued by the Messengers.

"It's over," Devoy said. "Ruined! Finished."

A figure rose from the shadows, a disheveled, gaunt woman in a dress. Danny stifled an exclamation. Devoy didn't see her as she made her way along the parapet, but a sweet smell drifted through Danny's mind, a honeyed voice. . . .

"It is a fine evening, is it not?" Nurse Flanagan said. Devoy turned with a start. "Things have changed a little since we last saw each other."

"You were dead. . . . Ambrose had you . . ." Devoy trailed off.

"Killed? The photograph was a fake. You disappoint me. Did you think a simple assassination attempt would succeed against me?"

"Of course not," Devoy said, regaining his composure. "I knew you would escape."

"I paid Fairman to bring me here. . . ."

"Not now," Devoy said impatiently. "Things are going against us on the battlefield, but there may be time to turn things around. This is what I want you to do. . . ."

"'Going against us'? There is no 'us,' not after your brother left me in that jail."

"Be quiet, woman!"

"I will not be quiet." Nurse Flanagan walked along the parapet toward him, swaying on her high heels, her hair hanging over her face, her makeup streaked.

"Damn you, woman!" Devoy snarled, gesturing to ward her away. Nurse Flanagan stepped sideways, her heel caught in the forgotten Treachery Trophy. She teetered on the edge.

"Narcusus!" She reached out and caught his hand. He tried to break free, but her grip was strong. She started to topple.

"Let go! Let go!" he shrieked. But it was too late. Nurse Flanagan fell like a stone. Devoy was jerked from his feet. One hand clutched at the parapet for a second, and then he was gone.

23

A SONG OF LOSS AND
UNBEARABLE LONGING

The defenders could not believe it: the attackers had fled, pursued to the edge of the sound and beyond by the Messengers and their Cherb allies. Those who remained turned to each other, numb with shock and sudden weariness. It was a great victory, but no one raised a cheer. Weapons were dropped; tired bodies slumped on whatever space they could find in the ruined apothecary. Others gazed aghast at the injured or at the silent bodies on the lawns below. It was not until Vandra stirred and moaned that Pearl stood up.

"It's not over," she said. "We have wounded to tend to. Shame on us, letting Vandra lie in the dirt after all she has given."

Several defenders sprang to Vandra's side, but it was Steff Pilkington who carried her to a bed.

Other defenders helped Jamshid care for the injured. Messengers returning from chasing the defeated Seraphim saw to their fellows, although some were beyond help. Fred Morton's body was lowered sadly to the ground. The little Cherb whose weight he had borne still had his arms around the Messenger's neck.

Wings fluttered in the apothecary and Gabriel landed, stern and tall, with a bloodstained sword at his side.

"I saw Conal hit by a crossbow bolt," he said. "He was bearing Ness on his back. They fell into the raging sea. They will do no more harm."

"And Longford and Nurse Flanagan fell. As did Devoy," Danny said, entering with Nala. He sat down heavily. "The Ring of Five is no more."

"Then we have victory," Jamshid said.

"Why doesn't it feel like it, then?"

They worked through the night tending to the wounded. Shortly after midnight Danny called a conference of all the staff and teachers in the library of the third landing. No one questioned his authority. The instructors sat down quietly. They were exhausted. Fighting and nursing the injured had tired them, of course, but it was Devoy's betrayal that put lead in their hearts.

"How could we not have seen it?" Spitfire said.

"He was very cunning," McGuinness said. "And no one knew anything of his history. He destroyed all records here in the library so that the curious could not delve back and find out about his relationship with Longford. He has been working on this since he was a boy of Danny's age."

"Everything was done for the opposite reason from that which was given," Pilkington broke in. "When he sent Danny to join the Ring, he said it was to infiltrate the Ring for the good of Wilsons. In fact, he wanted to use Danny to control the Ring. When he sent Danny after the Treaty Stone, it was to compete with his brother, to see who could get it first. Devoy would have found a way of breaking the stone himself if it had not fallen."

"And what of you, Steff?" the Storeman said. "Why did you fool us all as Brunholm? Was no one to be trusted?"

"Shortly before Danny's birth I unmasked the real Brunholm as a traitor. He tried to flee to Grist but fell from the bridge and drowned. I had to become him, manage his contacts, all the time working to unmask the real traitor, the deep mole, as we in the spying game refer to it. I dared not risk revealing myself, not even to Danny." He turned to his son. Danny met his eyes, his heart pounding.

"It was your mother and I who arranged your safe passage to the Upper World, who chose Stone and Pearl to care for you and who paid Nana to watch you until it became too dangerous to maintain the contact."

"You were behind everything?"

"There was less danger in the Upper World, Danny," a soft voice broke in. "The minute you were born I knew you were the Fifth." It was Grace.

"The siren . . . ," Valant began.

"A character I created many years ago, by imitating a

319

real siren who lived on a rock off the fortress of Grist. She has long since moved to a home for retired temptresses. But when I was young I recorded her song. Listen."

She took a small device from under her cloak. A sweet song of loss and unbearable longing filled the library.

"Turn it off!" Danny said harshly. "We have a lot of work to do. We have many injured, and enemy casualties to be dealt with as well. Valant, call Fairman and ask him to bring a message to the Upper World to the Phonemaker. Have him tell the prime minister that there is no longer any threat from the Lower World. It might help stop a war there."

Danny stood abruptly and swept out of the room. Steff and Grace looked silently after him. The others worked on into the night until they fell asleep where they stood.

It was almost dawn when Steff and Grace Pilkington entered the apothecary.

"Where is Danny?" Pilkington asked. Jamshid pointed. Danny sat in the shadows beside Vandra's bed, looking into her face.

"Should we . . . ," Grace began.

"No," Jamshid said, "she is not quite out of danger. Leave him. He has a lot to absorb."

The following week passed in a blur of rebuilding, dealing with the injured and making contact with the Upper World and Westwald. Danny set up base in the library of the third landing. Steff and Grace kept their distance, and Danny showed no sign of wanting to see them.

Toxique and Gabriel were Danny's lieutenants during

this period, and the sky over Wilsons was full of Messengers carrying information or flying sorties over Westwald and Grist to ensure that the Seraphim didn't return. Gabriel organized the remaining Cherbs and put Nala in charge of them so they would go back to Westwald and set up a government. Starling was to accompany them to reassure people that the Ring was not about to return.

Nala came to the library the night before his forces were due to depart. He was wearing a uniform, designed by Duddy, which was brown with blue piping. Danny rose from a table covered in papers to greet him.

"You boss now," Nala said with a grin.

"Not me." Danny shook his head. "But you are!"

Smyck and Exspectre were found locked in a shed at the back of the school along with several Cherbs. Smyck told how they had been put there by Conal. The Cherbs nodded in agreement.

"Conal keep room like shed in Grist," they said. "Cherbs call it Conal's larder."

Vandra's recovery took a long time. The venom she had ingested was old but persistent. Danny went to see her in the evening when he had time. On his third visit she put her hand on his arm.

"You have to see Les and Dixie. They can't leave the Butts." Danny grimaced. He couldn't bear the thought of what had happened to his friends.

At the end of the week the school was under control. The ravens had returned to their silent work as though nothing had happened, and pupils were starting to drift back. A new school structure had been set up, with

Valant at its head until a proper principal could be appointed. Valant took over Devoy's office, and Danny's work was transferred to him.

That evening Vandra was released. She went to the Roosts, where she met Toxique.

"Danny's gone!" he said.

"What do you mean, gone?"

"He's packed his bag, taken all his stuff! Fairman was about this afternoon, said he had a fare to pick up."

"He wouldn't have gone without saying goodbye," Vandra said. Toxique could see the tears in her eyes.

"He wouldn't have gone without saying goodbye to you," Toxique said.

"Is that your gift talking?" Vandra said.

"No," Toxique said gently, "it isn't."

"Well then," Vandra said, "I know where he might be."

Danny had in fact packed his case and started to walk in the direction of Tarnstone. As when anyone walked on the grounds of Wilsons, he seemed to find his way to the summerhouse. It was dusk, and he thought he could stay there for the night and strike out in the morning. He had prepared several disguises and could take a ship from Tarnstone. He had done his work and belonged nowhere now.

He sat in the window of the summerhouse watching the sun go down, wishing he had brought some food with him. Half an hour later he regretted that he hadn't brought extra blankets. He wrapped his coat around him and shivered. Why was it so cold, and why was ice creeping along the window seat beside him?

"Strike a light, Danny," a voice said.

"Oh, get out of the way, Les," another voice chimed in, and a candle sprang to life.

"Les, Dixie!" Danny said in surprise.

"Hiya," Dixie said. "We're allowed in the summerhouse, you know!"

"It used to be a portal to the Butts," Les explained.

"Couldn't let you take off without saying goodbye," Dixie said, "though I don't know where or why you're going."

"How could I stay here without you and Les, apart from everything else?"

"But you *wouldn't* be staying without me and Les. We're still here!"

"I kind of like being dead," Les said. "Took a bit of getting used to, mind."

"But you can talk to us all the time," Dixie said.

Les's chilly hand touched Danny's shoulder. "You can't use us as an excuse for leaving like this," he said.

"Did it ever occur to you that *we* might be lonely without *you*?" Dixie said. Danny felt his face turn red. He had thought only of himself.

"Someone's coming," Les said nervously.

"Are you sure we're allowed in the summerhouse?" Dixie said suspiciously.

"Of course!" Les said, speaking too quickly to be convincing. "But maybe we better—"

"You liar!" Dixie said. "You told me the Boatman said it was okay."

They started to fade from view, still arguing, though Les found time to direct a wink and a smile at Danny as Dixie told him off.

"Danny!"

Danny turned with a start. Steff and Grace were standing at the door.

"May we enter?" Grace asked.

"Come in," Danny said quietly. "How did you find me?"

"Vandra knew where you would be," Grace said. "She's a sensible girl."

Steff sat down on the window seat, looking at the thin film of ice on it.

"We've come to say sorry," he said. "Sorry for the way your life has been, but also to try to explain why it had to be that way."

"I know you don't think you abandoned me," Danny said, "but you did."

"The two worlds were in mortal danger! We had—" Steff began, but Grace cut him off.

"There are no words to explain how hard it was to give you up, Danny," Grace said, "and we have no right to demand your forgiveness. But we are spies. We met as spies. It's in our blood, the thing that binds us together, and we could no more refuse a mission than the sun could refuse to rise in the morning."

"And a spy can carry no baggage, Danny," Steff added.

"So I'm baggage now, am I?" Danny said.

Grace glared at Steff. "I'm sorry, Danny," Grace said. "He didn't mean it like that."

"He did," Danny said, "but that's okay. What I need to know is why you"—he looked at Steff—"were so nasty to me as Brunholm, and why you"—he turned to Grace—"were really sneaky as Vicky."

"When you're in deep cover," Steff said, "you have to *become* another person. Brunholm was a vain, sneaky brute, so I had to be as well. Even Devoy sometimes did good, because in a sense he had become a good man. But when I sent you into danger, I only did so believing that you would overcome it and come back a better person."

"You saw the 'S and G' signs."

"Yes, on the ring, and they were carved everywhere."

"We carved them so we didn't become like the Unknown Spy and his wife."

"You mean in deep cover so long they forgot who they were?"

"Exactly. Every time one of us saw it, we remembered who we were. It became a symbol of resistance as well, to help others."

"And the ring?"

"We thought you might falter, Danny. We wanted to give you a sense that we were still there, in some way, even if you thought us dead. The Boatman gave it to you. He was the only person who knew the truth."

They sat in silence for a long time. Then Grace stood up.

"Will you come back to Wilsons with us?" she said.

Danny nodded dumbly.

Steff lifted his bag, and as they walked back, Grace linked arms with Danny. He could smell her sweet, heavy perfume.

They walked together across the lawns and toward the front door. Fairman's taxi was there, its engine running.

"Who's it for?" Danny asked, puzzled.

"Not for us, Danny," Steff said. "He'll be taking us on our next mission, of course, but not this time."

"Next mission?" Danny said.

"Never mind," Grace said hastily, "it doesn't matter."

The front door opened and Agent Pearl came down the stone stairs. She was carrying a small bag. She looked up and saw Danny. A smile started to spread across her face, but it died when she saw him flanked by Steff and Grace.

"Where are you going?" Danny said.

"Back to the Upper World," Pearl said. "I have nothing to do here." She looked tired, her hair hanging over her face. "I was helping in the infirmary, but everyone is getting better. It's all so strange, Messengers and Blackpitt and this spooky building!"

She opened the door of the taxi. She put her bag in and came over to Danny.

"Goodbye, Danny. I'm glad you found your mum and dad. You deserve some happiness and looking after." She leaned over and kissed him on the forehead, her eyes glistening. She turned to Steff and Grace.

"Look after him," she said. "He's a wonderful boy."

Pearl turned back toward the cab. Fairman revved the engine.

"Thank you," Grace said softly. Pearl put one foot on the running board of the taxi. She looked hunched-over and defeated.

"Wait!" Danny said. He strode to her and took her arm.

"Grace might be my mother in name, but you are my *real* mother. You were the person who looked after me. You read to me and put me in the bath. You fought enemies to keep me safe, put yourself in harm's way for me and never asked for anything back. Even now."

Danny turned to Steff and Grace. "It's not that I don't admire who you are, but you were never there for me. You put yourselves and spying first. I'll always be proud to be Steff and Grace Pilkington's son, but Pearl cared for me."

Grace looked away. Pilkington was stunned. When Grace turned back, her face was composed. "It's as much as we could have expected, or deserved," she said. "I am proud to be your mother, and always will be."

"And I to be your father," Steff said.

"Will you stay here?" Danny said to Pearl. "It would be good to have you."

"Why not?" Pearl said. "If you want me to. There is nothing left for me, and somebody has to look after you." She smiled, tears trembling in her eyes.

"Make up your bleeding mind," Fairman growled.

"I'm not going."

"Well, somebody has to pay for my time!" Fairman said.

"Err, well," Steff Pilkington said, "if we were to go now, we might get a jump on the Traitor of the Three Gates. What do you think, dear?" Grace looked at him and shook her head.

"Go on," Danny said. "You know you want to." Grace smiled, then stepped forward and embraced Danny. Steff held the door of the taxi for her as he reached out his hand to shake Danny's.

"Very proud of you, my boy," he said gruffly, "very proud indeed. We'll be back."

The door closed and the taxi lurched forward. They watched until it reached the end of the driveway, then disappeared. Danny looked around and saw Vandra and Toxique standing at the top of the steps. There was a flicker and Dixie momentarily appeared beside them.

"Hi," Dixie said. "Did I miss something?"

"Dixie," Les yelled from a grating at ground level. "Come back. You're supposed to be dead!"

"Coming," Dixie said with a shrug. "Ciao, everybody." And she disappeared again.

"Anyone for Ravensdale and some food?" Pearl said.

"Yes," Danny said. "We have a lot to talk about."

"Can I come too?" Toxique asked.

"Of course," Pearl said warmly, and Toxique's normally white face turned pink with pleasure as she took his hand.

"And me?" Vandra said in a small voice.

"I would like that," Danny said, smiling. "I would really like that."

Nothing stirred on the lawns at the back of Wilsons. The school and the Roosts were asleep. Clouds scudded across the face of the moon, and the trees rustled. Then all was still again. Still except for a fluttering sound high in the sky that might have been the beat of wings. Still except for a shadow flitting across the front square that might have been a trick of the moonlight.

A raven perched above the front door put its head on one side, black eyes glinting. It gave a gentle caw and was answered from the trees. For as long as Wilsons stood, there would be spies. And for as long as there were shadows in the night, there would be watchers.

About the Author

EOIN MCNAMEE was born in County Down, Northern Ireland. *The Ghost Roads* is the third book in the Ring of Five trilogy; he is also the author of the Navigator trilogy for children, and he is critically acclaimed as a writer of novels for adults, the best known being *Resurrection Man,* which was made into a film. He was awarded the Macaulay Fellowship for Irish Literature and has also written two adult thrillers under the name John Creed.